PRAISE FOR
HELP WANTED

"How did the writer of a novel that precisely described the parties and bedrooms of literary Brooklyn transform into the writer of *Help Wanted*, a deeply political yet highly readable story about the lives of low-wage workers? The answer might be that the novels have more in common than is readily apparent, despite their very different settings; both of them capture a world and a moment in time in a way that's become unstylish in recent history and has a closer affinity with the works of George Eliot and Jane Austen than most novels published today." —Emily Gould, *New York Magazine*

"I doubt there are many authors who could write a literary critique of neoliberalism as breezy and almost sitcom-like as *Help Wanted*." —Michelle Goldberg, *New York Times*

"[Adelle] Waldman refreshes the social novel's insistence on the necessity of seeing past the conventional or obvious to a more fine-grained yet elusive reality.... *Help Wanted* washes labor in a stately, almost Steinbeckian light, emphasizing its difficulty but also its dignity." —Katy Waldman, *The New Yorker*

"Adelle Waldman applies her sharp sense for relational drama and dark comedy to the retail work space.... *Help Wanted* is structured around the collective, depicting the toll of capitalism on low-wage workers.... Waldman is skilled at building momentum and tension through intricacies of plot. The book shines whenever the group is together, concocting plans to better their working conditions, resisting and influencing one another in search of a shared sense of hope." —Alexandra Chang, *New York Times Book Review*

"Perhaps the most impressive thing about *Help Wanted* is that Waldman manages, in telling her small story, to describe not just the American economic prison but the global one. So: both a novel of manners and a systems novel, a book that shows us, perhaps, how intimately linked these apparently disparate genres were all along. It's a funny novel, as well as deeply humane and very angry. . . . [I]t also reads, with a frightening lack of irony, as a message from America itself. Help wanted. The question is, who's listening?" —Kevin Power, *Guardian*

"*Help Wanted* is a tragedy of circumstance. . . . As ever, Waldman is a sharp observer of the world, a writer whose attention to particulars only sharpens the big picture." —Jordan Kisner, *Atlantic*

"Graced with the psychological acuity that distinguished its predecessor." —Maureen Corrigan, NPR

"The dramatic irony instills this comic novel's small-time escapades with a potent and lingering feeling of injustice."
—Sam Sacks, *Wall Street Journal*

"Great workplace novels are few and far between . . . and great workplace novels that deal with social and economic class in our country are even rarer. However, Waldman adds a rare entry to the workplace canon with this wise, funny story of an upstate New York big-box store."
—Bethanne Patrick, *Los Angeles Times*

"A shrewd workplace comedy that never makes low-wage workers or the issues they face the punchline." —Shannon Carlin, *Time*

"The events in Adelle Waldman's fleet-footed novel *Help Wanted* take place at a box store of declining fortunes in upstate New York—a set-

ting that in Waldman's steady hands proves to be a crucible of ambition and survival."
—Taylor Antrim, *Vogue*

"Lively [and] humane."
—*Economist*

"Waldman observes her characters with the hilarious, remorseless precision real people use on real people. . . . Waldman's briskly roving point of view captures the constant squeeze on everyone."
—Tom Socca, *Air Mail*

"Reflective, wry. . . . If *The Office* had been centered on the warehouse crew at Dunder Mifflin, but without playing its workers entirely for laughs, it might have looked something like Waldman's book."
—Harvey Freedenberg, *Bookbeporter.com*

"An immersive, deeply affecting human drama."
—*Bookseller*

"The workplace dramedy of the year."—*Kirkus Reviews*, starred review

"With great compassion and humility. . . . Waldman shines a much-needed spotlight on the inequities of corporate retail policies and practices."
—*Booklist*, starred review

"A bracing and worthwhile glimpse of the high stakes faced by low-wage workers."
—*Publishers Weekly*

"Tightly plotted, slyly caustic and often very funny, it's hugely enjoyable."
—*Daily Mail* (UK)

"Sharply observed . . . Waldman's writing is richest and most humane as she traces each worker's private ambitions."
—*Telegraph* (UK)

"A smart satire of skulduggery and drudgery."   —*Times* (UK)

"Corporate hypocrisy and the futility of hard graft are skewered in this novel on working culture in a New York superstore. . . . [S]hows Waldman's gift for subtle, devastating satire."
—Max Liu, *Financial Times* (UK)

"*Help Wanted* isn't just smart and funny and wise. It's also important—vital, really—to our understanding of how and why the American dream is becoming increasingly inaccessible to working class Americans, even as that long-shot dream stubbornly refuses to die."
—Richard Russo, author of the North Bath trilogy and *Empire Falls*

"*Help Wanted* is like a great nineteenth-century novel about now, at once an effervescent workplace comedy and a profoundly human exploration of the psychic toll exacted by the labor market. The characters are so richly drawn—so full, under all their defenses, of the desire to be loved—that even the annoying ones will win your heart. Adelle Waldman is a master."   —Elif Batuman, author of *Either/Or*

"In *Help Wanted*, the tragic heroes of the gig economy, full of dreams and sob stories and what-if scenarios, concoct a plot to better their lives. Yet even as frustrations mount and their plot goes sideways, hope never dies. Adelle Waldman delivers both a brilliant diagnosis and a moving account of retail workers hidden in plain sight all around us, whose full humanity has never been so richly displayed or touchingly rendered."
—Joshua Ferris, author of *A Calling for Charlie Barnes*

"A serious moral inquiry into the lives of a group of people who work in a big-box store, *Help Wanted* is a novel about work, about the retail

industry in the age of Amazon, and about the effects of late capitalism on human relations. It is also hard to put down."
—Keith Gessen, author of *Raising Raffi*

"What a gorgeous and ingenious and heartfelt work *Help Wanted* is!"
—Michelle Orange, author of *Pure Flame*

"I can't think of a book more necessary. Adelle Waldman takes us into the universe of American labor with generosity and compassion. It has been a while since workers have been portrayed through the lens of a novelist with such insight and attention to the details of service industry life. Simply enthralling."
—Gary Shteyngart, author of *Our Country Friends*

"*Help Wanted* is a marvelous novel. We get to eavesdrop and follow and enjoy the misadventures of the motley cast working the four in the morning shift (unloading trucks at a big box store, a place none of these workers can afford). On one level this is about economics and gentrification; on another level it is about people struggling to keep themselves from drowning; meanwhile there are hijinks so funny you blow your tea out of your nose; there's a perfectly absurd plot straight out of *Catch-22*. We want everyone to get that lifesaving promotion. The worst thing about this novel is that I finished it and can't ever read it again for the first time. But now it is part of my life. I am thankful to Adelle Waldman for being brave and talented and bighearted enough to have created this gift."   —Charles Bock, author of *Alice & Oliver*

HELP WANTED

Also by Adelle Waldman

The Love Affairs of Nathaniel P.

HELP WANTED

A Novel

ADELLE WALDMAN

W. W. NORTON & COMPANY
Independent Publishers Since 1923

This is a work of fiction. Names, characters, places, and incidents are the products of the author's imagination or are used fictitiously. Any resemblance to actual events, locales, or persons, living or dead, is entirely coincidental.

Copyright © 2024 by Adelle Waldman

All rights reserved
Printed in the United States of America
First published as a Norton paperback 2025

For information about permission to reproduce selections from this book, write to Permissions, W. W. Norton & Company, Inc., 500 Fifth Avenue, New York, NY 10110

For information about special discounts for bulk purchases, please contact W. W. Norton Special Sales at specialsales@wwnorton.com or 800-233-4830

Manufacturing by Lakeside Book Company
Book design by Patrice Sheridan
Production manager: Julia Druskin

ISBN 978-1-324-10517-6 pbk.

W. W. Norton & Company, Inc., 500 Fifth Avenue, New York, N.Y. 10110
www.wwnorton.com

W. W. Norton & Company Ltd., 15 Carlisle Street, London W1D 3BS

10 9 8 7 6 5 4 3 2 1

To all retail workers

What makes life dreary is the want of motive.
—GEORGE ELIOT, *Daniel Deronda*

TOWN SQUARE STORE #1512
TEAM MOVEMENT

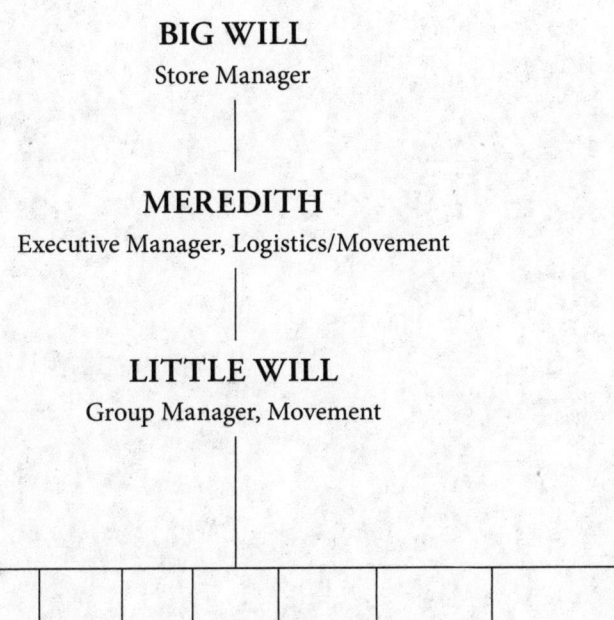

BIG WILL
Store Manager

MEREDITH
Executive Manager, Logistics/Movement

LITTLE WILL
Group Manager, Movement

NICOLE   RUBY   DIEGO   VAL   MILO   JOYCE   TRAVIS   RAYMOND   CALLIE

Movement Team Members

1

THE FIRST HINT something was up was so subtle that it barely registered. Just before the start of Monday's 4 a.m. shift, the members of Movement were in the employee area at the front of the store, waiting to clock in. Everyone was there—everyone, that is, except Meredith, the person at the center of the plot that was soon to take shape, its reason for being.

Nicole turned to Little Will, Movement's group manager. "She's still coming back today?" Nicole asked. "She hasn't been, like, fired?"

At twenty-three, Nicole was the youngest person in Movement.

"Nope," answered Little Will. "She texted me last night."

As if Nicole had demanded proof, he fished his phone from his pocket, tapped its screen several times, and passed the device to her. *I'll be a little late tomorrow*, read the message from "Meredith, boss." *I need a little rest after vacay, you know how it is!* The words were followed by two emojis: a beach ball and a glass of wine.

Nicole rolled her eyes. She was about to hand back Little Will's phone when a new text bubble appeared on the screen. She couldn't help but read it. *Hey man, I've got some news. Could be big for Movement. Coming in now, will tell you & M after the unload.* The text was from Big Will, the store manager.

"Huh," Nicole said. She gave the phone back to Little Will, then watched him as he read the text.

He was six foot one. He was only called Little Will to distinguish him from Big Will. Big Will was five eleven, but it was his grinning face, captured by a Polaroid, that sat at the top of the org chart taped to the wall of the break room at Town Square Store #1512 in Potterstown, NY. From Big Will's photo, seven spokes pointed diagonally down to the next layer of management, the store's executive managers. One of these was Meredith. Her photo, taken at a flattering three-quarter angle, showed her smiling coyly. Two months earlier, it had been pulled from the slot that said "Executive Manager for Sales—Hardlines" and reglued above the words "Executive Manager for Logistics (a.k.a. Movement)." A lone vertical line led down from Meredith's picture to Little Will's. His appeared to have been taken under duress. It had a startled mug-shot quality. As if to underline a point about his status, Little Will's title—group manager—wasn't capitalized. The rank-and-file members of Movement weren't pictured at all.

"Maybe Meredith really *is* getting fired?" Nicole said when Little Will looked up from his phone. She grinned hopefully.

She was pretty, in a fresh-faced, apple-cheeked, straight-from-the-farm way, the kind of dimpled white girl you could picture in ye olden days, in a gingham dress and braids as she milked a cow. To tamp down such associations, she slouched, wore baggy T-shirts and boxy pants that sat low on her hips, smoked constantly, avoided both the sun and foods that weren't heavily processed and/or white in color, and generally cultivated an air of boredom and free-floating hostility.

Little Will frowned. As a manager (albeit a low-level one), he tried to adhere to certain standards. "Let's not jump ahead of ourselves," he said.

Nicole looked at him with something close to pity. It wasn't only because he was too nice to talk shit even about Meredith. He'd missed multiple buttons on his shirt—a limp, faded, pill-covered flannel he kept balled up on the passenger seat of his car when he wasn't working. Swatches of white undershirt were visible between buttonholes. Little Will would have been ridiculous if he weren't so good-looking.

The digits on the two identical time clocks hanging on the opposite wall changed synchronously from 3:54 to 3:55. The text slipped from Nicole's mind as she joined the others.

After clocking in, a few people went straight to the sales floor. The rest headed to the warehouse. Movement was responsible for unloading the trucks that came from Town Square's corporate distribution center in western Pennsylvania and for getting the merchandise onto the store's shelves.

Nicole, who was in the warehouse group, walked with the others through the quiet store to Aisle E26 (lightbulbs), all the way in the back. At the end of the aisle, they passed through a set of double doors, marked EMPLOYEES ONLY.

The warehouse was even more dungeon-like than usual. With sunrise still a ways off, its small, dirty skylights were useless. The half dozen or so bare bulbs that hung from the high ceiling only dented the gloom. The air was thick and warm. There was never any AC back here, but with the store closed to customers, the HVAC system was on eco mode: no occasional blasts of cooled air wafted in from the sales floor. The truck was parked ass-out in the first of the warehouse's three loading docks. Every few seconds, high-pitched squeals tore through the dark space. The line—a long metal track that ferried merchandise through the warehouse—needed oiling.

Milo and Diego had arrived before the others, to set up. Milo was already in position, standing just inside the truck, and was raring to go—rotating his arms in their shoulder sockets, like a pitcher warming up.

Milo was the thrower. His job was to transfer boxes from the truck onto the line, then push them to the next person, who scanned them. At store #1512, this was Nicole. If her scanner said a box held backstock, she drew a slash on its label with a Sharpie before pushing the box down the line. Downstream from her, Travis, Raymond, Diego, Val, and the old guys were spread out along the line. Each one was responsible for picking certain categories of boxes off the line and putting them onto pallets waiting by their feet. Boxes that weren't theirs, they pushed to the next person, until the truck was empty.

Without waiting for the old guys to get to their posts at the back of the line, Milo began pushing boxes down the track.

Nicole's scanner intoned dully—*beep, beep, beeeeep*—as it hovered over a microwave, a box of DVDs, a bundle of six swim noodles tied together with twine, which for some reason—who knew or cared—elicited a longer and higher-pitched squawk. Nicole fell into a steady, almost somnambulant rhythm as she scanned and pushed, scanned and pushed. There came a cordless vacuum cleaner, an infant car seat, several packages of paper towels fused together with shrink-wrap, a box containing tubs of protein powder, an office chair, a dollhouse, kitty litter, curtain rods, an air conditioner, a box of mixed HBA (health and beauty aids), a flat-screen TV, baby wipes, a box of individually packaged, microwavable bowls of organic mac 'n' cheese, two Blu-ray players, a convection oven, four Android cell phones, a crate of jarred pasta sauce, a box of DVDs, a stack of Monopoly sets wrapped in cellophane, a white-noise machine, a mixed box of Chemical (cleaning supplies), a bundle of shrink-wrapped lampshades, more kitty litter, several cases of flavored seltzer water in 12-ounce aluminum cans, tiny cans of gourmet dog food, deodorant, double-A batteries, even more kitty litter—for decades, Potterstown had been hemorrhaging people, but judging by the fecal evidence, its cats were flourishing—dish soap, soap dishes, a drip coffeemaker, a Keurig coffeemaker, pots for planting, pots for cooking, rubber mats to put in the footwell of a car, crayons, laundry baskets, bookshelves, a half dozen bound American flags, shampoo, nail polish, wood polish, shoe polish.

When a pallet filled with boxes, Little Will used a jack to whisk it from its spot. Before taking it out to the sales floor to be unpacked—or "broken out," as they called it—he swapped an empty pallet in its place so the movement of the line wouldn't be interrupted, even for a moment. Corporate insisted the unload take no more than an hour. If they took even a minute longer, Meredith, as executive manager, had to submit a "failure report," as she called it. Having to do this guaranteed she'd be on the warpath for the rest of the morning. One time, after it happened, she'd sent Raymond home early, on the grounds—dubious, in Little Will's judgment—that Raymond was still drunk from the night before. (He'd just smelled of booze.) More recently, she'd gone off on Nicole, chewing her out and threatening to write her up for no reason at all.

Before taking a pallet of HBA to Joyce on the sales floor, Little Will glanced at his wrist. It was bare. He remembered that his watch battery had died a few days ago. He pulled his phone from his pocket: 4:09. *Shit.*

Although corporate permitted them to clock in five minutes earlier, Movement's shift officially started at four. They had to finish the unload by five.

Little Will rubbed his cheek. It was already stubbly. His shift began at three, an hour earlier than the others', and lasted eight hours and forty-five minutes. Then he went to his second job, landscaping. He showered and shaved at night, before going to bed.

"Jesus Christ!"

Back in the warehouse, Val's voice rose above the screech and clang of the line. Little Will turned to her. So did everyone else. With one hand, she held a large bag of kitty litter above her head, like the Statue of Liberty wielding her torch.

"This is soaked!" Val shouted, giving the kitty litter a little shake as the line came to a slow, whining stop. "C'mon, mofos! What's the use of kitty litter if it's wet?" With her free hand, she tapped the side of her head. "Think about it."

But she was grinning. There were few things Val liked more than an opportunity to display her competence.

"Drama queen," Milo muttered from the truck. Only Nicole heard.

She didn't respond. Nicole thought the idea of Milo calling anyone, even Val, dramatic was laughable. After three years of working next to Milo on the line, Nicole's precise level of irritation with him ebbed and flowed, but it rarely dipped below a six on a one-to-ten scale.

Val tossed the kitty litter into the Damaged pile (which, to Milo's point, she could have done immediately, without stopping the line). Boxes started to move again.

Nicole scanned and pushed three tightly bound tiki torches, an electric kettle, a box of Hawaiian Tropic sunscreen. Then items began coming faster, one right after the last, with barely an inch of space between them. Nicole scowled. She guessed Milo was timing himself, trying to see how quickly he could throw. *Dumbass.*

Nicole refused to be pressured. Ignoring the line of boxes that began to form behind her, she continued to work at the same pace as before. Why not? Meredith wasn't here to yell at her to go faster, screaming "Push, Nicole, push! Push like you mean it!" like some kind of demented midwife.

What did Nicole care if they missed the unload time? When it happened, Meredith disappeared into the ladies' room only to emerge fifteen minutes later with red eyes. "Allergies," she'd say if anyone asked. On the other hand, last time Meredith had taken out her disapointment or whatever on Nicole. In front of everyone, she'd called Nicole "slow," as in retarded, and imitated the supposedly imbecilic expression on Nicole's face. She also threatened to write her up, for a bad attitude. (Which really made no sense when you thought about it: if Nicole *were* retarded, then her slowness wouldn't be the result of her attitude, would it?) Still, Nicole was counting on her raise this year. She didn't want to get written up. And it had been horrible, being singled out like that. The worst part was that everyone had seen her take it, stand there stupidly while Meredith insulted her.

Reluctantly, Nicole began scanning and pushing a little more quickly. Then a phone alarm trilled.

"Forty-three!" Milo grinned triumphantly. "Tied my record for number of boxes pushed in a single minute."

Nicole knew it, she fucking knew it.

Nicole glanced at him. Tall and skinny, with hands and feet that looked too big for the limbs that sprouted them, Milo had a narrow, almost elfin face dominated by pink cheeks and a long, pink-tipped nose that twisted at the bottom, like a caterpillar executing a turn. On the back of his head, a glabrous, quarter-sized spot of pale white skin was surrounded by dark, spiky hairs, like a column of ants marching in a spiral formation. His bald spot was important symbolically. It was the only indication that he was, technically, a grown-up.

Nicole gave him a look so withering that his smile vanished. He slumped a little as he turned back to the boxes.

But Milo didn't stay down for long. A minute later, grocery items came rolling down the line: boxes of peanut butter, cereal, granola bars, single-serve Styrofoam cups of soup. They were followed by toilet paper. In spite of herself, Nicole grinned. When he wasn't trying to break his own records for speed, Milo amused himself by choosing boxes deliberately, to tell a "story." This was a classic: what comes in—food—followed by what comes out. Milo called his box stories "performance art." Milo was a dumbass, but Nicole had to admit she felt some affection for this aspect of his dumbassery.

She was still smiling as she pushed packages of toilet paper to Travis, who pushed them to Raymond. Raymond was responsible for Toys and Big D—large-scale domestic goods, i.e., furniture, mirrors, wall art, lamps, etc.—as well as Paper. Paper referred to disposable kitchen and bath products, including toilet paper. (Actual paper, for writing, was Office.)

Raymond was short. Soon, he had to stand on his toes and stretch his arms over his head to get the packages of Charmin and Scott onto the top of his rapidly rising stacks. The blue Town Square T-shirt he wore was too big for him, nearly knee-length, like a little girl's nightgown, and he hadn't shaved for several days—his beard was coming in unevenly, in scraggly, unhygienic-looking tufts. Raymond was a nice enough guy—at least he wasn't actively annoying like Milo—but he was runty and unfortunate, one of those people who give off an unmistakable whiff of loserishness.

A gigantic white cube careened down the line: twenty-seven packages of Quilted Northern toilet paper, each made up of sixteen individual rolls, stacked three rows deep and three rows high, the whole edifice held together with bands of shrink-wrap. It was like a moving snowbank. Raymond opened his arms wide and nearly dove into the ivory mass, pressing the side of his face into its only moderately pillowy surface while his outstretched arms hugged the cube. His short khaki-clad legs did a sort of shimmy as he attempted to set the giant cube gently next to the Paper pallet. He bungled it, knocking into one of the stacks on the pallet, sending small packages of toilet paper tumbling to the ground.

As she watched Raymond scramble after the fallen rolls, it occurred to Nicole that when she was in high school, she wouldn't have hung out with Raymond any more than she would have hung out with Milo. Not that she'd been in the popular crowd—not by a long shot. To be popular, you pretty much had to be rich or an athlete or both. Usually both. And pretty or not, Nicole had crooked teeth, wore the same black hoodie day after day, scowled constantly, and had acquired, due to a single fight, a reputation for toughness that made her scary to the rich kids in their college-track classes. Still, among Nicole's people—the stoners and summer school regulars—she had had a kind of status. That would not have been true of either Milo or Raymond, Nicole was sure, even if she hadn't gone to Potterstown High at the same time as either of them. (Raymond was twenty-seven, four years older than she was. And she wouldn't even have been in *kindergarten* when Milo graduated. Hard as it was to believe, Milo was thirty-seven.)

Nicole wondered now if working with them, hanging out with them—albeit mostly at the store—represented some sort of comedown, a gradual loosening of standards that she hadn't been fully conscious of until this moment, when it was too late to do anything about it. This bothered her. Nicole preferred to see her life as a success story, in which she advanced ever closer to achieving her goals. Since high school, she had moved out of her mother's house, gotten engaged, had a baby. She had a steady job, one she was good at. At her last performance review, Big Will had told her she was "very smart" and "smarter than she knew." He'd given her the highest raise allowed by corporate. Only 3 percent, but still. It was the highest anyone got. Hopefully he'd do the same this year—if Meredith didn't write her up.

Nicole sighed.

A Balloon Time home helium tank came down the line. (Milo had finally run out of toilet paper.) Nicole scanned the tank and pushed it to Travis. Then she scanned and pushed a glossy box bearing the image of the printer inside it. Three more printer boxes followed, like a family of ducks waddling single file. Travis collected the printers in his arms— the stack of boxes came up so high that he had to tilt his head to see around them—then jogged them to the cage.

As the new guy—he had only been on the job for a couple of months—Travis had naturally been stuck with the worst categories, Bulk and Softlines as well as Electronics, which, to prevent theft, had to be taken to a metal shelving unit that would be locked after the unload, a.k.a. the cage. Bulk items, like Electronics, couldn't just be dropped onto a pallet at your feet: they had to be taken to a designated area next to the fire exit, a kind of staging area for cribs, strollers, reclining chairs, and large, plastic storage containers. The problem with Softlines—clothes, shoes, and accessories—was just that the store got so many damn boxes of them. Nicole would know. After the unload, her job was to break out Softlines on the sales floor with Ruby.

As he ran back from the cage, Travis flashed Nicole a wry, close-lipped smile.

He was missing several top front teeth and made a point of keeping his upper lip pressed down over the gap where his teeth should have been. It worked. Not only were the missing teeth less noticeable than you'd think, but his perpetually close-lipped expression—combined with a reserved, ironic manner—lent him an air of cool, as if he were watching everyone at a remove. It jibed with the confident way he stood and wore his clothes. Unlike Raymond's, Travis's oversized T-shirt looked purposeful, stylish.

Travis, Nicole realized, was *exactly* the kind of person she would have been friends with in high school. This thought filled her with something like pride. But when she glanced at Travis again, she had the distracting sensation—not for the first time since he'd started working here—that she'd seen him somewhere before. She was trying once again to call up the memory when a Softlines box fell off the line. T-shirts spilled onto the floor by Travis's feet.

Little Will hurried over. Getting down on his knees—something almost no one else was willing to do (they saw it as undignified)—he began picking up shirts. He paused over a white V-neck, began rubbing at it, trying to remove some grime it had picked up on the ground but only managing to make the dark streak larger.

Little Will looked up at Travis. "I hope the people who shop here wash the clothes they buy before they wear them."

Travis merely raised an eyebrow, conveying by this means some sort of judgment, whether on Town Square for selling dirty clothes or on the people who shopped here, Nicole couldn't say.

Of course Travis didn't shop at Town Square himself. Almost no one who worked here did. Even with the employee discount—10 percent—the mass-produced knockoffs of trendy, boutique-type items Town Square sold were cheap only to people who shopped at actual boutiques. For some reason, these people got a kick out of imagining that they were shopping at a real discount store. The people who worked at Town Square shopped at Walmart, in the next shopping center over.

Little Will finished stuffing the shirts back in the box. When he stood up, Nicole realized something. He would have been in the popular crowd in high school. He would have been the nice one, the one always apologizing for the shitty things his asshole friends did, but still: he would have been popular. He'd played hockey, after all, and he was tall and well built with a Ken-doll face and thick, light brown hair only a few shades darker than his skin. (Because of all the time he spent outside landscaping, he was always tan.) Even Val—who wasn't into men, who was married to a woman—agreed that Little Will was "fucking hot, for a dude."

The thought of Little Will as popular bothered Nicole. She had thought the popular kids were rich, spoiled shits. Yet if Little Will had so much as looked at her back then, she knew she would have given him her virginity. She'd been a sucker for a certain kind of all-American guy.

She was still thinking about this when Milo bellowed, "Four twenty!" This was Milo's idea of wit. Nicole's level of irritation rose to a seven.

Little Will also groaned. Twenty minutes in, he thought, and the truck was significantly more than two-thirds full. And even if they made the unload time, what did it signify? They still wouldn't have time to break out all the boxes on the truck—nineteen hundred today—let alone make progress on the backlog that had built up over the last few weeks.

The warehouse was in terrible shape—overcrowded, untidy to the point of being dysfunctional. Hundreds of boxes that should have been taken out to the sales floor and unpacked had been stuck back here for weeks because the people of Movement hadn't had time to break them out. As a result, whole sections of the store were depleted, nearly empty. When Little Will's mother had stopped in the other day, she'd said the store reminded her of those pictures they used to show on TV of grocery stores in the Soviet Union with nothing on the shelves. "Funny how things come back around," she'd said.

But what could they do? The team was working as hard as they could. They simply didn't have enough hours for the workload. They needed money, a budget big enough for Little Will to schedule all thirteen members of Movement each truck day and schedule them to work longer, beyond their standard 4 a.m.-to-8 a.m. shift, at least until they were caught up. Unfortunately this wasn't Little Will's call to make. It was Meredith's.

Little Will told himself that he'd talk to her—again. Reason with her.

When Little Will left to take a pallet of Softlines boxes to the sales floor, Milo began dramatizing the human life cycle. He pushed out boxes of baby food and powdered formula, a crib mattress, a baby stroller. Then: a toddler car seat, a play kitchen, a stack of six sets of Candy Land bound together with cellophane, a children's bike with training wheels. For the teenage years, he chose a Nintendo Switch, a pair of speakers, motor oil, cans of Red Bull, and a box of condoms. Adulthood—a letdown in Milo's estimation—was a set of pots and pans, a box of Tide Pods, an alarm clock, a rake, dental floss, garbage bags, and heartburn medicine. Then for old age: cartons of denture cleaning tablets, an electric blanket, a deluxe walker. He looked around for his finale. He was forced to settle, somewhat anticlimactically, for a box of adult diapers. If only Town Square sold coffins.

By then, Milo was sweating, both from the heat—worse inside the truck than in the rest of the warehouse—and the pressure of performance. The others laughed when he tried to explain, but his "shows" were a lot of work. He had to think and act quickly, picking boxes from the limited selection accessible to him at any given moment. It required both mental and physical agility.

"Can I get a fan, Will?" he called when Little Will returned to the warehouse. "It's got to be ninety-five degrees in here. I'm, literally, dying."

"Sure thing." Little Will headed for the storeroom. "I guess summer's finally here," he said to no one in particular.

"Then why we not getting summer hours?" Diego asked. His tone made Little Will wince.

A compact black man from Honduras, Diego stood with his feet set apart and his shoulders pushed back, making himself as wide as possible, as if to compensate horizontally for a slight vertical deficit.

Little Will knew why Diego was mad. They all did.

Summer was the store's busy season. Potterstown was two hours north of New York City and tucked between the Catskill Mountains and the Hudson River. In the last few years, it had become an increasingly popular summer destination for a certain type of city person (the kind who eschewed—or was priced out of—the Hamptons). Starting around the end of May, city people began arriving with their wallets open—eager to stock their second homes and Airbnbs. This usually meant that store #1512's employees got as many hours as they wanted, at least up to thirty-nine a week (busy season or no, overtime was a no-go—"challenging time for retail," yada yada yada).

It was now mid-June.

"I can't remember the last time I got more than twenny hours," Diego continued. Because he was upset, his accent—Honduran, but with a lilt that made a lot of people think he was from one of the Caribbean islands—was even more pronounced than usual. "My phone got shut off. I can't get it turned on till we get paid on Friday."

Little Will looked down. "*I know*," he said to the floor. He looked back up at Diego. "I'm sorry. I'm going to talk to Mer—"

Before he finished, the warehouse doors were flung open with so much force that they banged against the walls on either side, the sound reverberating through the long, cavernous space. From between them, a slim, blond figure appeared, flouncing and smiling, as if the doors were stage curtains and this, her grand entrance.

"Hellooo!!!"

2

MEREDITH'S CHIN-LENGTH HAIR was freshly blow-dried, with only the tiniest bit of dampness clinging to its dark roots. Her lips were coated in pink gloss, and her eyes lined with pencil. She wore a close-fitting baby blue T-shirt and khaki-colored skinny jeans. Even executive managers had to adhere to the store's dress code.

As she made her way toward Little Will, the heels of her suede ankle boots tap-tap-tapped against the concrete floor. Little Will clutched the handle of his jack.

"How was—uh—Lake George?" he asked.

"Lake Placid," Meredith corrected. "Lake George is kind of, I don't know . . . ?" She scrunched up her face.

Before his dad's business went under, Little Will's family went to Lake George every summer. "Right," he said. "Right."

"So." Meredith smiled. "Talk to me about what?"

The guilty, panicked look that appeared in his org chart photo flit across Little Will's face. This was not the moment he would have chosen for the conversation he wanted to have.

"Will?" Meredith prodded.

"Sorry," he said. He smiled unnaturally. (He looked like a revivified corpse, Nicole thought.) "It's, um, about our, um, hours." Then, buoyed by the strength of his conviction, he began to speak more fluidly. "The store has been getting busier. Which you know. So of course the trucks are getting bigger. While you were gone, all five were upwards of eighteen hundred pieces. Two had more than two thousand. But we're working with the same budget we had all winter and spring, when we were dealing with thirty or forty percent fewer boxes. There's no way to get through a June workload on a March budget." He gestured at the warehouse's packed shelves and the overflow boxes, stacked on the ground, clogging up what should have been open arteries. "We need more money, to schedule more people each day and for longer hours."

Meredith's smile made her small, deep-set gray eyes become even smaller. "*Wiiiill*," she said. "I've told you, it's a matter of priorities. I wish we could do it all, but it's not in the cards right now. Our number one priority is staying on budget. That means working harder and smarter with the hours we have."

"I hear you," Little Will said. "It's just—well, the effect on the store?" He looked at her pleadingly. "Whole sections are empty. People can't buy what's not on the sales floor. We could be losing thousands, maybe tens of thousands of dollars in sales each day."

The boxes that came in off the trucks were disproportionately full of the store's most popular items—the things they'd sold out of, for which they needed replacements from the distribution center.

The implication that she was causing the store to lose money made Meredith's upturned nose quiver slightly.

"The store's sales are up for the month," she said. "And they're up this June from the same period in June last year. That's what matters—the trend, not the raw number. As long as sales are up, we're good. Okay?"

Little Will was about to point out how hard it was on the team, not getting the hours they counted on this time of year. "Besides, we have Callie starting tomorrow," Meredith said before he could.

She had, it was true, agreed to bring a new person on, to help Nicole and Ruby break out Softlines.

"Even so—" Little Will began, but he was speaking to the stripy blond highlights on the back of her head. She had already turned away.

Little Will wondered for perhaps the thousandth time why Meredith had asked to transfer from Sales to the warehouse, to Movement or Logistics or whatever you wanted to call it. (Several years earlier, on the advice of management consultants called in to help with hiring, corporate had changed the name of the department known as Logistics to Movement. Movement sounded more fun and modern and would appeal more to potential rank-and-file employees, the consultants said. But executive managers shrank from the change—for themselves. They felt that being executive manager of something called Movement sounded dinky, as if they worked for a yoga studio or a laxative company, and successfully lobbied corporate to retain their original titles.)

In attitude as well as appearance, Meredith was so clearly a front-of-the-store person. And though the transfer was technically a lateral move for her, Movement was at the bottom of the store's informal pecking order. It wasn't "customer-facing," it was where Irina from HR put people whose social skills were, in her words, "not ready for prime time."

While Little Will was absorbed in these thoughts, Meredith began walking toward the truck. She was almost there when the line began emitting a series of clanks and moans, the volume and complexity of which were at a pitch unusual even for such a sprawling and poorly cared-for apparatus. The noise called to mind a dying animal—or several, as if an extinction-level event were being visited upon a rabbit warren or fox den. For a moment, everyone in the room was transfixed—it seemed as if the entire line was on the verge of collapse, as if its many constituent parts were about to declare independence from one another, causing the whole thing to come clanging to the ground in a useless heap. Then, just as suddenly as it began, the cacophony ceased. The problem had apparently righted itself.

Meredith tittered uneasily, then began clapping her hands. "Okay, guys," she yelled, "we're all good here. Let's get back to work. It's four forty. Twenty minutes to go. So—game on! Let's crush this truck! Woo-hoo!"

Nicole pretended to shoot herself in the head, then quickly dropped her gun hand when Meredith turned toward her, on her way to the loading dock.

Her boots clattered like horseshoes on its metal surface.

By now, Milo was deep inside the truck. He'd worked his way through more than half the merchandise. Nicole had wheeled in additional sections of track to extend the line so that it reached the boxes in the back. At Meredith's approach, Milo began working faster, trying to replicate, or even improve on, his performance from earlier, when he'd been timing himself. He twisted, reached for the next box, pivoted, set the box on the line, swiveled back in a rapid but graceful, almost balletic motion. He wanted the boxes to come out in a continuous line, with no space between them.

Meredith watched him for a minute, then turned around and left the truck, without giving any indication she was impressed. On her way out, she approached Nicole, getting so close that Nicole could see the flakes of the pencil she had used to line her small eyes and smell the chemical whiff of her face powder. The only "beauty product" Nicole had used that morning was toothpaste.

Meredith thrust her hip toward Nicole's, tapping Nicole's khaki pants with her own, in a cross between a dance move and a lewd gesture of friendship. "Hi, love," she said. "How *are* you?"

When Meredith wasn't in one of her bad moods, Nicole's youth and good looks appealed to her. Nicole reminded her of herself when she was younger (albeit with better bone structure and worse grooming).

Nicole gave Meredith the smallest, coldest smile she could get away with, then turned to a large box—a mini fridge, for a college dorm room—rolling toward her. Nicole yawned as she scanned the fridge and nudged it to Travis. It had only traveled a few inches when Meredith bent forward and gave it a big, theatrical shove. "Boom chicka boom!" she called gaily.

She turned to Nicole. "See?" she said. "Just because a box is heavy doesn't mean it won't move fast. That's what the rollers are for. A little energy is all it takes."

She snapped her fingers twice, right up in Nicole's face.

Unable to slap Meredith's hand away, Nicole instead thought about quitting. But it wasn't exactly a good time. Her fiancé Marcus was currently between jobs, and her food stamp card hadn't refreshed at the beginning of the month like it was supposed to—in the past two days, she had tried it at three different grocery stores, to no avail. She had to go to Social Services right away—as in today—to get it fixed. Besides, where would she go? Town Square actually paid a bit better than most retailers.

Nicole scanned and pushed a stack of three chaise longues, held together by a plastic band. When they reached him, Travis lifted them over his head. Their weight made his body droop. His wiry torso formed the shape of a question mark as he ran the chairs to Bulk. When he returned, his face was shiny with sweat.

"You're working hard," Meredith said. "I like it!"

Travis smiled. It was a real, wide smile that briefly revealed his missing teeth and displaced his air of ironic detachment. It lasted only an instant. Then he closed his lips and looked at the ground. If Nicole hadn't been turned to him at that very second, she would have missed it entirely. But it was clear to her that Meredith's compliment pleased Travis. Nicole was surprised. Too-cool-for-school Travis didn't seem like he'd give a fuck.

Meredith walked over to Raymond. Leaning toward him so her nose was a few inches from his cheek, she inhaled deeply. She was trying to determine if he smelled of alcohol. Apparently she was satisfied that he did not, because she moved away, just as mini gas grills began coming down the line, dozens of them, entombed in their boxes.

Little Will had warned Diego they were coming—they were part of a display in Seasonal. Diego had set up a special pallet in anticipation.

Standing next to Diego, Meredith watched as he transferred the grills to the pallet. Under her hawklike stare, Diego felt his heart rate rise. Did she think he was going to steal one—slip it under his T-shirt? They weren't *that* mini.

Only after all the grills had been unloaded did Meredith turn to Val, who was hoisting a forty-pound bag of dog food over her shoulder.

The Pet pallet was crowded. Val dropped the bag on top of a large, plastic-covered dog bed. A rush of air farted from the mattress. Meredith's mouth formed a prim O of disapproval.

"Try to put the heaviest pieces on the bottom," she told Val. "It's more stable that way."

A few months earlier, Val had lost her temper in Big Will's office. She'd been written up as a result. Now, her cheeks—windows onto something, her mood, if not her soul—turned diaper-rash pink. But Val didn't tell Meredith that she was wrong. She didn't say anything at all. Meredith was sensitive about her ignorance of the warehouse—she wouldn't appreciate Val explaining that the line moved too fast to worry about arranging items perfectly. If you didn't want to miss any boxes, you threw everything on your pallet as quickly as possible and waited to organize the items until the line had stopped—which it did fairly frequently, when a box fell off or Nicole had to wheel more track to Milo.

Abruptly, Meredith began clapping a[gain].

"Come on, people!" she shouted. "I[t's not]. This isn't the time to start slacking. Do[n't get] your break soon enough."

Break was at six, more than an hou[r away].

Still, they began pushing faster.

Then an open-topped crate of pickles fell from the line. Gl[ass shat]tered against the concrete. The smell of brine rose through the warehouse. There was silence—the sound of ten people not saying "I told you so."

Even Milo knew that pushing too aggressively was counterproductive, causing bottlenecks and making boxes fall off the line. Milo worked fast to entertain himself; he knew the line would eventually get backed up and he'd have to wait for the rest of them to catch up. Meredith alone didn't get that the line naturally moved at the fastest sustainable pace. It was a pride thing. No one wanted the others to point to them as the person slowing everyone down. Even Nicole, who didn't like to look as if she were trying hard—it felt embarrassing—worked at the same pace as everyone else.

Little Will mopped up the pickle juice.

A small box filled with 2-ounce tubes of Astroglide personal lube rolled down the line. It was followed by a long procession of diapers: pull-ups, newborn-sized, organic, ones with Sesame Street characters, ones with princesses. One after another, they began rolling down the track. Milo had gone back to performance art. This was a concise morality play, about the outsized, years-long consequences of one small mistake.

Diapers were usually one of the first items loaded onto the truck at the distribution center, which meant they were among the last boxes to be unloaded. Their appearance generally signaled that the truck was nearly empty. Meredith perked up.

dn't realize that Milo had been performing. To render his eam of diapers, he had deliberately ignored many other boxes.

When Meredith peered into the truck, she saw how many boxes ere left. Her nose began to twitch. Like a rabbit on the scent of carrots, Raymond had said of her once. Like a rabbit on coke, Val had corrected. Meredith began to pace.

"Rabbit in distress," Val whispered to Diego after she walked past for the second or third time. He suppressed a laugh, but a croaking noise came out instead.

Meredith turned to him. On her face was the feral look she got right before she lashed out at someone. Diego felt a flash of anger toward Val for putting him in this position. He really didn't want to get written up. He needed his raise.

"*Really*, Diego?" Meredith began. "Really? You choose right now, when we're behind, to be disrespectful, that's just terrif—"

But a loud bang reverberated through the warehouse. It was Milo hitting the truck's side wall with the palm of his hand. Two more identical bangs followed. This was the signal that he had thrown the last box.

Only then did Diego's body unclench, his anger at Val recede.

Short and squat with red stripes on its sides—it contained books, from the publisher Penguin Random House—the last box seemed, in proportion to the number of eyes that turned to look at it, almost comically insignificant, like a limp penis overpowered by pubic hair.

The time was 4:59.

Meredith's face broke out into a wide, childlike smile.

Milo had said once that Meredith had a mind like an Etch A Sketch. With the equivalent of a shake, her moods changed, leaving no trace of what had been there before. (Even Nicole had chuckled at this. She allowed that Milo could be smart, funny even—when he was stoned. Weed lifted his thoughts from the mire of his self-involvement.)

Meredith turned to Nicole. Still smiling, she raised her hand to give

Nicole a high-five. Pretending not to see, Nicole immediately looked down at her scanner, began tapping furiously at its screen.

When Meredith realized she'd been left hanging, her face reddened. Her arm fell limply to her side.

A pale cone of green light from the device in Nicole's hands illuminated her pretty, wan, vitamin-starved face as she willed herself not to smile, at least not outwardly.

3

THE SALES FLOOR was dimly, almost romantically lit. Also quiet. The cleaners, Jesus and Maria, didn't arrive until six, and Plan-O, short for Plant Operations, not until seven. For now, Movement had the place to itself. Even with a thin, tinny stream of R&B playing from the speaker of her phone, Ruby—standing in the precise middle of the store, at the intersection where Women's, Baby, and Boys met—could hear the gentle whir of refrigerators all the way in Grocery.

Ruby was surrounded by ten blue Town Square shopping carts. Like spokes on a wheel, the carts pointed inward, with Ruby at the center. Next to her were several stacks of Softlines boxes. These had come off previous trucks. Ruby used the surface of an upturned box as a makeshift table on which to refold clothes that had gotten messed up in transit, then sorted the items by type into the carts arrayed around her.

She was folding a pale pink onesie when voices from the back of the store signaled that the people on the line had emerged from the warehouse. At the sound, Ruby reflexively smoothed her T-shirt and adjusted the rhinestone-studded reading glasses that were propped up on her head.

Ruby had once dreamed of being a singer or an actress. The blandness and masculinity of Town Square's requisite khakis and blue shirt depressed her. A nice scarf or cardigan or a playful accessory, like her glasses, went a long way toward dressing up the look.

"What?" Ruby asked when Nicole came shuffling down the corridor a moment later, looking pleased as could be.

But Nicole couldn't explain, not even to Ruby, who was her closest friend at the store. (Never mind that Ruby was forty-eight, the same age as Nicole's mom, and of a different race. Who cared? Nicole's fiancé Marcus was black too.) Still, if she told Ruby how happy leaving Meredith hanging had made her, she'd sound like she needed to get a life.

"I was just thinking about what a tool she is," Nicole said. There was no need to specify who "she" was.

Ruby wrinkled her forehead and puckered one side of her mouth, communicating both sympathy for Nicole and contempt for Meredith. Before she'd gone on vacation, Meredith had denied Ruby's request for a Saturday off to go visit her son, who was in prison in Coxsackie.

When she'd arrived, Ruby had set up a second cart circle for Nicole, next to her own. Now Nicole dragged several boxes to the center of her circle. Hers would be for adult clothes. Ruby liked doing kids'—baby especially—so Nicole, who didn't care, always took adult.

Nicole had barely started in on her first box when Meredith's loud and surprisingly unfeminine laugh broke out, from the rear corner of the store, somewhere near Electronics. But she was on the move—and coming closer. Seconds later, she rounded the corner from the central corridor.

"Hi, ladies!" she called. "Working hard? Good. Unfortunately, I can't stay and chat. I've been summoned by—well, I probably shouldn't say." She giggled, then continued toward the front of the store, only turning back to give them two thumbs-up.

Tool, Nicole thought.

Then she remembered the text on Little Will's phone. Big Will had said he would tell Little Will and Meredith his news after the unload. While they worked, Nicole told Ruby about the text.

Meanwhile, the store grew gradually brighter. Outside, the sun had risen—light filtered in through the store's wide glass customer entrance, bouncing off its white floors and glossy shelving units, reaching them even here, in the middle of the store. After a while, the store's loudspeaker crackled to life. Static filled the sales floor. Then the store manager began speaking. "Morning, Movement." Big Will's voice was smooth and sonorous, like a professional DJ's. "I've got an announcement to make. Can you all do me a big favor and set aside what you're doing for a bit? I'd like you all to come to the break room. Thanks, guys."

His tone was so lazily confident, almost self-satisfied, that you could picture him punctuating his words with a wink.

Nicole glanced at Ruby. "I told you."

Then she tilted her head to see over Ruby's shoulder. "Here come Tweedledee and Tweedledum."

Milo and Raymond were walking toward them, from Toys. Milo was so tall and skinny that, at his side, Raymond looked even shorter and runtier than usual, like a small dog, nipping at the heels of a bigger one.

Ruby and Nicole joined them.

A self-locking door separated the sales floor from the employee area. Milo tapped the four-digit code—2003, the year store #1512 had opened—into the keypad. They entered a set of rooms constructed on a different scale than the store itself, as if for a more diminutive and light-averse species. High ceilings and shiny white surfaces were replaced by a narrow, warren-like hallway with scuffed beige walls and gray linoleum tile. Past Big Will's office and the reception area, where the time clocks hung, was the break room: a large, windowless, bunker-like space bisected by an accordion curtain.

Big Will stood at the front of the room next to a wall-mounted flat-screen TV. Dressed in crisp khakis and a well-pressed light blue polo shirt, with just a bit of product smoothing his dark, wavy hair, he looked like a teen idol turned awards show emcee.

"Hi, Milo. Hey, Raymond. You look nice, Ruby. I like your glasses." Big Will pointed to the top of his head, to indicate that he meant the pair Ruby had pushed up on her head and not some other, absent pair.

From his coloring, Big Will could have been an Italian or a Jew, but Will was actually short for Guillermo. He was Hispanic. His diffuse, nonthreatening air of diversity, combined with his good looks and his youth—Big Will was twenty-nine—coincided exactly with corporate's Platonic ideal of a store manager. For several years running, they'd included a photo of him in their annual report. Last year, he was shown smiling kindly as he helped a disabled veteran in a wheelchair retrieve a roll of paper towels from an upper shelf. The year before that, he was standing on a ladder in Seasonal, looking cheerful but respectful as he fastened a cardboard menorah to the top of a Hanukkah display.

"What's up, Will?" Ruby asked. "We all getting raises or what?"

Big Will's smile grew even wider, to show that he didn't in the least resent her joke, as he simultaneously tilted his head and lifted his eyebrows in a manner that suggested regret. "I wish, Ruby," he said. "I wish."

That he was convincing—that you believed, in the moment, that he did in fact feel aggrieved on their account—was part of what made Big Will a popular manager. They all knew that he was unlikely to go to bat for them against corporate on anything that really mattered. They liked him anyway. He was like the guy in the teen movie who drives the fancy red sports car and wears mirrored sunglasses and gets all the girls.

When he leveled his charm in your direction, he was hard to resist, and whatever else might be said of him, Big Will made a point of chatting up everyone, even Jesus and Maria, who, technically, weren't even on the payroll. (They were subcontractors, hired by a third-party cleaning firm less particular about workers' immigration status than the Town Square Corp.—TSC on the New York Stock Exchange.)

In the corner of the break room, Nicole began filling the coffeepot. One of the perks of being in Movement was free coffee. No other department got it. Town Square even provided milk and sugar, requisitioned from Grocery. Nicole almost always made the coffee. That it tasted better when she did was one of the few things everyone in Movement agreed on.

The last members of Movement filed in and took seats at the tables scattered throughout the room. Big Will looked around. The diversity of race, gender, and ethnicity in the faces before him would have filled the headmaster of an elite private school with envy.

"Thanks for coming, guys," Big Will said, his bleached white teeth glinting under the fluorescent lights. "There's a reason I called you all in. As some of you know, I'm from Connecticut. My family is still there. So is my fiancée."

"You finally getting married, Will?" Val broke in. "Going to start making babies?"

Ever since Val and her wife had a baby a few months earlier, Val had become very vocally pro-procreation.

"Don't wait too long," Joyce chimed in.

Big Will touched the carefully trimmed mustache he grew for gravitas, to make himself look less like the UConn student he so recently had been.

"Maybe soon, ladies," he said. "Maybe soon. But that's not why I asked you all to come in. We've got some store business that's even more pressing than my personal life, if you can believe it." At this, a few people tittered, a testament to Big Will's charisma rather than to the inherent humor of his remark. "What I called you in to tell you," he continued, "is that I've asked for—and been given—a transfer to the West Hartford store, to be its new store manager. I'm moving to Connecticut!"

More than one person gasped.

Big Will was part of the store. He seemed to imbue the place with something of himself—his good looks, his glamour—making store #1512 better than other Town Square stores with normal, middle-aged managers of middling (or lower) levels of attractiveness and charm.

Val recovered first. "Congrats!" she yelled. Others began to clap and whoop.

They all knew that the transfer was a promotion.

Potterstown had yet to recover from the departure of IBM, once its largest employer. These days, Potterstown was as much museum as city, its past glory evident less in its people—many of whom walked around with something of a shell-shocked look, as if modernity itself had caught them unawares—than in the fine old buildings that had outlived the purposes for which they'd been built. The domed, neoclassical former Potterstown National Bank, for example, was now a struggling coffee shop. A former shirt factory housed an organic bakery called Kneads that was, like the coffee shop, geared toward part-timers from New York. For most of its full-time residents, Potterstown's center of gravity had moved from downtown to the surrounding ring of strip malls, in which liquor stores, kidney dialysis centers, dollar stores, cigarette discounters, and military recruitment offices flourished. If it weren't for the influx of city people each summer, Potterstown would be in far worse straits, like so many of the truly depressed towns farther upstate—towns that didn't even have a Walmart, let alone a Town Square; even with the city people, store #1512 was a low-volume store, a training store, where corporate sent new managers to cut their teeth. The highest-grossing and most profitable stores—the ones they sent their best managers to—were located in places whose fortunes had risen in recent years in inverse proportion to the nation's Potterstowns. Affluent suburbs, places like Westchester County and northern New Jersey. And Connecticut. West Hartford was the big time.

"Thanks, guys," Big Will said when the clapping died down. He leaned forward and began speaking in a lower voice. "By the way, no one else knows yet. I came in early because I wanted to tell you guys first."

This elicited smiles.

That Big Will thought to flatter them by not only telling them first but telling them that he was telling them first was typical of his instinct for popularity (a perennial source of resentment among the people of Movement was that, because they were excluded from the Huddle—a daily meeting of front-of-the-store workers that took place after their shift ended—they were last to find out store news). It didn't matter that Big Will wasn't, technically, telling the truth. Until a few hours ago, he'd planned to come in at his regular time and announce his departure at the Huddle. But he'd woken up just after three, his mind racing with move- and transfer-related tasks. When he realized he wasn't going to fall back asleep, he decided he might as well get a jump on the day when the store was quiet and he was unlikely to be interrupted. Only when he was in the shower had he gotten the idea to call Movement in right away.

"I wanted you guys to know that you're important to me," he said. His expression turned somber, like that of a television news reporter interviewing a hurricane victim. He leaned one arm on an old, broken foosball table, the sole remnant of an initiative, briefly taken up in the dot-com era, to make work fun. "I'm going to miss you, each and every one of you," he said, panning the room with his eyes.

Then—as if the news program had switched over to a feel-good story about a heroic local dog or a kid whose lemonade stand raised enough money to fund his cancer treatment—his face became cheerful again. "You're probably wondering who's going to take over here as store manager."

They were not. At least Nicole wasn't. She couldn't speak for anyone else, but she had been too busy processing the fact that Big Will was leaving to wonder who would take his place. Now she noticed that while Big Will had been talking, Little Will and Meredith had entered the room. Standing by the door, Meredith was rocking her weight from one bootie-clad foot to the other while making weird, fishlike, puckering movements with her lips.

She was, Nicole realized, trying to keep from smiling.

"Nothing is official yet," Big Will continued, "but corporate wants to go with an internal candidate, someone who is already at the store. An executive manager."

Nicole felt a sudden chill.

"Multiple candidates are being considered," Big Will went on, "and you can probably guess who they—" He abruptly stopped speaking and turned to Meredith. She'd started to cough, to cover the grin that had momentarily flashed on her face. "You okay, Mer?" he asked, a hint of disapproval in his narrowed eyes.

Meredith colored. "I'm fine," she said. She smiled tightly. "Allergy season."

Of course Meredith was thrilled, Nicole thought. Starting pay for store managers was $110K.

A few weeks ago, in one of her friendly moods, Meredith had told Nicole that her "life goal" was to make six figures before she turned forty in three years. "What's yours?" she had asked Nicole, as if they'd agreed to exchange confidences. Not to punch you in the face, Nicole had wanted to say. She wasn't about to tell Meredith how much she wanted a car of her own, so she didn't have to borrow the Dingmobile, a.k.a. her mom's minivan. What right did Meredith have to know her business?

Now Nicole turned to Little Will, hoping to find some kind of sign that she was misreading the situation, that what she thought was happening wasn't actually.

What she saw was not reassuring. The expression on his face was pinched, almost pained, as if he were in the before part of a pharmaceutical commercial, with a camera training in on his face while a disembodied voice asked, "Are you clinically depressed? Effervesa can help."

Fuck, Nicole thought. *Fuck, fuck, fuck.*

"Corporate is going to do this a little differently than usual," Big Will went on. "Since we're already stretched thin, they're going to act quickly. A committee is coming in early next week to evaluate the state of the store, see how we're doing. They're also going to decide who to put in place as store manager. But here's the thing. They want to talk to you guys individually, to hear what you think. They want to make sure that you're all behind their choice. After all, it's your store too."

Big Will flashed a meaningful grin, as he usually did after uttering a platitude.

He asked if anyone had questions. Nicole eyed the coffeepot—which by now was hissing and sputtering wildly, like a small animal trying to scare off a larger predator—while the people who always asked questions, the ones who thought not having a question would be a humiliating acknowledgment of their own cosmic insignificance and eventual nonexistence, raised their hands.

Joyce asked how corporate would go about "finding out what we think." As she spoke, she made quote marks with her hands, to suggest this was an inherently dubious undertaking.

A white woman in her late fifties, Joyce was the kind of person who, no matter where in America she lived, would be described as a local: she wore (when not at work) starched jeans (never sweatpants) and spotless, unfaded sweatshirts, with a turtleneck underneath in the winter; her shoulder-length brown hair was only lightly teased—her bangs were not sprayed into gravity-defying wings but fell straight over her forehead.

"Interviews," Big Will told her now. "The team from corporate will schedule confidential, one-on-one interviews with each of you, and before you jump in, Val"—Big Will saw that Val was dying to interrupt—"the answer is yes. You will be paid for the time you're being interviewed." Everyone—including Val herself—laughed at Big Will's ability to anticipate her objection.

"And the interviews will decide who's promoted?" Val asked.

"They'll be a factor. A major factor."

Ruby—whose question-asking proclivities Nicole only overlooked on the grounds that Ruby was her good friend—wanted to know if they were talking to everyone at the store: "All hundred and fifty employees?"

"Good question, Ruby," Big Will said. "They're only talking individually to the members of select departments, people with the most insight into the executive managers being considered."

"So if they're talking to us," Ruby said, "they must be considering—"

"I see what you're getting at," Big Will broke in, stopping Ruby so gracefully, and with such a conspiratorial smile, that Ruby felt more like she'd been complimented on her quickness than cut off. "For the sake of discretion, I'm not going to say more at the moment. We want to respect the candidates' privacy."

Nicole almost snorted. Meredith was no longer even trying to hide her glee—she was grinning like she'd just been given an Academy Award. But maybe Meredith was getting ahead of herself. Nicole thought about what Big Will had said about the interviews, about how corporate wanted to know what they thought. It sounded like Meredith's promotion wasn't exactly a done deal.

By now, the smell of fresh coffee filled the room. "I guess it's about time you guys took your break," Big Will said.

That was all they needed. Chair legs scraped against linoleum tile as the members of Movement beelined for the coffeemaker.

As he watched them, Big Will felt a twinge of guilt. A week earlier, he'd gotten an email from corporate, marked "confidential (for store managers only)," about an analysis corporate had commissioned on the feasibility of automating much of Movement's workload.

From his perch at the front of the room, Big Will smiled uneasily. He didn't like the thought of people losing their jobs. But then corporate was always commissioning reports and analyses. Most came to nothing. This one probably would too.

4

OUTSIDE THE EMPLOYEE DOOR, two blue benches faced the parking lot. The smokers—Nicole, Ruby, Milo, Raymond, Travis, Val, and Diego—gathered in front of them.

Nicole pulled a hand-rolled cigarette from the silver case Marcus had given her for Christmas. Without turning her head, she took the light Travis offered. Her gaze was directed elsewhere.

Store #1512 was situated on the top of a large foothill, directly facing the Catskills. The wide, open view from its parking lot regularly made city people sigh with delight. When Nicole had arrived for work a few hours earlier, the mountains had been shrouded in darkness—only the illuminated blue block letters spelling out Town Square on the building's exterior had been visible. Now, in the light of the new morning, the jagged range glimmered green-gold against a crisp, almost lucent blue sky.

Nicole turned to the others. "Well," she said as a plume of smoke rushed out between her lips. "Meredith thinks she's going to be promoted. It's actually funny when you think about it. All I can say is, don't count your chickens. I can't wait until my interview. I'm going to sink her."

"Do you really think you'll be able to stop this?" Raymond looked skeptical. "I don't know. Did you guys see how miserable Little Will looked in there? I've got a bad feeling about this."

Raymond's eye started to twitch. He had a congenital condition that prevented his left eye from opening all the way and made it appear hazy. When he was anxious, it also blinked frantically.

"Big Will won't let them make her store manager," Ruby assured Raymond. "He ain't stupid."

Diego turned to Ruby. "Woman. You heard Big Will. He practically said right out that she was going to get the job."

"They'll promote her, all right," Milo agreed. "I don't doubt it for a second. Every manager who gets promoted at this store has exactly one thing in common. It's not competence, it's not intelligence. Nope, what they have in common is that they hate me. Meredith has that going for her, so yeah, they'll give her the job."

Milo laughed.

When people first met Milo, they assumed he had a good sense of humor because he laughed loudly and often. It took a while before they realized he mostly laughed at his own jokes, and even longer before they realized that many of these weren't actually jokes at all but appeals for pity he tried to pass off as humor.

"Have you guys—" Raymond started to ask at the same moment as Nicole began, "If they—"

Raymond ceded the floor to Nicole.

"—*do* promote her," she continued, "I'm quitting. No fucking way I'm going to stay here if she's store manager."

Never mind about her food stamp card or Marcus being between jobs or that she'd been at Town Square for three years, longer than any other job she'd had. Never mind that her current bank balance was less than thirty dollars or that her mother—from whom she was going to have to borrow cash if she couldn't get her card fixed—would tell her it was irresponsible to quit without having another job lined up. Didn't matter. Nicole simply couldn't work at a store that Meredith was in charge of, and that was that.

"Right?" Nicole looked at the others.

No one spoke. Or even met her eye. Suddenly they were all entirely absorbed in their cigarettes and their coffee.

"I would have to think about it some more," Ruby said finally.

"What were you going to say?" Val asked Raymond. "A minute ago?"

"What?" Raymond asked, scratching his cheek. "Oh. Yeah. Did you guys see how she got up in my face and sniffed my breath? Again? It's bullshit—I came in smelling like booze *one* time, the day after my birthday, and she acts like I'm an alcoholic."

Diego made a face. "You are."

As if Diego was one to talk. Raymond gave Diego the finger.

Nicole grinned. "Hold on," she said. "Everyone knows Meredith doesn't like Diego—she's always acting like he's going to steal something, right? And she doesn't like Raymond *Santos*. Maybe she's prejudiced. Maybe she doesn't like *people of color*."

They all snickered.

The joke was at Raymond's expense. Although his father was Filipino, Raymond didn't look Asian. His hair was dark—at least it had been before he started going prematurely gray—but his skin was more sallow than brown. The others liked to accuse him of only claiming to be a minority to get affirmative action. "The only way you could get Town Square to hire your sorry ass," according to Diego, who, being both black *and* Hispanic himself, felt he should know.

Raymond laughed too. Nicole sometimes wondered if it was because of his eye condition that Raymond was so easygoing—that and being short. Perhaps, growing up, he'd just gotten used to being ragged on. Nicole wouldn't have been so tolerant in his place.

"It's not that," said Milo irritably. (Jokes by people other than himself tended to grate on his nerves.) "Meredith ignores me, and I'm as white as can be." He held up his arm, as if the others might not have noticed his skin color before now. "She doesn't even say hello to me. It's as if I'm not even a person to her, as if the truck just throws itself."

At this, Milo laughed.

Nicole sighed. Her cigarette had gone out. She rolled her own because loose tobacco was cheaper, but they weren't as smooth as regular ones and didn't stay lit as well.

She nodded at Travis's lighter. He handed it to her, then went back to squinting into the distance.

He was looking beyond the parking lot, toward Potterstown—or rather at the lush, green valley into which it was tucked, rendering it nearly invisible from here on the hill. If he held his head just so, Travis saw almost nothing but trees. Aside from a tall, spidery water tower, its rusted cylinder glowing burnt ochre in the early-morning sunlight, and the hulking façade of a Hampton Inn rising monumentally from the greenery, like Sleeping Beauty's castle from the brambles, you'd never know there was an entire city between where they stood and the mountains spread along the horizon.

Travis never joined in when the others complained about Meredith.

"Guys," said Val. *"Guys."*

Val's sandy brown hair was razor cut on the sides but several inches longer on top. When the others turned to her, she pushed the longer hair from the top of her head straight back so it looked slicked down, as if she were an old-timey salesman. This made her wide, pink cheeks look even wider. Val was a funny combination of childish and practical, a daydreamer, but also the kind of person who'd be good at evacuating people during a mass casualty event.

"What if we're thinking about this all wrong?" she said now. "What if we should *want* Meredith to get promoted? What if—"

"What you smoking, girl?" Diego said.

Val ignored him. "Remember when Brian left?" Brian was the executive manager for Logistics before Meredith. "Before Meredith put in for this job, no one else wanted it. No one who was eligible. Corporate was going to make an exemption for Little Will, give him executive manager for Logistics, even though he didn't have a college degree. When she put in for the job out of the blue, Meredith messed that up for him."

The others had heard this—from Val.

Val liked to hang around outside Big Will's office, ostensibly reading the flyers hanging on the bulletin board in the hall, which told of things like an upcoming seventy-cent increase in the state minimum wage and the company's support for employees who wanted the day off to attend the Pride March in New York City. ("Are they also going to pay for my gas and tolls to get down there?" Val had asked Big Will the day that particular flyer was posted. He'd chuckled. "Don't ever change, Val," he said. "Remind me again, what is it you call milk?" Val grinned proudly. "Cow-titty juice," she said. Val had grown up on a farm. The wailing of mother pigs whose babies had been taken away turned her vegetarian at eleven; at fourteen, the moans of cows made to lactate constantly turned her full vegan.) But the truth was Val learned a lot from hanging out by the bulletin board. Big Will liked to keep his office door open as much as possible. Often he failed to close it even when he was on the phone, discussing store business with his boss Ryan, the district manager. Val had excellent hearing—which she attributed to her plant-based diet.

"If Meredith were promoted to store manager," she said to the others now, "there'd be no one standing in Little Will's way. He could have her job. Can you imagine how much better our lives would be if Little Will were executive manager of Logistics, if he were our boss—our real boss? Not Meredith's lackey but fully in charge?"

The others looked skeptical. They all liked Little Will as much as any boss they'd ever had—well, all of them except for Milo, who had his own issues. Still. That didn't mean they liked him enough to want Meredith to be promoted for his sake.

"Sure," Raymond said. "Having Little Will as our actual boss would be good. I'll admit that. But good enough? To make up for Meredith being store manager?"

"Hell no," Nicole said.

Val began gesticulating with her arms. "How much difference does it even make to us who the store manager is day-to-day?" she asked. "We deal a lot more with our group manager and the executive manager of Logistics. Think about it. Until today, when's the last time Big Will came in before seven thirty? Most days, we see him on our way out the door, if we see him at all. Now, think about that—what if we barely saw Meredith?"

Val could see from their faces that her words were starting to have an effect. She grinned. "Uh-huh," said, nodding. "Now you're getting it."

But Ruby waved a finger in the air.

"Hold up a minute," she said. "What about a few weeks ago when I wanted to go up and visit my son and Meredith said I couldn't have the day off because I didn't request it in time? I went to Big Will. Remember? I explained to him how my sister only just offered to give me a ride to Coxsackie. He said, 'Yeah, Ruby, I get it. Don't worry. You go see your son. I'll talk to Meredith.' And he did—he put it right."

Ruby didn't mention that she still hadn't gotten to see her son. That had nothing to do with Meredith. Her son had an odd BIN number.

It turned out that only prisoners with even BIN numbers could have visitors that day. Ruby hadn't realized until the evening before her sister was scheduled to drive her.

Ruby turned from Val to the others, as if addressing them rather than Val. "What would have happened if Meredith had been the big boss? If we didn't have someone over her that we could go to?"

Like spectators at a tennis match, the others looked back at Val.

"If Little Will were our executive manager, you wouldn't have needed to go over his head," Val said. "Little Will would never have put you in that position."

Ruby touched the gold scrunchie that held her hair in a stubby bun at the back of her head. "Huh," she said. "I see what you mean."

"Wait," Travis said.

Travis so rarely joined their conversations during break that the others turned to him in surprise.

His expression was focused, as if he were adding up a long column of numbers in his head. "If Little Will were promoted," he said slowly, "they'd have to promote someone to take *his* job, right? To be our group manager? Who would that be?"

Val had been waiting for someone to pick up on this.

"That's right," she said. "If Meredith gets promoted, so does Little Will. And voilà, his job opens up. As far as who gets it, it could be anyone—any one of us." At this, someone—Nicole couldn't tell who—drew in their breath audibly. "It would definitely go to one of us," Val continued. "Group manager of Movement always goes to someone already in Movement."

Now this, they all felt, was something. A big something.

Hourly pay for group managers was only several dollars per hour higher than that of rank-and-file workers—a fact corporate liked to point out to the media, to demonstrate its "egalitarian" ethos—but group managers wound up making about $40K a year. In contrast, rank-and-file workers made between $10K and $25K. The difference was in the number of hours group managers worked. Managers were guaranteed forty hours a week, whereas rank-and-file workers might get as little as a single four-hour shift a week during the slow, winter season. Plus, managers were guaranteed benefits—health insurance, 401(k), paid vacation, sick days—that rank-and-file workers were eligible for only if they worked more than twenty-five hours a week for a full year—which sounded fair enough until you realized that corporate gamed the system. Some people consistently worked close to forty hours a week during the summer, then saw their hours cut sharply in the final months of the year, bringing their average for the year to just under twenty-five. As Milo had pointed out last year, the company clearly did it on purpose because at the same time as it was cutting regular workers' hours, it hired additional temporary workers for the holidays.

What would it be like to have a predictable income? Nicole wondered now. One large enough so that her bank balance didn't fall precipitously close to zero between paychecks? If a problem with her food stamp card didn't send her into a panic about how she and Marcus were going to feed their daughter until payday?

And Nicole was lucky. Unlike a lot of people, she could ask her mom for help if she had to. Her mom would grumble, but she'd lend her forty bucks for groceries. Still, Nicole hated asking. Her mom loved to point out that when she was Nicole's age, *she* was married, not just engaged, and had two kids *and* a car of her own *and* a house. *She* hadn't needed—or gotten—help from anyone. But—as Nicole tried to point out—her mom grew up in a different time. Potterstown had been different. She had made good money assembling keyboards for a company that sold to IBM. When IBM shut its Potterstown location—as well as most others in the state—the company her mom worked for moved to Mexico, but by then she and Nicole's dad had already bought their house. They owned two cars. Yet when Nicole pointed out that things were different now, her mom looked at her as if she were failing to "take responsibility."

But what if her mother was right? Nicole thought. What if she had failed until now to make her own opportunities, or whatever? And what if *this* was her chance?

She thought again of her last performance review—of what Big Will had said, about her intelligence. That had to mean something. And if she did get the job, it would change everything. She could get a car, get married, become fully independent, be a real adult just like her mom at her age.

Nicole's hopes usually revolved around far more modest possibilities, things like picking up an extra shift, making an extra forty or fifty dollars. She began to feel almost dizzy with possibility.

Then she remembered the second part of what Big Will had said at that performance review.

After he told her that she was smarter than she realized, he said that she didn't "work to her full potential"—that there was room for her to "grow." She should focus on "showing more initiative," whatever the fuck that meant when your job is to scan and unpack boxes.

With that thought, Nicole was back in reality. She wouldn't get promoted. Big Will and the other managers didn't see her that way. They'd give group manager to someone like Val, who put on such a big show of taking the job seriously. Or else they'd give it to Diego, who had a way about him, an air of competence and authority that people responded to.

Nicole looked around. The others were gazing dreamily, still absorbed in their own stupid fantasies of promotion.

"You're all crazy," she said. "C-R-A-Z-Y, crazy if you think we should help that beyotch get promoted."

Surprised by Nicole's tone, Val whipped her head to face her. "How else are we going to get her off our backs?" she asked. "Do you have a better idea? Other than quitting?"

Nicole put her hands on her hips. "How about we tell the truth about what she's like, how incompetent she is? Maybe they'll do something—like *fire* her."

Val sighed. "They won't fire her. You know that."

It was true. After Meredith had gone after Nicole, Raymond had gone to Big Will, told him about the way Meredith had called her slow and imitated Nicole by standing with her mouth open and an expression that suggested Nicole was retarded. "Intellectually disabled," Big Will had said quickly, instinctively looking around to make sure no one was near enough to hear. "That's the term now." But he'd agreed with Raymond that Meredith had behaved badly. He said he'd talk to her. Only nothing changed—except that since then Meredith seemed to dislike Raymond even more than she had before. Raymond said that was why she'd started sniffing him, although Nicole didn't buy that part. He really had reeked the day after his birthday.

"Just because it didn't work that one time doesn't mean we can't try again," Nicole said. "If we all went to Big Will—"

"It won't work," Val cut in. "Corporate paid for Meredith to go to college through its tuition assistance program. They spent a lot of money on her. They aren't going to fire her just because some roaches didn't like her."

"Roaches" was what other employees called the people who worked Movement, because they descended on the store in the dark of night, then scattered at eight, when the customers arrived.

"Fine," Nicole conceded. "But what if Meredith does get promoted, and they give Meredith's job to someone else and Little Will stays group manager?" Nicole looked at Val accusingly. "Then all you've done is help her get store manager. Did you even think about that?"

Val shook her head pityingly, as if Nicole really were "intellectually disabled."

"You have to read between the lines," she said. "Big Will said they want to act fast. They aren't going to have time to bring on someone from a whole different store to take over Logistics. And who, among our executive managers, would want Meredith's job? Remember, a lot of people don't want to work in the warehouse and they don't want Movement's hours. Except for Meredith, no one internal wanted it a few months ago. What's changed? No one new has come in."

Nicole had no answer. For her, it was instinctual, moral. Meredith didn't deserve to be rewarded. She deserved to be punished.

While Nicole was silent, Val turned back to the others. "The real worry," she said, "is that they'll promote Anita to store manager instead of Meredith. She's the competition."

Anita was the store's executive manager for Softlines Sales. She was one of those competent, professional, and not particularly charismatic managers whose primary passion was for covering her own ass. But she didn't alienate people the way Meredith did, and she basically got the job done the way corporate wanted it to be done, to the extent that that was possible, given that corporate was erratic, unpredictable, and didn't give managers enough money to fully enact most of its plans. She also had several more years at the executive manager level than Meredith.

"Anita is the only other likely candidate among the current executive managers," Val continued. "*That's* what we have to prevent, Anita getting the job. Otherwise we'll be stuck with Meredith for *years*."

Someone actually gasped. They all realized how disappointing such an outcome—the continuation of the status quo—would be. That was how far they'd come already.

"I feel like my head is going to explode," Raymond said. "I mean, it seems crazy to want Meredith to get promoted. But I hear what you're saying, Val. I do."

Diego looked at Raymond curiously. Diego might rag on Raymond, but he had once told Nicole that Raymond had good judgment, said he was smart about people, good at predicting what they would do and at anticipating outcomes. Nicole had been semi blown away by this. She'd never thought about Raymond in anything like those terms. To her, Raymond was marginally less annoying than Milo, but he was still just short, loserish Raymond, with his unattractive facial hair and unfortunate eye condition. A dork, in other words.

"What does it even matter what we think?" Ruby asked. "In the end, they'll do what they want to do. They always do. It won't have anything to do with what we want. I know."

Ruby had been working service jobs since she was sixteen, more than thirty years.

Val suppressed a sigh of impatience. "You heard Big Will," she said. "They're coming here. They're going to interview us. They'll ask us about Meredith as a manager. Do you think they want to give store manager to a person everyone hates when they could give it to Anita, who no one loves but no one hates either? We can either tell them the truth—that Meredith sucks donkey dick—and basically force them to give the job to Anita. Or we can keep our mouths shut."

"Or tell them that Meredith is really smart and good at her job and a pleasure to work with," Raymond said, grinning.

Even Milo laughed at this. Everybody did, except Nicole, who stamped out her cigarette. It was just about time to go inside.

Val seemed oblivious to the time. "The thing is, though, Raymond's right," she said. "If we really want to do this, that's exactly what we should say. So—" Val looked around. "Who's in?"

Raymond nodded. So did Milo. Even Travis shrugged some sort of assent. Val turned to Nicole.

Nicole made a face. "Not me. No fucking way."

"Suit yourself."

Val turned to Diego.

He nodded. "You convinced me, V."

Val grinned. "Ruby?"

Ruby glanced apologetically at Nicole. Then she turned to Val. "I'm willing to give it a try."

Val's smile became radiant.

Nicole turned on her heel. She was halfway back to the store when, with her back still turned to the others, she raised her right hand above her head and gave them the finger. "Fuck you all," she called.

5

THE MINI GAS GRILLS that Diego had set aside during the unload were for a display in Seasonal. Val spent the hour and forty-five minutes that remained on the shift after break assembling the display, the centerpiece of which was a person-sized cardboard cutout of a hot dog, complete with arms and legs and wearing a pair of oversized sunglasses.

As she slotted pieces of cardboard together, Val began to hum. She couldn't believe what had just happened.

Val had wanted to be group manager of Movement forever, for as long as she had been working here. It was quite possibly her dream job—if you didn't count stupid childhood fantasies like rock star or astronaut. She was an active person, perhaps even (according to her mother and several elementary school teachers) a hyperactive one. She liked being physical, working with her hands, being part of a team. She wouldn't be happy sitting at a desk all day in an office—which in Potterstown these days generally meant the call center at UnitedHealthcare. (Val knew all about it—her wife Liz worked there.) Val also liked being in charge. And she knew she was good at it—

decisive but fair, capable of listening to others and changing her mind when necessary.

She might once have had other aspirations, but her life had taken a decisive turn when she was seventeen. She had run away from home. For a while, she'd lived in her car. Even after she'd gotten on her feet—found a job, a place to live—she had struggled. For years, she had been both depressed and wild, self-destructive. It wasn't until Val met Liz in her mid-twenties that everything changed. In the past five years, Val had gotten married, gotten her GED, had a baby. She'd reconciled with her grandmother—now she and Liz took care of her and lived in her house. Val even saw her mom sometimes—without her dad's knowledge. He was the reason she'd left home in the first place. He was the kind of person who'd get drunk with his buddies and go out to the coop and shoot his own chickens. For fun. He also didn't like gay people.

In many ways, Val was happier now than she'd ever imagined being. There was just this one thing that gnawed at her, especially in the past year, as her thirtieth birthday approached. She yearned for professional recognition, some kind of acknowledgment that she was a valued member of society, a person with something to offer, not just a deadbeat who worked an entry-level job at a big-box store, the kind of person who was the butt of jokes on late-night TV shows.

She wasn't a snob. She knew firsthand how many smart, hardworking people were prevented by circumstances outside their control from achieving what they were capable of. Still. The fact that she was still just a rank-and-file employee bothered her. It affected so many parts of her life. Since their son was born, Liz had been on her about making friends. Liz had long wanted them to have more lesbian friends, but now she also wanted mom friends or even—the holy grail—dyke mom friends. Val usually pooh-poohed this—"We have each other; what more do we need?" she'd say—but on some level she knew there was truth to what Liz had long insisted: that Val's aversion to making friends stemmed from the shame she felt about her job, her fear of being judged.

At her last performance review, Big Will had told her that she had the skills and experience to be promoted—he'd pretty much promised that the next "suitable" management position would be hers. Val had been ecstatic. The money would enable her and Liz to give their son so much: books, toys, good food, high-quality child care so he wasn't always stuck in the house with Val's grandma playing talk shows and *The People's Court* at top volume. Val and Liz wouldn't have to work opposing shifts in order for one of them to be home with him.

As group manager, Val could also, if she wanted, do what Meredith had done: use Town Square's tuition assistance program (once available to all employees, now limited to managers only) to get her degree. Maybe astronaut wasn't out of the question—or at least some kind of engineer. *Maybe.* Val liked to think she was smart, but she didn't really know if she could hack college. Before she'd dropped out of high school, her academic performance had been uneven. But even if she didn't go back to school, she'd have options. Other employers would look at her differently because she'd proven herself at Town Square; she would be eligible for a whole other category of job. On another level, getting the job she'd long wanted, while being married to the woman she loved with a child of her own, would be hugely symbolic—it would mean that she'd successfully corrected course, come full circle, that her father hadn't had the power to permanently mess up her life.

But after the performance review, weeks had gone by. Then months. Nothing happened. Eventually Val came to understand. Store #1512 had 150 employees, only fourteen of whom were group managers. Of those, only three had positions that were what Big Will would consider "suitable" for Val, i.e., based in the warehouse: group manager of Movement and two group manager positions in Plan-O, a larger department that, among other things, shared responsibility with Movement for setting up displays and oversaw the warehouse during the day, after Movement left. But group managers—from any department—rarely left. Where would they go? This was Potterstown. Full-time jobs with benefits were in short supply.

The more time passed, the more Val realized that she was no better off than she'd been before Big Will had said what he had. In a way, she was actually worse off. Before, she felt that she had some control—that if she kicked ass, worked as hard as she could, she'd get promoted. Now she knew that the thing she wanted most was out of her hands, entirely dependent on circumstances that had nothing to do with her.

That's where things had stood until this morning. Big Will's announcement changed everything, brought all the hopes she had nurtured after the performance review back to life.

As Val slotted the hot dog's body into the base, she began to sing, belting out *"Ch-ch-ch-changes!"*

Jesus and Maria, the cleaners, were pushing their cart of supplies down the corridor. They looked at her curiously. Val realized she should play it cool. She hadn't told the others what Big Will had said at her performance review. At the time, she hadn't told them because she wasn't an asshole—she hadn't wanted to brag. But now she couldn't tell them.

She turned back to the hot dog.

Seasonal was all the way in the rear corner of the store, as far from the main entrance as any place on the sales floor. From here, you could barely tell it was light outside. But Val knew it was after seven because the first group of Plan-O people were on the sales floor. Like the sound of crickets on a summer night, the dull *beep-beep-beep* of their scanners as they searched for items corporate had designated as "clearance" came from everywhere and nowhere.

Per corporate's instructions, the hot dog was to be placed on a pedestal of mini gas grills. While she walked to the warehouse to get the grills, the keys on her key ring—a large carabiner she attached to her belt loop—jangled. Liz had once described Val's style as "janitor chic." She'd been joking about the "chic" part.

Val passed Men's. She noticed that the metal racks that held socks—or should hold them—were practically empty.

She sighed. It was Meredith's fault the section was in such bad shape. The socks that should be here were still in the warehouse, waiting to be unpacked. Convincing corporate that Meredith was store-manager material was not going to be easy. Val would have to think hard, anticipate what corporate would look for. At least the others were—mostly—on board. She would have to keep them focused, committed. She needed to strategize.

It was 7:45 when she returned to Seasonal with the grills. Only fifteen minutes left on the shift to arrange the grills in a pyramid. If she left this last component unfinished, someone from Plan-O would do it, then take all the credit, as if they had built the whole display.

As she stacked grills, something occurred to Val, something terrible: What if Big Will had changed his mind about promoting her? Because of the "incident"—that's what Big Will always called it—in his office (which had, as a matter of fact, been triggered by this very issue, her belief that Plan-O people were taking credit for her work). At the time, Val had been feeling so low, so hopeless about ever getting promoted, that she'd snapped. She yelled at Big Will and Svetlana from HR, complained about how unfair it was. Of course, her outburst hadn't accomplished a damn thing, except get her written up. That was bad enough—she could say goodbye to her raise for the coming year. But that was nothing compared to the fear that came over her now: What if the job she'd been working toward for so long finally opened up, only for Big Will to decide that she no longer deserved it?

But no—Big Will wouldn't do that, would he?

Val finished setting up the grills. She placed the hot dog on top of the pyramid just as the store's overhead lights flickered. This was followed by a familiar click from the front of the store. The doors to the customer entrance had been unlocked. When the lights came back on a second later, they were in their bright, daytime setting.

Store #1512 was open for business. It was time for the roaches—Val included—to scatter.

6

THAT NIGHT DIEGO dreamt of snow.

Not as he knew it to be now—dirty, inconvenient, depressing—but as it had seemed to him when he experienced it for the first time. He was sixteen and on an airplane from Honduras to JFK, by way of Mexico City. The flight descended into New York City at dusk. As darkness fell, the glittering Manhattan skyline appeared in the small airplane window, at first askew, and then, as the plane finished turning, upright: a thousand buildings lighting up before his eyes. Then came the snow: millions of tiny diamonds, twinkling in the beams of the plane's landing lights as it approached the pavement. Diego felt he was not merely moving to a new place but entering a magical realm, one he, like almost everyone he knew, associated mainly with those most magical phenomena of all, movies and television.

The sound of his alarm jarred him from his dream. It was 2:30.

Diego pressed the off button quickly so the sound didn't wake his girlfriend, snoring lightly beside him. Then he lay back on his pillow.

He thought about the moment he stepped outside for the first time, in the United States, after he and his father had retrieved his bags from the luggage carousel. Even the weight of his suitcase—filled with packages from his grandparents and aunts to his father—as he heaved it down the pavement to the terminal bus stop, a snakelike torrent of cars and buses honking and wheezing next to them, added to the strange unreality of those moments. When they stepped out from under the overhang, he inhaled. The white powder tickled his nose. It smelled clean but also like cardboard.

In bed, Diego felt for a moment as if he were that kid again: the cheeky, confident boy who had nonetheless lived in abject terror of humiliating himself, of saying or doing the wrong thing and being laughed at—but who also hadn't doubted for a second that he'd be a success in the USA. The hard part, he had thought, had been getting here.

It was the second time he'd moved to a new country. Diego had been born in Belize, but his mother was unstable, unable to care for him. When he was two, his paternal grandparents brought him to Belize, where they lived. His father was a sailor who traveled the world, but eventually he married an American woman and sent for Diego to join them in the Bronx. At the time, Diego had spoken almost no English. For years after he arrived, his stepmother said she couldn't understand him, that it sounded like he was talking through a mouthful of rocks. Diego had acquired the habit of saying little, unless he felt sure he was among friends.

Or when he was drinking. Alcohol had always made his self-consciousness evaporate.

The digits on the alarm clock read 2:40. He must have drifted off. He couldn't linger any longer. He and Milo started at 3:30, half an hour before the others, to set up the line. And he had no ride today.

Diego showered quickly, then returned to the bedroom with a

towel around his waist. A drawer at the bottom of his dresser gaped open, blocking the narrow alleyway around the bed. He'd found the dresser on the side of the road—it was too big for the bedroom, but free was free. Every time Diego stepped over the busted drawer to get to his side of the bed, he told himself he'd fix it soon. From the drawer above the broken one, he selected a Town Square shirt.

Some people wore the same shirt day after day, only changing their undershirts. Not Diego. Whenever any of the store's executive managers unlocked the closet where they were kept, he asked for another. Most of the time they found it easier to say yes. In four years, he had acquired seven. Even in those periods when his girlfriend stayed in bed all day and Diego did all the laundry and the cooking himself, he always had a clean, neatly folded one ready.

A full-length mirror hung in the hallway between their bedroom and his girlfriend's son's room so Diego could see himself in the mornings without disturbing his girlfriend, who was bipolar. To stay healthy, she needed proper sleep, as well as meds.

He tucked in his shirt carefully, making sure it was even. He wasn't one of those jokers who wore oversized shirts—he liked to look respectable, trustworthy. His glance moved upward to his face. His expression was canny, expectant, the look on a comedian's face right after he'd delivered a punch line. Then he smiled. His teeth were his worst feature. They were yellowing and widely spaced and jutted in different directions like antennae covering all navigational bases. Not that this hurt him with women. Diego'd always been popular. Too popular perhaps. His problem had always been staying faithful.

A half flight of stairs led up from their basement apartment to the building's outer door.

Even at this hour, the air was warm as he made his way through the grounds of the complex. Sunset Gardens consisted of sixteen three-and-a-half-story redbrick apartment buildings built in the 1960s. Because it accepted Section 8 and was just off the two-mile stretch of highway where almost all of Potterstown's big-box stores were located, a lot of people who worked retail lived there. Nevertheless, the walk to Town Square was unpleasant. The highway, 11W, consisted of four tight lanes for cars and no sidewalks. The tiny strip of asphalt designated as a shoulder was just wide enough for the telephone poles that still lined the road.

At this hour, the few cars that passed treated the road like an interstate, roaring by at fifty-five, sixty, even seventy miles an hour, sometimes leaving in their wake a blast of bass from their stereos. Every year several pedestrians were killed on this part of 11W, usually at night, almost always restaurant or retail workers walking to or from work. Diego thought of those people a lot when he walked to work.

Back in the Bronx, not having a car hadn't mattered. Diego'd taken the subway to his job at a Duane Reade drugstore on the Upper East Side. He had worked there for seven years. He had excelled: his manager said he could work at any Duane Reade in the city, anytime—that's how strong his reference would be, a "calling card," he'd called it. But there had been nowhere to move up at Duane Reade, not with Diego's accent and limited English writing skills. Over the years, things had come up, opportunities, or what he'd thought were opportunities—a guy he'd worked with in a corporate dining room said he'd teach Diego to be a chef, a friend of a friend had offered to sell him a coffee cart so Diego could go into business for himself. But nothing had panned out. Moving to Potterstown had been his ex's idea—a better life, she'd said. But after a couple of years here, she found out Diego was cheating on her. She moved back to the Bronx. Diego stayed. He liked it here, liked the space and the trees.

He walked by a largely abandoned shopping center from the 1960s with weeds growing through cracks in the parking lot. Land here was so cheap that when a building became outdated, its owners often didn't bother to tear it down. They just built a new one next door. What's a half mile of dead space to people in cars?

Finally, Diego reached the driveway that led up the hill to the Catskills Mall and Town Square. The store was attached to the mall, though not really of it—you could only get from store to mall through a single door in Customer Experience. As he walked up the drive, Diego quickened his pace—he had to, if he was going to make it on time. Little Will wouldn't give him a hard time, but it was a point of pride with Diego that he was never late.

He walked diagonally across the large, nearly empty parking lot—the only cars in the lot at this hour were Little Will's and Milo's. The employee entrance—a nondescript beige door—was located several hundred feet from the big customer entrance. When he reached it, he was huffing, but it was worth it. It was 3:28.

Diego pressed his face against the small window cut into the top of the door as he knocked—pounded. Through the glass, his eyes met Little Will's. The reception area was bright, gold-hued compared to the dark night. For a moment, Diego felt like the Little Match Girl, from the story. Then there was a click. Little Will had hit the electronic unlock button under the reception desk. Diego pushed the door open.

Little Will and Milo could tell immediately that he'd walked.

"Why didn't you text me?" Milo asked cheerfully. He gulped the remains of a fluorescent blue energy drink and tossed the empty plastic bottle in the bin. "I would've picked you up."

Diego scowled. "My phone is shut off, remember? You pick me up on Thursday, okay?"

"Okay," Milo said. "But don't blame me. How was I supposed to know you needed a ride?"

Diego didn't feel like conceding the point. He just shrugged.

Milo's large, black, old-man shoes flapped against the store's linoleum tile as he and Diego walked to the warehouse. Milo headed straight for the truck. Little Will had already opened the rear door. Milo gazed at the disorderly sea of boxes that had been not so much stacked as thrown inside at the distribution center.

Milo scrunched up his face in contemplation. "I'd say nineteen hundred pieces."

Diego could have told him it didn't matter: however many boxes were in the truck, they'd unload them. Tomorrow they'd do it again. But after four years of working together, Diego knew that Milo needed to feel like a person who'd accrued expertise, even if his expertise was in guessing at a number he could just as well have read off the shipment report.

The two of them began rolling out sections of track from the back of the warehouse. Then they connected the sections to one another. For several minutes, the only sounds in the room were the rolling of wheels and steel rods being shoved into eyebolts. *Whoosh-bang, whoosh-bang.* Then Milo started complaining about how he hadn't had a girlfriend since his ex, the mother of his younger daughter, left him.

"Two years," he said. "Can you believe it? I feel like I'm going to lose my mind."

Diego couldn't imagine going two years without sleeping with a woman. "You need to stop trying so hard, man," he said. "That's your problem."

That's what Diego always told Milo.

Once the line was assembled, they began laying out empty pallets on the ground next to it. Milo began telling a long story about how he'd been lying in bed the night before, in the heat of his attic bedroom. He had realized he wanted a glass of cold water, wanted it more than he'd ever wanted anything in his life. He would have given away everything he had in the whole world for water. The only thing he wouldn't do was to get up from his bed and walk down to the kitchen to get one.

Diego only half listened. He guessed Milo was planning to turn this pointless story into a "comic" monologue for his YouTube channel. But Diego realized his mood had improved. Milo's presence, their morning routine, the familiar sawdust smell of the warehouse, and even the work itself—the sense of mastery he felt over it—eased the rawness he'd felt ever since he'd woken up, his head swirling with memories of being sixteen.

Also: Val's plan. He'd been so absorbed in his past that he'd briefly forgotten about it.

Diego knew Val assumed she'd be the one to get promoted, but he liked his own chances. He was the person Little Will usually delegated to—like the day before, when he'd asked Diego to deal with the shipment of mini gas grills during the unload. He was also mature, stayed away from a lot of the nonsense the others got up to. Plus, there was his performance record, his punctuality, the fact that he never missed a day of work, even when he was sick.

With the regular, predictable income of a group manager, he could get an auto loan. With a car, he could work other jobs after his shift at Town Square. His friend Kelso worked for a company up near Woodstock that assembled and installed high-end ceiling fans. A small shop, it didn't offer benefits and the work wasn't always regular, but the hourly pay—$17—was better than what Town Square paid. Kelso said they were looking for strong, reliable men who could work on an as-needed basis. Problem was, Diego couldn't get up there now. The place was in the sticks.

With a second job, he could move his girlfriend and her son out of the airless basement apartment in Sunset Gardens, into a place with a yard or even just a porch of their own. It would be good for the boy. For

Diego too. This was the reason he'd agreed to move to Potterstown in the first place: he had imagined a spot of land that was his, somewhere where he could drink a beer and look at the sky.

THE OLD GUYS, having never fully acclimated to the automobile age, tended to allot fifteen minutes more than necessary for their commutes. They were, as a result, usually first to show up for the four o'clock shift. But today Val arrived almost as early as they did.

She was fastening her name tag onto her shirt when she heard a rap at the door. The sound was quieter and more tentative than the zealous banging with which most people in Movement chose to announce their presence, as if every second they spent standing outside were an affront to their dignity.

Instead of using the buzzer under the reception desk, Little Will walked over and opened the door. "Welcome, Callie," he said. "Come on in."

Val had forgotten about the new girl.

She was young—although not quite as young as Nicole, maybe twenty-six or twenty-seven—and white. Pretty, too, with blunt-cut straight hair that was dyed an almost white blond. Her roots were visible, but they weren't the kind of roots that looked trashy—or fussy, like Meredith's. Callie's hair looked purposeful, a little punk. Otherwise her appearance was conventional and neat. Her sneakers looked new, and she was wearing a pale blue polo shirt instead of the Town Square T-shirts most employees wore because you could get them for free—if you knew to ask. She probably hadn't known to ask.

Little Will handed Callie a box cutter. He made the joke he made to every new employee: "Hold on to it—it's the only thing Town Square will ever give you." The others filtered in, arriving in something pretty close to descending order of age, while he showed Callie the lockers, the coat closet, and the cabinet behind the reception desk where scanners and walkie-talkies were stored and charged.

He had finished by the time everyone arrived. He cleared his throat. "I've got something I want to tell you," he said. "I know the situation with our hours has been hard on everyone. At long last, I have some good news. Corporate is freeing up some funds. You're all going to start getting more hours—a lot more."

He paused to let his words sink in.

"We're going to get serious about cleaning up the store," he continued. "For the next week or so, anyone who wants to work, whether or not you're on the schedule now, can come in. Plus we'll work Sunday, for anyone who wants to. And most importantly we're going to do overnights. Starting tomorrow night, we'll work from midnight until eight every night, until we get this place in order."

Ruby raised her arms in exultation. "*Money, money, money,*" she sang. Today, she was wearing a silver scrunchie with white stripes and a cardigan with a faux-fur collar.

"They made us wait long enough, didn't they," Joyce said.

Little Will started to respond, but Joyce cut him off.

"And what?" she continued. "We're supposed to be grateful because they're 'giving' us more work—for, what, a week?" Joyce turned abruptly to Callie, whose existence she had until now given no indication of noticing. "You're new," she said. "You should know what you're getting into. You're part-time?"

"Ye—" Callie started to say.

"Of course you are," Joyce said in a tone that suggested Callie had interrupted her. "Everyone is nowadays. That's so corporate can preserve its 'flexibility'—that means it can cut our hours whenever it wants. Well, what about my car payments? Are they flexible? That's what I'd like to know."

As Joyce laughed at her own joke, Val could already hear, in her mind, what Joyce would say next: *When I started here, it was different.*

"When this store opened fifteen years ago, things were different," Joyce said. "Working full-time, forty hours a week, wasn't some big privilege—something you had to beg for. It was standard. That meant you could work here and live on what you made. You wouldn't be rich, but you could live. If you wanted to make more, you could work overtime. Not anymore. Let me tell you—"

Joyce stabbed a finger toward Callie, who was trying hard to look indifferent, but couldn't quite manage it: her expression was strained, and her face had colored slightly. If she had really been a blonde, she would have been bright red, Val thought.

"These days," Joyce went on, "corporate would sooner let you steal from the register than make time and a half."

She paused—either for emphasis or a breath. One of the old guys tried to seize the moment. "It's because of the illegal immig—" he began at the same time as Travis started to say, "It's because of China—"

Travis had spent time in prison. A guy there had explained to him about trade and the loss of manufacturing jobs.

Joyce had no intention of letting either man hijack her moment. "When it comes to overtime," she continued over them, "corporate is so paranoid that they won't let you work more than thirty-nine hours—they don't want to risk coming within sixty minutes of having to pay overtime, like it's a disease that they've got to keep a safe distance from." She chuckled again, with that extra gusto with which people laugh at their own jokes. "Used to be, corporate cared about getting things done right. Every night, before the closers left, everything in the store was put away, all clothes were properly zoned. Didn't matter how much it cost as long as it was done right. I was proud to work here. Now look at this place. It's a dump. Honestly, if I had known where things were heading, I would have kept cleaning houses full-time. I made more per hour, but I thought, I should do this, you know, for job security, for benefits." She snorted. "I've never been smart. At least I've been here long enough that my benefits are grandfathered in. It's you young people I feel sorry for."

She looked from Raymond to Nicole to Travis to Val, each of whom instinctively averted their eyes.

Joyce had a way of making them feel stupid, as if they were suckers for working at Town Square, for putting up with conditions she tolerated only because she was nearing retirement. Raymond once said that it was like when you've decided to stay with your shitty girlfriend—because she says she's pregnant or something—and then, once you've moved in together, everyone starts telling you about all the guys she cheated on you with, which maybe you sort of knew about but didn't want to have rubbed in your face. (Val thought his choice of comparison might say as much about Raymond's personal life as it did about Joyce's.)

"Don't you feel bad for them, Will?" Joyce asked.

Little Will, whose head had been bowed, looked up.

"I hear what you're saying, Joyce," he said. "I think you know—I think all of you know—that if it were up to me, we'd do a lot of things differently"—Joyce was about to interrupt, to clarify that she didn't mean *him*, she knew it wasn't *his* fault, but this time Little Will spoke over her. "At least we're going to be working more from here on out. Better late than never, right?"

When Joyce shrugged, Val saw the opening she'd been waiting for.

"This is about the people from corporate coming to check out the store, isn't it, Will?" she asked.

Val didn't actually need confirmation—obviously the extra hours had materialized because Meredith now cared about cleaning up the store—but it was important to her that the others knew she had figured it out right away, before anyone else. "I mean, we've been behind for months, and Meredith hasn't given a shit until now."

"Yeah," Raymond said, and they all glanced at him because his voice sounded weird—raspy and harsh. "It's terrific that for months there was no money to do anything, and we were all screwed. Then Meredith is up for promotion, and just like that, there's money to make the store look good."

Little Will began fiddling with one of the buttons on his shirt, which he'd only now realized was misbuttoned—again. He was irritated with himself. He had meant to deliver the good news in such a way that people would be happy. Clearly he'd screwed up. Or maybe it was an impossible task. They weren't stupid.

"I can't say that corporate's upcoming visit has nothing to do with it," he said after a moment. "I don't know, is the answer. I'm not privy to most of Meredith's conversations with Big Will or with corporate. I'm just passing along the information I get. Meredith called me last night. Late." He made a wry face.

A few people snickered. It was no secret that Meredith had a habit of hassling Little Will with texts and phone calls in the evenings, when he was trying to sleep. With his two jobs he went to bed early.

"But before anyone gets too bent out of shape about the timing," he continued, "keep in mind that hours are always short in the winter and spring. That's not Meredith's fault. It's just the way it is. It always feels like it takes too long for summer hours to start—we stood here and had this same conversation last year. Maybe it was a couple of weeks earlier, but maybe it wasn't and it just feels that way. I don't know. The important thing is the money we've all been waiting for is finally here. That's a good thing."

He nodded, then glanced at the time clocks. "Meanwhile, it's already three minutes to four. How about you guys clock in so you can start getting paid?"

7

"HEY, HEY, HEY!"

A few minutes later, the sound of Meredith's voice made everyone look up from the line. It was five after four, a good fifteen or twenty minutes before she usually put in an appearance.

Registering the surprise on their faces, Meredith giggled, then made a mock-accusing face. "I know you guys like to give me a hard time for coming in 'late,' but you always seem to forget that while you leave at eight, I'm here all day, until three or even four o'clo—"

"We'd stay too if we were paid to," Raymond cut in. He spoke in the same harsh, raspy voice he'd used earlier, in the employee area. Val figured he was hungover.

Raymond turned to Diego. "My health insurance got cut off because they wouldn't give me enough hours, no matter how many times I requested more"—he began speaking more quietly—"but she wants a fucking medal for doing her job."

Diego glared at Raymond, willing him to shut the fuck up before he got them both in trouble. But Meredith took it in stride.

"I'm on salary, Raymond," she said. "That means, I don't get paid any extra for working long hours. Meanwhile, this isn't the time or place for complaints. If you have an issue with your benefits, schedule a meeting with Svetlana in HR, okay? Now"—she turned to the others—"I'm sure Little Will has told you all that I've gotten us the okay to do some serious overnighting."

Nicole glanced at Milo, who had—whatever his flaws—attended three semesters of college. "Is *overnighting* even a word?" she whispered.

Milo shook his head, Meredith went on. "Honestly, I'm a little nervous. We never did overnights in Sales, except on Black Friday and Christmas. But I know you all like doing them and you get a lot done, so we're going to give it a try." She paused, as if waiting for applause to break out. "Okay then," she said when the silence became intolerable. "Let's get this show going. Bring it on, Milo! Woo-hoo!" She was standing near Travis, which was perhaps why she turned to him. "Come on, Travis! Gotta feed that baby!" She laughed merrily, pleased with herself for remembering that Travis had a newborn at home. With so many people to manage, she often had a hard time keeping track of all their personal lives.

Travis looked at her in confusion. The necessity of feeding his six-week-old daughter didn't quite strike him as a laughing matter. He gave her one of his hard-to-read, ironic smiles.

Val turned to Meredith. "So, we're going to focus on getting the store into shape before corporate comes?" she asked, smiling and cocking her head submissively. "Getting through the backlog?"

Being nice to Meredith wasn't crucial, but there was no harm in it.

"That's the plan," Meredith said. A sigh of anxiety escaped her.

"Oh, don't worry," Val assured her. "We'll clean this place up, no problem. A few overnights, and this place will be tip-top." Val nudged Diego with her elbow. "Right, D.?"

Diego—whose face had been blank, expressionless—seemed to

spring to life. "Oh, yeah," he said, smiling. "No problem. Like Val said. Tip-top."

But he couldn't quite pull it off. His neck had disappeared into his shoulders, and his smile was hollow, as if he were a hostage in a proof-of-life of photo.

Meredith didn't notice. She wandered off, toward the back of the line, where the old guys, in what constituted Movement's version of chivalry, sorted Grocery. (The pace was slower back there. All the non-Grocery boxes had been weeded out already.)

When Meredith was gone, Nicole shook her head at Val. Val turned to meet her eye. Nicole lifted her chin, puckered her lips, and made a series of quiet little kisses. Val smiled and bowed, as if receiving accolades.

A chorus of "What?"s and "What'd you say?"s rose from the back of the line. Meredith always forgot that the old guys turned their hearing aids off for the unload.

Meredith gave up trying to talk to the old guys. She began examining the tri-level industrial shelving units that lined the warehouse's walls. She pulled a little notebook out of her back pocket and began making little ticks in it.

She was trying to figure out exactly how big the backlog was. If she knew how many pallets they needed to break out in the next few days, she could divide the number of pallets by the number of overnights and set concrete goals for each shift. That would go a long way toward alleviating her anxiety. But it wasn't as easy as it sounded.

When Meredith looked around, all she saw were boxes. Some were brown, Town Square–issued boxes with the company logo printed on the side. Others were manufacturers' boxes with their own logos printed on them. Still others were consumer-ready boxes bearing full-color photos of convection ovens or air mattresses. But to Meredith they were all—fundamentally—just boxes. By contrast, most people in Movement had worked in the warehouse for years. They possessed finely developed mental maps of the place and knew at a glance which boxes belonged—which were rightfully stored here because they were backstock, here because they weren't yet needed on the sales floor—and which ones were just parked in a random spot because they hadn't yet been broken out.

Meredith could theoretically ask someone more knowledgeable to count the number of pallets in the backlog, but she was reluctant. She didn't want to reveal the extent of her ignorance. After just two months in Logistics, her authority was still so precarious.

The irony, she thought as she began to pace, walking parallel to the line, was that until yesterday Little Will's constant badgering about the backlog had bothered her far more than the thing itself. Unlike unload times, which had to be reported daily, the existence of the backlog was unknown to anyone outside the store. The only way corporate would find out about the backlog was with a surprise site visit. And those were rare. In practice, corporate almost always gave advance notice. On the other hand, managers' ability to operate within budget was pretty much the most important metric used to evaluate performance and determine raises and promotions. You didn't have to be a genius to understand that corporate's willful blindness to conditions in the store, compared with its hyperattentiveness to the budget, was a way of telegraphing to managers what they should prioritize if they wanted to be successful.

Little Will didn't get it. He'd go on and on about lost sales, no matter how many times she explained to him that it wasn't the raw number that mattered but the trend line, the fact that sales were going up. Frankly, if sales went up too much, it'd be that much harder to ensure that next month's number was better than this month's, which meant they were setting themselves up for failure. Perhaps if he'd gone to college—studied business, like she had—he'd understand better.

Almost as bad was when he'd try to make her feel guilty about the team, their finances, how they were used to getting more hours by this time of year. But Town Square was a business, not a jobs program. They had to make decisions on that basis. Besides, anyone who wanted to could get a second job. Or quit if they didn't like conditions here. And wasn't this what welfare, Medicaid, food stamps, etc., were for? People like Meredith paid taxes to provide a safety net for those who needed it. Why should she then be made to feel bad about doing her job the way corporate expected it to be done?

But none of this mattered now that corporate was not only coming—but coming for the express purpose of checking up on her management of Logistics.

Meredith had invested years of her life in Town Square. After high school, she had attended fashion school in New York City, but in the end she'd left without a degree. After that, she had worked for several years at an upscale boutique in a nearby resort town. She'd risen to manager. From there, there was no place to move up—the boutique's owner wouldn't even consider making her a partner. That was when Meredith decided to get in at a big company, someplace where there were no limits to her advancement.

She'd come to Town Square as group manager of Electronics Sales and immediately began taking classes at night, using the company's tuition assistance program. Once she had her degree and was eligible, she was promoted to executive manager of Hardlines Sales. A year and a half later, she'd requested the transfer to Logistics. No one had understood why she'd done it—they assumed that it was for the $5,000 raise she'd negotiated along with her transfer. But though the raise was nice—it brought her salary up to $85K—that wasn't the reason. Meredith had realized that warehouse experience would make her better rounded, a more attractive candidate for the job she really wanted: store manager.

She'd made the case to corporate that she was the right person to lead Movement, regardless of her lack of warehouse experience. She wasn't—she had argued in her interview—bogged down by habit like people who'd come up in Logistics. And she was energetic and resourceful, the kind of person who wasn't afraid to break some eggs in order to make an omelet. She would reinvigorate the department, increase productivity. Corporate had eaten it up, not only giving her the transfer and the raise but praising her "initiative" and "drive" and designating her as "fast track" for future promotion. That was why Meredith had known—as soon as Big Will called her into his office yesterday and told her the news of his departure—that the top job was very likely hers.

She just had to clear the backlog before corporate came. The overnights would kill her budget, of course, but what choice did she have? She would resort to plan B: explain to corporate that the reason she'd had to go over budget was that her predecessor had left the department in such bad shape. There was certainly truth in that. The team she'd inherited left much to be desired. In the week before she'd gone on vacation, they had missed the unload time *three* times.

Oh god. Just the thought of filing another failure report made Meredith hope she'd remembered to bring her migraine medicine with her today.

Her pitch to corporate had, after all, rested on her claim that she could do better than her more experienced predecessors. The fact that under her management, Movement had missed the unload time more often than it had previously hurt her case. On the other hand, she'd only been in Movement for two months. A learning curve was to be expected. She'd probably be okay—as long as she could show improvement. They simply couldn't have another miss between now and corporate's visit.

She stopped pacing and clapped her hands. "Keep up the pace!"

she yelled. "Just because I'm not on the line with you isn't an excuse to slack. Don't take advantage!"

MEANWHILE, IN SOFTLINES, Callie picked up a pink sports bra. She was about to put it on a rack with other bras.

"Uh-uh," Ruby said. "It's Girls. Not Women's. Look at the tag. 'Pink Lemonade' is a Kids brand. Put it on the Girls rack."

Ruby was teaching Callie how to break out hanging clothes. She started with hanging because it was easier than folded. Hanging clothes arrived at the store already on hangers and only had to be sorted onto wheeled hanging racks before being put away.

Callie put the sports bra on the Girls rack.

"You got to pay attention," Ruby said.

Callie picked a black dress from the box. She turned toward one of the Women's racks.

"Nope," Ruby said. "That's the 'Forever' rack. That dress is 'Body & Mind.' Remember, women's clothes are separated by brand, except for lingerie, bathing suits, and pajamas. Those each have their own racks, no matter what brand. Got it?"

Ruby looked squarely at Callie. She felt it was important to show newcomers that they were not on equal footing with her. She had also noticed Callie's car in the lot this morning when she and Nicole pulled in. The only car in the employee parking area not familiar to Ruby, it was a red Mazda 2.0, only a year or two old. Ruby had peered in. The interior was sparkly clean, just like the exterior. Even the car seat in the back looked like it had been freshly vacuumed for crumbs. As a person with no car—Nicole gave her a ride to work most days—not even a crappy one like the Dingmobile, Ruby felt the burden was on the person with the nice car to prove she wasn't a snob.

"How old's your kid?" Ruby asked after a minute.

Callie looked up from the Men's cargo shorts she was hanging. "How'd—"

"I saw a car seat in your car," Ruby said. "When I came in this morning."

"Oh."

Callie still looked a little confused, but she let it go. She told Ruby that her daughter was two and that she was in the middle of a divorce. She and her daughter were living with her mom—"until the divorce is finalized. When I finish school, we'll get our own place, hopefully. I should start getting regular child support, too, once the divorce goes through."

It seemed to Ruby as if Callie repeated the word "divorce" more than she needed to—as if Callie wanted to make extra sure Ruby knew she didn't have her kid out of wedlock. *Well, ain't you special*, Ruby wanted to say. Ruby had been married once too. Worst decision of her life. Her ex-husband was abusive, a piece of work—Ruby and her three kids had had to leave with nothing but the clothes on their backs.

"What you in school for?" Ruby asked when she pushed Callie a new box.

Callie said she was studying to become a "sleep technologist."

"A *what*?"

Callie said she was learning how to read scans of people's brains as they slept. In order to help them with insomnia and other sleep disorders. It was a growing field, she said. A lot of high-end treatment centers were opening up, especially in wealthy areas, closer to the city.

Ruby had the fluid features of a comic actor. She raised one eyebrow and pressed her lips together. "You tell those rich people to come in here and break out boxes at four a.m.," she said, pursing her lips into a ball before continuing. "They do this for a couple of hours before they go to their other jobs, like I do, and I guarantee you, they'll start sleeping just fine."

"Speaking of sleep," Callie said when Ruby stopped laughing at her joke, "no one told me anything about overnights when I interviewed."

Her tone annoyed Ruby. Ruby didn't like complainers.

"Oh, overnights aren't so bad," Ruby said. "We have fun. You'll see."

"It's not that—it's just, well, it's hard for me to nap during the day. Between my daughter and my mother's chemo—she can't really drive, so I take her. And I've got my classes and the homework."

"You ain't the only one with a life, you know," Ruby snapped. "I work at ShopRite most evenings. Everyone has things to do. We make it work one way or another."

Ruby didn't tell Callie she mostly did get a nap in after she got home from her shift at Town Square, or that she usually needed a beer to help her fall asleep since by then she'd been up and about for five or six hours and it was the middle of the morning, and no blanket draped over the blinds could entirely block the sunlight that poured in through her bedroom window. Nor did Ruby tell Callie that generally she worked a second job only during the winter, when hours were short at Town Square. If they were finally going to start getting summer hours, Ruby would put in her notice at ShopRite so she'd have more availability for Town Square. It was a no-brainer. She not only liked it better here, they paid her $1.70 an hour more.

"They're 'Forever Vintage,'" Ruby said instead, taking the pair of capri pants Callie was holding and hanging them up herself.

Maybe she was being too hard on the girl. But Ruby wasn't in the greatest mood.

After she'd left Town Square yesterday, she had spent hours thinking about the group manager job. If she got it, she'd be able to pay her back bills—she still owed for heat last winter, among other things. She'd also be able to buy for her son, so he'd be provided for when he got out of prison, ready to make a fresh start, train for a career like he should have done years ago (he was smart, perhaps the smartest of her three kids).

It wasn't crazy. Ruby had management experience. Before she came to Town Square, she had been an assistant manager at LOL Burger down the road. She had loved that job. The high point of her professional life had been when the company opened a new location down in Wappingers Falls. They'd sent her there for a whole month to help hire and train staff, put her up in a hotel and everything, gave her vouchers for her meals—the works. She had never felt so energized or worked so hard. And fast food was different, she knew, but why shouldn't she be a manager at a Town Square? She'd been at the store for five years, hadn't she? And Big Will liked her. They had a nice rapport.

Ruby let herself imagine what it would be like, to be group manager—she envisioned being sent to special management conferences and training programs. She'd always wanted to fly in an airplane, maybe she would. Maybe she'd meet a man, a fellow manager—a peer.

It wasn't until she was at ShopRite that Ruby realized she'd never get the job. She wasn't eligible. Town Square required a high school diploma or GED for all management positions. How she had let herself forget that, even for a few hours, she didn't know. It wasn't like her to be so careless.

Callie was holding up a small white dress with a ruffled skirt, staring at it stupidly as if she expected the answer to simply come to her via divine inspiration. And yet Callie, with her college classes, was more likely to get promoted than she'd ever be.

"It's Baby," Ruby snapped. "Toddler sizes go on the Baby rack."

8

"YOU'VE BEEN HERE a long time, right?" Travis asked Milo.

Milo snorted derisively. "You could say that. Eight years. Longer than anyone in Movement. Not counting Little Will."

Milo's objection had been to the phrase "long time," which seemed to him altogether too generic and anodyne to convey the vastness of his tenure.

Milo was breaking out Toys after the unload.

Travis nodded. "Right. So, what do *you* make of Val's plan? Is she right that Little Will will get promoted if Meredith does?"

Being new, Travis lacked the institutional knowledge to judge Val's predictions.

Milo studied Travis. Travis's interest surprised him. Because Travis so rarely took part in the group's conversations about Meredith during break, they all assumed he didn't much care about the store, that he had too much else going on in his life.

"Val's probably not wrong," Milo said finally. "Not about Little

Will moving up if Meredith does. Little Will will see to it that he comes out on top. He always does."

Travis couldn't conceal his surprise.

"Little Will's a lot more ambitious than people realize," Milo explained.

"Really? I—"

"I know," Milo cut him off. "Everyone thinks he's *so nice*." Milo's tone suggested it was tiresome for him to have to constantly contend with this misimpression, but when he continued, he sounded almost excited. "I'll tell you the whole story and you can judge for yourself."

Regardless of how often the people closest to him failed to see things in what Milo considered the correct light, he instinctively expected new people to take his side—at least if they had all the facts.

"Little Will and I started here together," he began. "We were seasonal hires. He and I were the only two of that year's batch to be hired on as permanent employees after the holidays." He paused, then added, "Out of more than twenty people."

Milo stopped talking. It took Travis a second to realize that he was expected to react to this statement. Dutifully, Travis raised his eyebrows, made himself look impressed. As if Travis had put another quarter in the slot (as an ex-con, Travis had a lot of experience with pay phones), Milo continued.

"This was back when getting hired as a permanent employee was a big deal," he said. "It was during the recession. It wasn't like now, where any jackass can get hired."

Travis smiled, assuming that since he was a recent hire, Milo had meant to make a good-natured crack at his expense. But it hadn't occurred to Milo that his words might reflect on Travis. Milo's own reality was generally too vivid and overpowering for him to imagine other people's.

"I'm seven years older than Little Will," Milo went on. "And I'm only one semester short of having a college degree—which is more college than Little Will has, let me tell you. I've worked white-collar jobs—I was at UnitedHealthcare before I came here. So. You tell me. Why did they make him group manager four years ago and not me?"

Travis had a few guesses, but he shook his head politely. Milo's voice became confidential, almost a whisper. "What I think Little Will must have done is make sure that corporate knew that I'm the best thrower at the store. I think he made them think that they couldn't afford to promote me because they needed me to throw the truck. And it worked. They promoted him, and now I'm the only thrower." Milo nodded for emphasis before continuing. "At most Town Square stores, they alternate—one person throws for half an hour and then another person subs in—but I guess they like my throwing because they have me do the whole truck."

While Milo was talking, Raymond had walked over to the pallet. He got there in time to catch much of what Milo had just said. He waited until Milo was looking in the other direction, then met Travis's eye and shook his head, to indicate Travis should disregard what Milo's words.

Milo was one of Raymond's closest friends, and he was, in Raymond's opinion, a smart person. Milo's knowledge of certain subjects—Ultimate Fighting, the World Wrestling Federation, Adam Sandler movies, cartoons from the 1980s and 1990s—was encyclopedic. But there were some topics on which Milo was less reliable. These included his mother, the professors and administrators of Ulster Community College, his father, his old boss at UnitedHealthcare. And Little Will.

Grateful, Travis nodded at Raymond. He realized he would have been better off asking Raymond about Val's plan. (Lack of institutional knowledge indeed.)

The group was wrong in thinking that Travis didn't care about the store. He cared a great deal. The reason he didn't join in their conversation during break was that their conversations were usually about Meredith, and Travis believed complaining about your boss all the time was the first stop on the road to loserdom. He knew all about that road from his father.

In prison, Travis had had ample time to think seriously about what kind of life he wanted to have when he got out. What he hadn't counted on was being unable to find a job. He had been released in the middle of the Great Recession. This had been followed by what people were then calling the "jobless recovery." The name sounded right to Travis. For years, he hadn't been able to find anything except gig work. He'd pretty much given up when, a few months ago, on a whim, he'd put in yet another application to Town Square, his third or fourth since moving back to Potterstown. He and his girlfriend Jeanie had been paying their phone bill at the Verizon store in the Catskills Mall when, almost out of nowhere, the idea had occurred to him to give it one more try. He had by then been rejected so many times, by so many employers, that he could hardly believe when this application landed him an interview and ultimately a job offer. In retrospect, the fact that he'd even put in an application on that particular day felt like fate, a sign someone up there was looking out for him.

And now there was this plan. Meredith was strange—what was up with that "joke" about him having to feed his baby?—but he could tell she liked him. That had to count for something.

Now that he was here, Travis had every intention of rising within the company.

RAYMOND DIDN'T NEED a scanner to know that the Spider-Man-themed Lego sets belonged in Aisle B13, Shelf 4, Row 3, Space 2.

Raymond and Milo broke out Toys together almost every day, and Raymond paid special attention to things his five-year-old son would like, even if he maintained that the best toys were the ones left over from his own 1990s childhood. Even the exact same ones—Operation, Lego, Etch A Sketch—had been better back then. Today's stuff was junky, disposable. Take the game Chutes and Ladders, which Town Square sold for as little as five bucks on special. It probably cost four times as much when Raymond was a kid. But his childhood set was still in good shape. The new boards were so flimsy they might as well be made out of cereal boxes. They wouldn't last a year, let alone more than three decades.

As he worked, Raymond realized that the Advil he'd taken earlier had finally kicked in.

Contra Val, he hadn't been hungover this morning. That would have been better. He and his girlfriend Cristina had gotten into an hours-long screaming fight last night, and when he woke in the morning, his throat had been killing him. Every time he'd swallowed, he felt as if a razor blade were cutting into him from the inside.

Now that the pain had finally receded, Raymond's thoughts turned—almost of their own volition—to the last thing he wanted to think about, the fight itself, as if some invisible mechanism ensured that when one source of unhappiness lifted, another fell, and that he was always at least somewhat miserable.

It had begun not long after his shift at Town Square ended the day before. Raymond had gone down to the basement of his mother's duplex to clean the boiler. On his way upstairs afterward, he found a letter from the electric company in the mailbox. The letter warned that their power would be cut off if the outstanding balance wasn't paid immediately. Raymond had stared at the paper. It made no sense. Cristina had paid the bill. And the one before it. But according to this notice, nothing had been paid for months. It took Raymond about ten seconds to understand that Cristina had spent the money on pills. When she got home from work, Raymond confronted her. She didn't bother to deny it. She told Raymond that he was the reason she'd started taking the pills. It was because he was still in love with his ex, she said. How did he think that made her feel?

Raymond was temperamentally prone to feel guilty, to assume things were his fault. And there was, he knew, something in what Cristina said. He did think about Steph a lot. But in that moment he had been too angry to acknowledge any mitigating factors. "Funny," he'd said, "I thought you started taking the pills because you hurt your back. Or was that a lie too?"

Then they were off. Over the course of hours, the fight had expanded into a greatest-hits album of their grievances, but no matter how many other issues were introduced—and no matter how cruelly Cristina imitated his blinking or referred to his stupidity in imagining that Steph would want to get back with him—Raymond kept coming back to the fact that he'd have to use almost all the money in his savings account to pay the $447.57 they owed the electric company. What else could he do? It was his mother's house—where he and Cristina lived rent-free (in exchange, Raymond did all the maintenance for their unit, as well as for the tenants who lived in the upstairs apartment). It meant they wouldn't have the money to have their son's sixth birthday at Chuck E. Cheese. Raymond was furious. His own Chuck E. Cheese birthday party, when he turned six, had been one of the highlights, maybe *the* highlight, of his childhood. He'd wanted to give that to Lance.

The next box Raymond picked up was packed with Barbies. Raymond headed to Aisle B14, a.k.a. girl toys. Amid the riot of pink packaging, he tried to put the fight out of his mind. For almost the first time since he'd found the letter from the electric company, he began to think about Val's plan.

Raymond's instinct was to assume that he'd never get the group manager job, that it would go to Diego or Val, but not him. Cristina often said Raymond had "low self-esteem." She might have a point. Raymond knew that Little Will thought highly of him. Little Will said he was a hard worker, a good problem-solver. That was why Little Will sometimes asked him to do landscaping gigs with him. It was on one such gig that Little Will had told him—in confidence—about something that had happened with Val, in Big Will's office, an incident for which she'd been written up.

Maybe Val wasn't a shoo-in. Maybe Raymond did have a chance.

Raymond was still thinking about this a few minutes later, when he and Milo and Travis headed to the front of the store for break. Little Will jogged over to them. "I wanted to check with you guys about overnights," he said.

They played it cool, shrugging, scrunching up their faces, pulling out their phones, as if they had to consider impossibly busy schedules, but ultimately they all said yes to all four planned overnights, all available shifts.

Raymond began doing the math in his head. With the extra hours, maybe, just maybe, they'd manage to swing Chuck E. Cheese after all.

OUTSIDE, VAL TOLD the smokers that she had come up with a name for their group. "We're 'pro-Mer.' You know, because we're for promoting Meredith."

Val had gotten the idea from something she'd seen the week before, when she took her grandma to the doctor. On the TV in the waiting room, the newspeople were talking about a group called Antifa. The newspeople clearly didn't like them, but the group immediately appealed to Val. She had spent several years working as a bouncer at a club and retained an instinctual faith in physical strength as a tool for good.

"We'll have our first official 'pro-Mer' meeting tomorrow night, when we come in for the overnight," she told the others. Then she glanced at Nicole. "It's only for people who are in. Obviously."

For an instant, Nicole stared at Val in disbelief. Then she turned and walked off, taking her coffee and cigarette to a distant bench by the customer entrance. She had better things to do than listen to those losers anyway.

She took out her phone and typed in the URL for St. John's Episcopal Church. At Social Services the day before, they'd told her that the problem with her card was due to a clerical error. Her daughter's birth date had been entered into the system incorrectly—a zero was missing before her birth month. For some reason, this had only triggered a problem now, eight months after her birth. The woman who was helping Nicole fixed the error, but she said it would probably be several days before the changes went through and the card would work. "What am I supposed to do until then?" Nicole had asked. It wasn't her fault that someone made a clerical error. The woman helping her mentioned the food pantry at the church. Nicole had had to admit this was helpful. If Nicole looked under the seats of the Dingmobile and searched her apartment, she could scrounge up a bunch of change. Add that to the twenty dollars she could withdraw from her bank account and they should be able to get enough formula, diapers, and ramen to get them through the next few days, just until Friday, when the food pantry operated. They'd be okay.

And then . . . the overnights would translate into a nice fat paycheck two weeks from Friday. Now that was a nice prospect.

Overnights were Nicole's favorite way to pick up extra hours, far preferable to staying on during the day, after Movement's regular shift.

It wasn't just that on an overnight you could get away with things like listening to music on headphones while you worked. At night, when Movement had the store to itself, Nicole had a sort of status. She wasn't only the young, pretty one, she was also respected, even feared—at least by Milo and Raymond. But when she stayed on during the day, Nicole felt like Cinderella, transformed back into her shitty clothes. Literally. Her work clothes might as well be rags, given how dirty and ill-fitting they were. The college kids who worked Checkout and the prissy women in Sales looked through her, as if there was something embarrassing about her very existence. But what was she supposed to do? Go out and buy fancy work shirts or pants that fit her at precisely the weight she was now, eight months after giving birth? No. She didn't even have enough money to go to the Laundromat multiple times a week to make sure that the work clothes she did have were clean—and why should she? They were just going to get caked in warehouse grime as soon as she got here.

Nicole's cigarette went out. She set her coffee on the bench next to her and dug into the pocket of her pants for matches. Then she glanced over at the others, huddled together in their usual spot. Someone must have made a joke because they all started laughing. Nicole turned back to her phone.

NOT ALL OF THEM were laughing. Milo's lips were pursed in an almost feminine expression of disapproval. Pro-Mer this, pro-Mer that, he thought. What were they, a sports team that they needed a name?

The name wasn't what really bothered him, though. As the thrower—the person who literally stood at the head of the line—Milo saw himself as the de facto leader of Movement, second only to Little Will. That was bad enough. Val's assumption of leadership was pretty near intolerable.

On the other hand, he wasn't against Val's plan. Last night he'd imagined telling his dad that he'd been promoted.

Milo didn't see his dad much. His dad was remarried, with a second family. He was busy. But surely he would want to know that his eldest son was in management. Maybe he'd even take Milo out for a drink to celebrate with his friends, the guys he played with in his Christian rock cover band. It would be nice. Still, Milo didn't *need* the promotion as much as the others. He lived with his mother rent-free (luckily for her: his mother was unbelievably irresponsible—she would have lost the house a few years ago if Milo hadn't set up a payment plan for back taxes she'd long ignored). He also had a pretty lucrative side gig going, buying things that looked antique at garage sales and reselling them on eBay. (After a couple of unpleasant customer interactions, he'd added a stronger disclaimer stating clearly that returns would not be issued, regardless of whether the items turned out to be real antiques.)

The morning was, once again, bright and sunny. Light bounced off the shimmering black asphalt of the parking lot. Blinking, Milo turned his head. His gaze fell on the employee bike rack. Travis's bike—a black Schwinn ten-speed—was its sole occupant. Everyone else in Movement either had a car, got a ride, or walked. He glanced at the cluster of cars in the lot. He noticed one he didn't recognize. For a moment, he was puzzled. Then he realized that the little red Mazda must belong to the new person, whatever her name was. Milo hadn't seen her yet—she hadn't worked the line, and he was already in the warehouse, setting up with Diego, when she and the others arrived.

Beyond the parking lot, a giraffe-shaped Toys "R" Us sign still poked up from the shopping center next door, even though the store had been shut for months. When Milo was growing up, a local radio station had run a contest in which the prize was a half-hour shopping spree at the store, in which you could fill an entire shopping cart with as much merchandise as you could fit. Milo must have spent hundreds of hours fantasizing about what it would be like to win.

He took one last drag on his cigarette. Then they went in for their morning meeting, which usually took place after break, not before. Yesterday had been an exception, because of Big Will's announcement. Milo liked the daily meeting, even if there wasn't usually that much to say. Being a person whose attendance was required at meetings made him feel important, like a white-collar worker. It reminded him of working at United.

By a long-standing tradition of unknown origin, the members of Movement, like Orthodox Jews at synagogue, segregated by gender when they sat down in the break room, with the women on one side and the men on the other. (In high school, Milo had written a report on the Jews.) Milo took a seat next to Raymond at a table in the back, near the vending machines.

When they were all there, Little Will congratulated them on making the unload time and thanked them for their willingness to do overnights. Then he told them that corporate had sent out a reminder that employees were not to put cigarettes out on the ground but dispose of them in the standing ashtrays provided.

He turned to Meredith. "Anything else?"

She shook her head no.

Milo remained in his seat as the others began filing out.

His attention was directed to a fixed point on the other side of the break room. Where the new girl was sitting by herself. Callie—now he remembered Little Will saying that's what her name was.

She was the prettiest girl Milo had seen in ages. (Milo didn't count Nicole, whom he thought too mean to be considered truly pretty.) Callie looked nice, kind, a little shy as she looked around, clearly a little lost. Ruby and Nicole, her companions in Softlines, were talking animatedly to each other. They walked right past her. Callie paused a moment, then trotted out of the break room after them.

Only then did Milo get up. His whole mood had changed.

Raymond was already at the Toy pallet.

"New girl's cute," Milo said as he picked up a box.

"Yeah."

Raymond sounded indifferent. This wasn't because he didn't think Callie was good-looking, nor because he had his hands full with Cristina. He had taken one look at Callie and assumed she had a boyfriend or husband.

"Namajunas or Tate?" Milo asked.

Raymond looked blank for a moment. Then he got it. "Neither. VanZant."

Paige VanZant was a fierce—and very attractive—blond female Ultimate Fighter. Raymond and Milo had spent many hours determining which fighter everyone at store #1512 most resembled.

Milo grinned. "Good call."

He continued to think about Callie as he shelved box after box of jigsaw puzzles and board games. It wasn't just that she was pretty. He liked her hair, with the playful roots. She seemed likely to be creative, or at least like the kind of person who appreciates creativity. Someone who might get him. Not just his performance art with the boxes—that was kid stuff—but the comic monologues he posted online and, more recently, a series of web videos where he used toys to enact complex scenarios, such as a revolt of his two-year-old daughter's unicorns and ponies against her princesses, an uprising ultimately put down by Milo's own 1980s-era toy soldiers. The story was a dark parable about the insufficiency of idealism against superior weaponry.

Milo longed to be with someone who got him, who didn't just care about money or sex or good looks, who appreciated his mind—someone he could in turn dote on, shower with affection.

The other night, while watching *The Simpsons*, he had had a revelation: The show was not just comedy. It was also a love story. No matter what Homer did, no matter how foolish or humiliating his behavior, Marge never stopped loving him, never stopped seeing the best in him. Milo had never experienced that kind of love, but he hungered for it. With someone who believed in him, he felt sure he could do so much, be so much.

9

"MARK MY WORDS, she won't even show up for the overnights."

Ruby was talking to Nicole. The two of them were breaking out Maternity for the last part of the shift. "Trust me," she continued, "she'll make Little Will do all the work, while she sleeps in."

As Ruby spoke the last words, Nicole's face went blank, as if an invisible curtain had fallen in front of her. Ruby understood. Meredith was coming.

A moment later, Meredith popped out from behind a pregnant mannequin with a pair of elastic-waisted pants over its baby bump.

"Speak of the devil," Ruby said. "We were just talkin' 'bout you."

Meredith laughed. "Good things, I hope."

The smile that appeared on Ruby's face was not intended to put Meredith at ease.

For a split second it looked as if Meredith's nose might start to twitch. Then she got a grip. "Well, anyway," she said. Then something seemed to occur to her. She swiveled her head around. "Where's Callie?"

Ruby said that for the last part of the shift, she and Nicole had sent Callie to shelve swimsuits.

Meredith shrugged. "Well, I came to talk to you in particular, Ruby."

"Me?"

Meredith nodded. While they'd ultimately made the unload that morning, finishing with two minutes to spare, at 4:58 (something everyone but Meredith attributed to the fact that she was too busy scribbling in her little notebook to mess up their rhythm with her aggressive pushing), Meredith didn't like how close they'd cut it. She had decided that the best way to ensure that they made the unload time every day between now and Monday was to have an extra pair of hands on the line.

"I'd like you to start working the line in the mornings, Ruby. Just like Nicole. When you're done, you can come out here and break out Softlines the way you usually do."

Meredith smiled magnanimously, as if she were bestowing some sort of prize on Ruby.

Maternity was in the front of the store, near the main entrance. The light coming in through the glass created a halo effect around Ruby as she put a hand on her hip.

"No," she said.

"What?" Meredith asked.

"No."

Meredith looked confused. "What do you mean, 'no'?"

"What do you mean, what do I mean? You know what 'no' means, don't you?"

Nicole, pretending to be absorbed in zoning a rack of sundresses, tried to swallow a laugh but only partly succeeded. Meredith shot her a look. Nicole immediately bowed her head.

"I don't work in the warehouse in the summer," Ruby continued. "That's a fact. Big Will knows that. Little Will knows that. Everyone knows it. You the only one who don't. Apparently. It's on account of my asthma."

"Your asthma!"

Meredith gaped. Ruby smoked at least a pack a day. Even arriving for the 4 a.m. shift, she smelled like an ashtray. And she wanted special treatment on account of asthma?

"Uh-huh," Ruby said. "The heat and the dust in the warehouse aggravate it. Especially in the summer."

Meredith shut her eyes. She tilted her face downward and brought her fingertips to her forehead. For a second, she looked like a stressed-out housewife from one of those old commercials, a woman whose misery could only be alleviated by a new vacuum cleaner or a different brand of bubble bath.

"Ruby," she said finally, "if you've really got asthma, and if it prevents you from doing parts of the job, then you need to bring a doctor's note. Otherwise you've got to do what you're asked to do. That's part of being on a team."

"You want me to bring a doctor's note?" Ruby gave Meredith a fixed stare. "After five years? Why don't you just ask Big Will? He'll tell you."

"The policy is to bring a doctor's note," Meredith repeated.

The sigh that emerged from Ruby's lips was aria-like. "Fine," she said. "I'll go see my doctor. Maybe I'll have to miss work, but I'll bring you a note if that's what you want. Now 'scuse us. It's almost time for us to go home. We got to start cleaning up."

Meredith opened her mouth to say something—perhaps to suggest Ruby find a time to see her doctor when she was not scheduled to work or to point out that 7:42 was early to start cleaning up.

Ruby didn't wait to find out. "C'mon, Nicole."

Nicole ran after her, grinning like a little girl.

She loved that Ruby had left Meredith with her mouth hanging open. She loved Ruby generally. Ruby had what Nicole's mother called "presence." She made other people react to her, not the other way around.

THE FIRST THING Big Will noticed when he sat down at his desk was a yellow Post-it note. He'd stuck it to the edge of his computer screen the day before. "Prefers mornings, early," it read. Underneath was a name and phone number.

He stared at the piece of paper for several seconds. With any luck, this would be the last call he'd make to an irate customer before he left Potterstown.

Colleen from Customer Experience had given him the rundown yesterday. The woman had bought some baby food that turned out to have been expired. She was given a full refund, plus a $10 off coupon for her trouble, but had remained indignant, giving Colleen an earful about how the store had gone downhill.

Big Will set his hand on the receiver, but instead of lifting it from its cradle and making the call, he paused. How he would love to tell this woman that she was right: the store *had* gone downhill. He, too, would like nothing more than for things to go back to how they were when he started, seven and a half years ago, when Town Square staffed stores at almost twice the current level. Short of that, he would settle for an upgrade of the company's outdated inventory management system, one that would send them push alerts about items nearing their expiration dates, making the process of removing those products from the shelves less time- and labor-intensive. Unfortunately, Town Square couldn't afford to do that either. And whose fault was that? Hers.

Town Square had once been known for its customer service. When its founder opened his first store in St. Louis in 1907, he had, like an early Henry Ford, made a policy of paying employees generously and treating them well. The idea was to attract and retain the best workers, who'd ensure that customers had a high-quality experience. Even as Town Square grew into a powerhouse—one of the nation's top five retailers—it continued to operate according to the same principle, paying workers above the market rate, striving to become an "employer of choice" wherever it operated. This had been key to its success, with both customers and the media, which treated Town Square as a darling, an example of "nice" and "principled" big-box retail.

Then came along a certain niche digital bookstore. Barely on Town Square's radar when store #1512 opened its doors in 2003—the Seattle-based retailer seemed hardly distinguishable from so many of the dot-com start-ups that had come and gone—it rapidly accrued a remarkable logistical and technological capability, which it had no intention of limiting to the mere purveying of books. With breathtaking agility, it expanded into all facets of retail. In less than a decade, what had initially been an interesting phenomenon had grown into an existential threat, not just to Town Square but to all traditional retailers. The online retailer—this was how Town Square executives always referred to its competitor, as if this bookstore-that-wasn't-really-a-bookstore had occult powers by which the utterance of its name would make it grow stronger—enjoyed several key advantages, above and beyond not having to bear the cost of maintaining a network of physical stores. For one, it wasn't saddled with the legacy costs—pensions and benefits—that stemmed from decades of being a good employer. Second, because it was seen as a tech company, its investors were willing to accept losses year after year, something Town Square's dividend-happy shareholders, like those of most well-established public companies, wouldn't tolerate. The leniency of the online retailer's investors allowed it to offer unsustainably low prices (at a loss) and fast, free shipping (also at a loss), enabling it to cut deeply into the market share of those retailers who were unimaginatively expected—by the very same investors—to make a profit. Meanwhile, the online retailer used its giant war chest to invest mind-bogglingly large sums of money into state-of-the-art inventory management systems that allowed it to not only track things like expiration dates—child's play—but also to record in real time the exact location of every item in its vast network of warehouses and to track the productivity of every employee—employees who were frequently paid less than Town Square employees, even though the jobs were far more demanding physically. The online retailer could do that because it didn't need to locate its warehouses in the kinds of places where its best customers lived—it put them in areas that had been bleeding jobs for years, where people were grateful for any work at all, no matter how taxing and low-paid. As a result, the online retailer's labor cost per dollar of revenue was significantly lower than that of its brick-and-mortar competitors, especially ones like Town Square that had made a point of treating their workers well.

Naturally, these things had made the online retailer extremely popular with stock analysts, the business press, and the chattering classes generally, all of whom cheered "progress!" as it decimated the retail industry, leaving in its wake hundreds of thousands of laid-off workers as well as a vast network of abandoned storefronts and derelict shopping centers (a fitting complement, perhaps, to the derelict Main Streets that the chain retailers had themselves ushered in a generation earlier).

Unlike many of its tottering, dead, or near-dead competitors—Kmart, Sears, JCPenney, Macy's, Bed Bath & Beyond, Men's Wearhouse, Payless, Pier One, Toys "R" Us—Town Square had held on. It had its hip, "fun" product lines—the mass-produced knockoffs of trendy boutique-type items that the store was known for. Nevertheless, the online retailer was daily attracting more and more dollars from just the kind of customers Town Square had long counted on: middle-class, college-educated shoppers who found Walmart depressing and didn't mind paying a little more for a better experience (on average, 7 percent more for identical items, more for Town Square's proprietary lines of clothing and home goods). Unfortunately, for Town Square, it turned out that these well-heeled customers liked low prices as much as the next person—just as long as they didn't have to physically go to Walmart and rub shoulders with the kind of people who regularly shopped there. They had no problem with an *online* discount store, particularly one that for a very long time was not only free of Walmart's whiff of seediness but actually retained a certain cachet from its origins as a tech start-up, as if it were another cool import from a cool part of the country, like strong coffee and grunge music.

To compete, Town Square had no choice but to cut costs—reduce staffing levels, curtail employee benefits, make nearly all nonmanagerial employees part-time, eliminate overtime, shrink programs like tuition assistance, and look into automation. And, yes, the prospect of more automation—beyond the self-checkout lanes that had become de rigueur—bothered Big Will. But he got it. Corporate was doing what it had to do. Would the company's employees be better off if Town Square went out of business—or sold itself to a private equity firm that would bleed it dry and then force it to declare bankruptcy, like Toys "R" Us? (Although, from Big Will's perspective, Toys "R" Us's demise was not entirely unwelcome. After it closed, store #1512 enjoyed an immediate and, so far, sustained 30 percent bump in its sales of toys.)

Still, he thought—as he finally lifted the phone from the cradle and began dialing—it was a little much that the very same people who now shop at Town Square only when they wanted something right away, who gave most of their money to the online retailer (so convenient! such good prices!), had the nerve to complain that Town Square wasn't what it once was. No shit, Sherlock. Expired baby food was the least of it.

"Hello!" he said into the receiver. "Will Flores from Town Square here. May I speak to Erin?"

Erin was polite but shrill. "I take as a given that the store isn't what it used to be," she told him. "That's been true for years. But when you start selling baby food that might have gone bad to underslept new parents—parents who care enough about their children to pay more for organic products—a line has been crossed." It was obvious from her tone that she believed in the justice of her cause, that she felt herself to be acting nobly. Must be nice, Big Will thought. He was just glad Colleen from Customer Experience had brought this to his attention. This woman was the type who might have taken her complaint to social media. It could have turned into a big to-do, which was the last thing Big Will needed right now, when he was—finally—on the cusp of getting the transfer he'd spent years waiting for.

As she yammered on, Big Will murmured phrases of sympathy and agreement: "Yes . . . I understand . . . I couldn't agree more . . . Mm-hmm." Only when she seemed to be winding down did he take the initiative. "I can't tell you how glad I am that you brought this to my attention," he assured her. "As store manager, I want to let you know personally that I'm doing everything in my power to ensure that it doesn't happen again."

He was in the middle of telling her that he'd like to send her a $20 gift card—"not a coupon but an actual gift card"—when Meredith came banging into his office.

Big Will raised his index finger, indicating that she should be quiet. "Thank you again for letting me know," he said into the phone. "Have a great day. Thank you. Bye-bye. Thanks again. Bye now."

By the time Big Will set the phone down, Meredith had collapsed onto the black pleather love seat across from his desk. (The "date-rape chair," Val called it, not because she suspected Big Will of such behavior—on the contrary, he was extremely prim and proper, as if he sensed a need to overcompensate for his frat boy looks—but because it reminded her of the backseats of those big 1980s cars in teen movies.)

To Big Will's annoyance, Meredith had shut the door behind her. Per corporate's suggested "best practices," he almost always kept the door open. He suppressed a sigh.

"What's up, Mer?"

"Oh my god," she said. "How do you deal with Ruby? I just can't."

Big Will inhaled slowly through his nose. This wasn't the first run-in Meredith had had with Ruby. But he willed himself to speak calmly. "What happened?"

"Well." Meredith tossed her head so her chin-length hair fanned out around her face. "I decided this morning that we could use another body on the line. As you know, we're cutting it close with the unload time almost every day. And I thought Ruby would be perfect. She knows the store and how everything works. There wouldn't be a learning curve."

Big Will nodded. "Okay . . ."

"So I told her that I wanted her on the line. I said, 'Ruby, we need you.' And she said no. Not 'Oh, I'm sorry, I'd rather not, and here's why . . .' She just stared at me and shook her head and said 'no.'" Meredith threw up her hands. "Completely insubord—" she began, remembering too late that the word "insubordinate" was out of favor with corporate. "I mean, it's not at all what you'd expect from a team player," she corrected. "Anyway, she just stood there, with her hands on her hips, looking at me defiantly. Meanwhile, Nicole was watching and actually laughed when Ruby refused. Honestly, I like Nicole, but sometimes . . ." Meredith shook her head, remembering the way Nicole had refused to return her high-five the day before. "In any case, I asked Ruby why, and she goes, 'It's because of my asthma.'"

Meredith's imitation of Ruby was poor—overdone. She gave Ruby a bit of a southern accent, even though Ruby was from New Jersey. This was quite possibly racist. (All things considered, Big Will thought, it was probably for the best that Meredith had shut the door.)

"Clearly she was just being stubborn," Meredith continued. "She doesn't want to adjust, doesn't want to have to make any changes." She paused, waiting for Big Will to agree. "Right?"

But Big Will was looking up at the drop ceiling above his desk. In the past three years, he'd become deeply familiar with the shapes of the overlapping yellow and gray stains that hovered above his head.

Meredith had been foolish to say no to Ruby a few weeks ago, when she wanted the day off to visit her son in prison. Meredith could easily have found someone to cover for Ruby. The people of Movement were desperate for more hours—which for months Meredith had refused to give them. (And, okay, Big Will did appreciate Meredith holding the line so firmly there—not all managers would have been so steadfast. Her commitment to staying on budget made both of them look good in corporate's eyes.) But there had been no upside to denying Ruby's request. Whoever took Ruby's shift would have appreciated the extra hours—Meredith would have generated goodwill, made two people happy, at no expense to the company or to her budget. Instead she had dug in her heels "on principle": she wanted, she said, to set a new tone, show that Movement was going to start operating in a more orderly fashion. Stupid.

And now this.

Big Will dropped his gaze from the ceiling. "It's not about asthma," he said.

His tone made Meredith's smile disappear.

"Ruby has trouble reading," he continued. "She compensates by memorizing—she knows where just about everything in the store goes just by looking at it, without reading the locations off a scanner. It's actually quite impressive—she knows the store better than I do, better than any of us managers, I'm willing to bet. But she'd have a hard time on the line. A cardboard box is a cardboard box. She can't tell what's inside just from looking at it. You have to read the labels. And you have to read fast. I'm willing to bet that Ruby is worried that if she tried to work the line people would realize what a hard time she has."

"Oh!" Meredith said. "I had no idea."

"Do you want to know how I know this?" Big Will asked. He didn't give Meredith a chance to answer. "It's because Ruby and I have a good relationship. She feels comfortable with me. She had trouble with some of the written tests corporate administers periodically, and she confided in me."

Meredith nodded slowly. For a moment, Big Will hoped it would be an "aha" moment for her, about the importance of having solid relationships with the people she managed. Then she opened her mouth.

"I've only been working with her for a couple of months. I mean, I couldn't have known. Right?" He didn't answer, and she rephrased her question. "How could I have known?"

This was what pushed Big Will over the edge. *Of course* Meredith skipped over the part about taking responsibility and went straight to demanding reassurance that she wasn't to blame. With Meredith everything was both always about her and never her fault.

"No, you couldn't have known," he said, pressing both hands on the desk in front of him and speaking loudly. "But you do know that Ruby has been here for five years. And you know that Little Will, who has managed Movement for years, likes her because she's good at her job, and she's reliable. Knowing that, you could have *maybe* thought about approaching her differently—you could have maybe tried *asking* her if she wanted to work the line. You could have paid attention when she said no, asked why as if you really wanted the answer, instead of immediately assuming bad faith. You could have defused the situation instead of escalating it."

Meredith felt as if she'd been slapped.

He didn't understand, she thought. Ruby was different with him, jokey and teasing, telling him how skinny he looked, how he must miss his "boo" in Connecticut. Of course *he* thought Ruby was harmless.

"I just don't get why you alienate your team like this," he continued. "You make everything, every interaction, about you, about whether or not they're being 'insubordinate,' whether they respect you. In college, did you learn anything about managing people, anything at all? How about tight labor markets?"

How many times had Big Will tried to tell Meredith that in a city like Potterstown, finding people willing to work as an executive manager, for $80K or $85K, wasn't exactly a challenge? Finding good, reliable rank-and-file workers was a different story. Ten years ago, five years ago, it was different. For years after the financial crisis and Great Recession, the store had multiple applicants for every job opening. But that had all changed in the past couple of years. It was increasingly hard to find and hold on to good people—people who showed up every day, week after week, year after year, who knew the store and how it operated and were willing to put up with low pay and erratic scheduling and fluctuating hours, people who didn't mind coming in at 4 a.m. and were willing to do overnights when needed and work holidays. The team Meredith inherited might not be perfect—if they were, they wouldn't be working here, for what Town Square paid them—but they got the job done every morning, unloading and unpacking between fifteen hundred and two thousand boxes—about as many boxes as it took to move five large houses. If they started to quit on her, Meredith would see what trouble really looked like.

"I know you want them to be more productive," he said. "I know that's your 'mandate' from corporate, or whatever. But it's a balancing act. They won't be more productive if they leave. You've got to keep them happy where you can, *especially* if you're also asking them to work harder, to do things differently." He paused, then added, "Especially if you want to be store manager."

What Meredith heard was: team members are always right, kiss their asses, blah, blah, blah. Big Will had said it all before. It was bullshit then and it was bullshit now. He *never* gave her any credit for the efforts she made. What about the time she bought the whole team breakfast from the Starbucks in the store's lobby? And okay, that hadn't been exactly by choice. She'd learned it was the birthday of one of the old guys and said she'd buy him a pastry. Then Milo pointed out that it had been his birthday a few days' earlier, and he hadn't gotten anything. So Meredith said she'd get Milo one too. Then Ruby started listing other members of the team who'd had birthdays since Meredith had started in Logistics. Finally, Meredith gave up and said they could each get one pastry *or* coffee drink. The whole thing had cost her more than fifty dollars in the end.

Why didn't Big Will mention that? How many other managers would have done that?

She lifted her chin defiantly. "Frankly I think it's ironic that you're lecturing me about being a good manager, considering the way you've been speaking to me. To be honest, I don't think it's appropriate."

She looked at him squarely, trying to convey, without uttering the words, that she had options: she could complain to Svetlana in HR that he bullied her. In the current climate, Svetlana would have to take such an accusation seriously, send it up to corporate.

"You were the one," she continued, "who warned me that the people of Movement were insular and hostile to newcomers and that they might be especially skeptical of a woman in my role. And yet when I come to you with a problem, instead of offering support, you attack me. You know how hard I've been working—how many ten- and twelve-hours days I've been putting in. Some days I don't see my son at all. I leave the house before he wakes up and come home after he's gone to bed. But instead of appreciating that, it's like you don't have my back *at all*."

Big Will stared at her in disbelief. As if he didn't want her to get her work done in eight or nine or ten hours like all the other executive managers did, like he—mostly—had done when he had her *exact same job*—executive manager of Logistics—before he'd been promoted to store manager? But somehow overseeing the unload and the breakout process and getting the displays up and approving the weekly schedules and dealing with the vendors and all the rest took Meredith eleven or twelve hours. And that was *his* fault?

But the first flush of his anger had faded, and Big Will was beginning to feel increasingly unhappy with himself for having lost his temper. She wasn't *entirely* wrong. He shouldn't have raised his voice or said what he had about her not having learned anything in college. It was a mean, inappropriate thing to say—something he'd rather she didn't report to Svetlana in HR.

"I'm sorry, Mer," he said. "I said some things I shouldn't have. I messed up. Okay? I'm sorry. I'm just frustrated. If you want this promotion as much as you say, you simply have to *try* to get along with the team. The transfer to Movement was supposed to be your fresh start, yes?"

Big Will was trying to placate Meredith, but he miscalculated. To her, his words were a dig, an unpleasant reminder that she had racked up an unusually high number of complaints from subordinates over the years. In Meredith's mind, her move from Sales to Logistics had been exclusively about increasing her breadth of experience in order to make her a better candidate for store manager. The concept of a "fresh start"—with its implication that she needed one—had nothing to do with it.

She remained silent.

"Having good relationships is especially important now," Big Will said, almost pleadingly. "With corporate coming to interview the team. If there were ever a time to try to approach them gently . . . I mean, what do you want them to say about you next week when they're asked? You need them to be on your side."

But Meredith wasn't disposed to take advice from him just now. She could deal with her team, thank you very much.

"And I do have your back," he continued. "Don't worry about Ruby. I'll talk to her. Meanwhile, why don't you tap someone else for the line? How about the new girl? Callie? She's young, and she looks fit."

Meredith nodded. She was still mad, but she was beginning to see that there was no advantage in prolonging this fight—or making a formal complaint. Not now, not when what she really wanted—the promotion to store manager—was on the table.

"Okay," she said.

"So, we're cool?" Big Will asked.

She shrugged. "We're cool."

When Meredith left his office, it was almost eight. Big Will needed to get out to the sales floor soon, lead the Huddle. But he needed a moment. He went back to staring at the stains on the ceiling. He focused on a somewhat triangular one that had long reminded him—sacrilegiously?—of the Virgin Mary.

He was in a bind. No matter what he thought of Meredith, he had no choice but to support her bid for store manager. He'd put certain things in writing when he'd recommended her promotion to executive manager. He'd had to. The promotion to executive manager was considered a very significant jump in status. Executive managers were designated as corporate, not store-level, employees. The positions were salaried and came with a more generous benefits plan, commensurate with what mid-tier white-collar workers generally received. They had power over budgets and were also, unlike lower-level managers, eligible for performance-based bonuses.

The majority of executive managers joined the company as recent college or business school graduates, through its management training program, which recruited directly from universities. This had been Big Will's path. But corporate also wanted to demonstrate that it provided opportunities for members of the communities it served: it liked to report to the media and government that a certain percentage of its upper-level employees started on the lower rungs. Store managers were strongly encouraged to seek out store-level employees suitable for promotion to executive manager. The problem was corporate was also very picky about whom it deemed suitable. But Meredith had studied at a fancy fashion school in New York City (she'd dropped out, but still). She dressed nicely. She used words like "mandate." She came across as middle class—that is, she knew more about home equity loans than Section 8 vouchers, more about the health benefits of kale than about the ins and outs of the federal food stamp program. She was, in other words, the kind of person the people of corporate felt comfortable with, the kind of person in whom they felt intuitive confidence.

And so Big Will had described her, in writing, as "one of the most enthusiastic and committed managers I've ever worked with." He said she was "smart and motivated and would make an excellent upper-level manager." He had meant it at the time—at least he thought he had. In any case, his instinct about corporate had proved correct. He'd gotten a $1,000 bonus for "recognizing and cultivating internal talent," which he'd intended to use to pay down his student loan principal but which he had actually spent on tickets to a Giants game (a gift to himself) and a night at an upscale hotel & spa in northwestern Connecticut (a gift to his fiancée, Caitlin, which he'd deemed advisable after she'd reacted less than favorably to his going to the Giants game without her).

Now, though, Big Will wished he could give back the money, unsee the football game, un-exfoliate Caitlin's skin, un-have the sex in the hotel's well-appointed king-size bed, if it meant that he'd never put all those positive things about Meredith in writing. He had started to suspect Meredith was incapable of improving as a manager. She lacked something, tact or savvy. She seemed wholly unable to generate goodwill in the people she managed.

But what could he do? He'd been so emphatic—now corporate saw her as his protégée. An about-face, an admission to corporate that he'd made a mistake in championing her, would reflect poorly on him—and at the worst possible moment.

Big Will had been waiting for this transfer for three long years, since the day he arrived at store #1512. It wasn't just that Caitlin and his family were in Connecticut. He hated Potterstown—hated its crumbling infrastructure and decrepit housing stock, hated the aura of urban menace that permeated its downtown (in spite of Potterstown being too small to be considered an actual city), hated the lack of free street parking in its historic, supposedly charming uptown neighborhood. (Big Will didn't care for coffee shops located in drafty old banks or bakeries with overly cute names.) He liked new buildings, big, wide boulevards, modern shopping centers with high-end retail, and clean, spacious restaurants with ample (free) parking. A well-to-do suburb was his ideal.

He was done sowing his oats—if that was a remotely accurate way to describe his life in Potterstown these last few years, in which he spent most nights in an underfurnished apartment in a shitty complex, watching sports or playing video games by himself while drinking more than was good for him. Big Will was ready, so ready, to start the next phase of his life. He and Caitlin were looking at houses in Connecticut this weekend. New construction was his dream, but it was likely beyond their budget. That was okay—he'd be content with an older ranch or split-level on a nice, safe street, a place with a big yard for the kids they wanted to have soon. He imagined a swing set and a trampoline in the backyard and big, boisterous Sunday night dinners with his parents and Caitlin's dad and their younger sisters and brothers.

This was the life he wanted, the life he'd always wanted, what he'd been working toward since he'd entered Town Square's training program from UConn. And if his transfer went smoothly—and he did well in West Hartford—in a few years he'd likely be considered for district- and regional-level jobs. (Then new construction *would* be feasible.)

No, he thought as he finally got up and began walking to the sales floor for the Huddle. He simply couldn't afford to make trouble now, create problems by raising questions about the very manager he'd spent the past three years building up.

10

FLECKS OF DUST shimmered in the long columns of light that streamed in through the warehouse skylights. Little Will was reminded of the way light slanted through the stained-glass windows of St. Joseph's, where his family had gone when he was growing up.

By now, the line had been disassembled. The truck was bare except for a few tarps and some coils of rope. The warehouse was empty, still.

At the bottom of the loading dock were the Town Square boxes Movement had emptied that morning—several hundred of them, flattened and thrown into large, messy piles. Little Will got down on his knees. He began counting out stacks of twenty boxes each, tying the stacks together with twine and then tossing them into the truck. The boxes would be reused at the distribution center.

He worked quietly, methodically. This was Little Will's favorite part of the workday.

When he let himself into the store at three each morning, the warehouse was black—tomb-like, save for the glow of two red EXIT signs. Then the team arrived, filling the space with energy and life. After the truck was unloaded, the clatter of voices and bodies moved to the sales floor until it, too, teemed with activity. When the team left at eight, the bustle receded. But this second quiet was different, satisfying—to Little Will it felt earned. At an hour when most people were just getting in their cars to go to work, his team had completed the task they'd set out to do.

Still. Had you told him a decade ago that this would be his life, Little Will wouldn't have believed you. In high school, he had been on track for a hockey scholarship, but he didn't play as well as he should have his final year and in the end it didn't come to pass. He decided to stay home, work for his dad at Saunders & Son, a carpet-and-tile store that Little Will's grandfather had opened shortly after the Second World War. Then came the financial crisis. The store didn't make it. Not long after, Little Will landed at Town Square as a seasonal worker. He'd meant for it to be short-term, something to do until he figured out what came next. But he was depressed, angry about hockey and his dad, who'd been devastated by the store's failure and whose health had deteriorated rapidly, as if Saunders & Son hadn't merely been his life in a metaphorical sense, but had literally been part of his lifeblood.

Several years passed before Little Will got it together, made a new plan. He decided to go to college to become a gym teacher. He was accepted into SUNY Empire in Albany. But when he told his boss at Town Square, he had been thrown for a loop: he was offered the position of group manager of Movement.

By then, Little Will had met his fiancée. They'd only been together a few months, but they already knew they wanted to get married. And they wanted kids. College would have taken years, left them in debt, and was uncertain anyway. Little Will was dyslexic. He had never been a great student. He wasn't even sure he'd make it through college. Even if he did, who knew if he'd be able to get a teaching job locally, and he couldn't leave his mother to take sole care of his father, who was by then wheelchair-bound and increasingly irascible. Little Will had taken the bird in hand, the full-time job with benefits. He toyed briefly with the idea of using Town Square's tuition assistance program to go back to school, but he soon learned that the program had recently been narrowed so that the money could be applied only to degrees related to the employee's job at Town Square. A degree in physical education wouldn't cut it. At least, as group manager of Movement, his hours would be predictable. He'd work mornings, leaving him free in the afternoons to build his landscaping business. It had been his fiancée's idea to name the new business Saunders & Son, after the store.

The two of them had made a five-year plan. They would live in the basement of Little Will's parents' house and save up for a down payment on a house of their own; when their combined income from his landscaping business and her salary teaching preschool was sufficient to support them, Little Will would quit Town Square. But four years had passed, and they were barely any closer to being able to afford a house. Real estate prices had shot up in the past several years. Little Will suspected the five-year plan would become a ten-year plan, that it would be a long time, if ever, before he could quit Town Square. When they had a baby, his fiancée would probably quit working for a while—they'd need his health insurance more than ever.

Little Will threw a stack of boxes into the truck. He used more force than was necessary: it landed with a satisfying thwack.

He had nothing against retail in principle. Just Town Square. He despised its ethos of corner-cutting (the Potemkin approach to store maintenance—cleaning stores only when upper-level visitors were expected—was a case in point), its willingness to cheat employees in any way that was technically not illegal (and call it "performing its fiduciary duty to stockholders"), its arbitrary rules, such as its insistence that the unload take no more than an hour, regardless of the size of the truck and no matter how little difference it made to finish at 5:01 rather than 5:00. Corporate didn't trust its own workers, was what it came down to—the big shots thought that without a hard deadline, its employees wouldn't work efficiently, which showed just how little corporate understood the people it employed. And then there was Meredith. More than any other executive manager Little Will had ever worked with, she seemed like the walking, talking embodiment of everything he disliked most about Town Square.

Little Will's own ideas about business had been absorbed from his father, who never would have dreamed of, say, cutting an employee's hours to avoid paying for their health insurance. His father had felt an obligation to the people who worked for him, many of whom had been with him for decades. He would sooner have cut off his own insurance than done that to one of them. Some people would say that this "softheartedness" was the reason Saunders & Son went under, that his father wasn't a savvy enough businessman. But it wasn't true. For decades—through recessions, gas shortages, periods of inflation, real estate depreciation, the departure of IBM—the store had survived, supporting their family and its ten or so employees. It would have continued to do so if the housing and lending markets hadn't collapsed simultaneously in 2008. That was the rub, both things happening at once. If Saunders & Son had gotten a loan to tide it over until home sales picked up, it would not only have regained its footing quickly but would be doing better than ever. All those second-home buyers from the city who had recently bid up prices around here, making it hard for Little Will to afford a house, would have been excellent customers for a high-quality, service-oriented carpet-and-tile store.

The last bundle of boxes hit the bottom of the truck so forcefully that it slid all the way to the rear wall, then pitched forward a dozen feet. But the twine held; the stack remained intact. Little Will pulled the door to the truck shut. Later one of the drivers from the distribution center would come with a fresh trailer. He'd hitch this one to his cab and take it back to Pennsylvania.

The truck taken care of, Little Will brought the thirty or so garbage bags of packaging Movement had amassed over the course of the morning to the dumpster out back.

His final task before he went up front to do paperwork—vendor invoices, schedules, budgets, etc.—was to take care of the manufacturers' boxes Movement had emptied. Unlike the Town Square boxes, these didn't get reused. There were several pallets' worth. He loaded them onto pallets and brought them to the baling machine, dropping them in in large armfuls. When all the boxes were in the chamber, he inserted his key and turned the dial. A few seconds passed before the rumbling began, the machine's large metal plate pushing downward, transforming the unruly mass of cardboard into a dense, brick-like rectangle.

On his way out of the warehouse, Little Will automatically reached out his arm and turned the light switch to the off position. With so much sunlight pouring in, it made no discernible difference.

11

AFTER YEARS OF declining sales, corporate had compressed store #1512's Entertainment section into a single aisle, dedicated to books. (In contrast to CDs, DVDs, and magazines, whose sales had all plummeted, books had held up surprisingly well in the digital age.) The shelving units that had lined Entertainment's other three aisles had been removed—in their place, a new, more open section had been set up to house large-scale toys: puppet theaters, child-sized kitchen sets, motorized cars, and anything else too big to be displayed to full advantage in the packed lanes of the regular toy section.

Val chose Toys for Rich Kids—she refused to call the new section anything else—for the first official pro-Mer meeting, at half past midnight on Wednesday night/Thursday morning, just after the start of their first overnight. Val's initial idea had been to meet inside a child-sized plastic playhouse at the back of the section, but she had quickly discovered she could barely get her own ass through its narrow door. Even if they could all fit inside, it was so small and airless, they'd probably suffocate. She, Ruby, Travis, Raymond, Diego, and Milo had gathered instead in the alley behind the playhouse. At least they didn't have to worry about Meredith catching them. Meredith had told Little Will she'd be late, arriving close to three.

The sales floor was dark. The red and blue and green indicator lights of the display devices in Electronics created a celestial haze that made a trio of headless male mannequins in the middle distance look like a boy band that had been guillotined. Val's wide, pale face seemed to glow when she stepped forward and opened the meeting.

"There are three things we need to do," she said. "Number one, we've got to clean up the store. If corporate sees the real state of things, it'll be all over for Meredith. So we've got to do what it takes to make it happen, no matter how hard we have to work. Remember, it's not for her—it's for us. We've got four days to get this place into shape. Four."

With that, Val pulled out a slightly torn felt Advent calendar she'd found in the storeroom drawer, a treasure trove of no-longer-salable religious junk that for Christian reasons some manager had felt queasy about tossing.

Val picked up a tiny beige-colored Baby Jesus attached to the calendar with an elastic string and started to place him in the pocket marked 21.

"Why don't you put him in 4?" Ruby asked. "I mean, we ain't counting to Christmas, are we? Wouldn't it be more clear if you counted down to zero instead of up to 25? Then we'd know exactly how many days are left."

Val felt a wave of defensiveness rise up in her. She squelched it. Ruby had a point. "Good idea," she said.

She moved Baby Jesus to the pocket labeled 4.

When she looked up, Milo was staring at her suspiciously, as if she were trying to pull something over on them.

He held up a fist. "Corporate comes on Monday," he said, and began opening his fingers one by one. "Today is Wednesday. Tomorrow is Thursday, then Friday, Saturday, and Sunday." All his fingers were now extended. "That's five days."

"It's after midnight," Val explained. "Technically it's now Thursday. Tomorrow's overnight is Friday, the next day is Saturday, and the last overnight is Sunday. So, four shifts between now and when corporate comes."

But Val realized now that the Advent calendar had been a stupid idea. She'd thought that having a prop would create a sense of occasion, but they all knew how long it was between now and Monday. She balled up the calendar.

"It doesn't matter. The point is, we don't have much time. Okay, on to item number tw—"

Ruby let out a loud yawn. "Excuse me," she said.

"—*number two*," Val repeated. "We need to think about how to take down Anita. She's Meredith's only rival, and she's got a real shot. She has four years at the executive manager level, to Meredith's two, and she—"

"—doesn't suck at her job," finished Raymond. His voice sounded even worse than it had the day before.

"You okay?" Ruby asked. "You sound sic—"

"*Anyway*," Val said over her, tapping on her watch face to indicate that they didn't have time for small talk. "My idea is that we'll mess up the stuff on the display tables in her sections before corporate comes."

"Hold up," Travis said, taking a step back and nearly bumping into a model sewing machine that had, literally, been displayed on the store's rear wall since Val started at the store three and a half years ago. It had looked like an antique even then.

Travis raised his arms in front of him, as if to physically stop whatever was coming. "I'm not comfortable doing anything that I could get fired for," he said.

The others had no idea how hard it had been for him to get this job.

Val thought everyone needed to focus on the big picture, not get fixated on details. But when she answered Travis, her voice was calm and empathetic. "I hear you," she said. "We'll keep you out of anything shady. You won't have to mess up any tables, I promise."

"I don't even get it," Ruby said. "You seen the tables in Softlines lately? We don't need to mess them up. They already a mess."

"They are now," Val agreed, "but I promise you, Anita will clean them up before corporate comes. Just like Meredith is having us get through the backlog. What we're going to do is wait until she cleans them up to mess them up again. See what I mean?" When Ruby nodded, Val continued. "Do any of you have any other ideas for messing with Anita?"

No one did.

Val said they should keep thinking. "Remember. Anita is Meredith's only competition. It might make all the difference. Okay. Number three. We need certain key people on board—or at least neutral."

Val picked up a legal pad she'd stashed on the roof of the playhouse. On its first page she'd drawn three columns, labeled "pro-Mer," "anti-Mer," and "unknown." Underneath she'd written in names.

She held out the notebook and waited as the others scanned the lists, looking instinctively for their own names first. Only after they found themselves did they check to see where others had landed.

"What about Callie?" Milo asked. "She isn't in any of the columns."

"Callie?" Val made a face. "Even if they bother to interview her, she won't have anything to say. She'll have been here less than a week."

"But—" Milo started to say.

Val cut him off. "*The people* we need to deal with are Nicole, Joyce, and the old guys. And I don't think we need to worry about the old guys. Meredith doesn't rag on them the way she rags on us. I doubt they care one way or the other who our manager is. I don't think we can risk letting them in on it. Just in case. We don't want anyone to go blabbing to Big Will."

Val looked around, checking that they were all paying attention. "This is serious. I don't think there's a specific rule that we're breaking. But if Big Will knew, or any manager—even Little Will—knew what we were up to, they wouldn't like it. They'd say we were trying to game the system, that the point of the interviews is to tell the truth and that we aren't supposed to coordinate our answers."

Val could sense from a certain shift in their posture that most of the others hadn't thought about this before.

"Don't worry," she reassured them. "There's no reason for them to ever know."

Raymond grinned. "Even if they did catch us meeting like this," he said, "the last thing they'd think is that we were trying to help Meredith. They'd probably think we were trying to start a union."

They all laughed.

"Lordy!" Ruby said. "Don't even joke. Then we'd really be in trouble."

Corporate wasn't playing when it came to unions. The year before, someone in Harvest—the team responsible for fresh produce and perishables—was fired for "time theft" after he'd been spotted talking briefly to a union organizer during his shift.

"Right," Val said. "Good thing we're *not* forming a union. *Now.* Back to what I was saying. We're left with Joyce and Nicole. They're the ones who could help us—or hurt us. Especially Nicole."

Val had been thinking a lot about Nicole, the problem she might pose. She thought Nicole was one of those smart people whose intelligence has no outlet, at least none that were productive. It was easy to imagine Nicole applying all her cleverness to the project of fucking Meredith over. She would know that she couldn't let on that she hated Meredith or sound like she had an ax to grind. No, she would dress neatly, with her long hair in a demure braid down her back, sit with her hands clasped primly in her lap, and gaze sadly at the interviewers as she told them—her voice dripping with regret—that Meredith was incompetent, ignorant of the warehouse, and had a management style that was alienating and bad for morale.

She could destroy the pro-Mer cause.

"I'll talk to Joyce," Val said, "but Ruby, I was thinking maybe you could talk to Nicole? See if you can persuade her to join us—or at least to keep quiet when corporate comes."

Ruby's eyes widened. "Me?"

Ruby wasn't a true believer in this project. She still believed that corporate would do what it wanted in the end, regardless of what they said or did. She had only come to this meeting for fun, because it was something to do that was different. And she and Nicole had tacitly agreed to disagree on the subject of Val's plan. Ruby didn't want to start pressuring her friend now, not for something so pointless.

"I'll talk to Nicole," Diego said.

Val was surprised. They all were. It was strange enough Diego was here at all. He usually looked down on their little schemes and jokes, called them immature. (Nicole had determined that in high school, Diego would have been the older boyfriend, the guy who sometimes hung out with her and her friends on account of the girl he was dating but was too aloof and superior to be taken for one of them.)

But Diego really wanted this promotion. He also had a high opinion of his own powers of persuasion, at least where women were concerned.

"That's great," Val said. "Let me know how it goes. In the meantime"—she turned to Ruby—"until we know if she's on our side, I don't want anyone to say anything to Nicole about what we're planning. If she's not with us, she's against us."

Ruby sucked in her breath. "Nicole wouldn't—"

"I know she wouldn't," Val interrupted. "That's not what I'm saying. But it's only right that we discuss our plans only with people who're in. We're all taking a risk." She turned to Travis and added, "A small risk, but a risk all the same."

Of course, Val knew perfectly well that Nicole wouldn't rat them out. But Val thought being frozen out might frustrate Nicole. She might join them just so she wasn't excluded.

"Fine," Ruby said.

"Okay. Anyone have anything else?"

Raymond stepped forward.

"There is one thing that's been bothering me."

"Oh?"

"Do you ever get the feeling that Big Will doesn't actually like Meredith? I wonder if he even wants her to get the job."

Val snorted. "Oh, yeah, he does. Remember he pushed for her to get promoted to executive manager. If it weren't for him, she'd still be a plain old group manager, making half of what she does now. *Of course* he likes her."

Raymond nodded. "Makes sense."

To avoid being spotted, they left Rich Kid Toys one at a time. As she watched the others leave, Val felt a twinge of something. Was it guilt? She wondered at moments if she was an asshole for not telling them that Big Will had pretty much promised her the promotion.

On the other hand, she hadn't told them about getting written up either. She'd been embarrassed. So maybe it was a wash.

12

"*PSST.* NICOLE."

Diego's voice was breathy, almost a hiss.

"I need to talk to you."

Nicole sighed, as if this was a big ask, but she followed Diego. He led her to an alcove in Domestics, next to a display table covered with decorative candles and bowls of potpourri.

"It's about Meredith," Diego began.

He was only a couple of inches taller than Nicole, but he was a lot broader, especially above the waist. He lifted weights, but he focused so disproportionately on his shoulders and chest that his body had a triangular aspect, like a genie tethered to a tiny bottle. The breadth of his upper body was accentuated by the snug fit of his Town Square T-shirt, which—now as always—he wore tucked into his belted khaki pants. He had, Nicole knew, a real hang-up about not looking sloppy or ghetto. Yet Diego was cool. No one who met him would think otherwise. Maybe that was why Nicole didn't screw up her face or tell him she didn't want to talk about Meredith, the way she would have if he'd been Raymond or Milo. Something about Diego made her act differently with him than she did with those doofuses, who were downright scared of her—crumpling before her eyes if she was even the tiniest bit mean to them. (And, really, it was impossible not to be, sometimes.)

"Look," Diego said, picking up a squat, cylindrical candle from the display table. "I know you don't like her. I don't like her either. None of us do. And maybe Val gets on your nerves some. That's fair. But I want you to ask yourself something. What good is going to come from telling the people from corporate what you think of her?"

Nicole started to answer, but Diego held up the hand in which he held the candle. "Let me say what I got to say."

"Oh-*kaaay*." The whine in her voice made her sound even younger than she was.

"See, what I think is that it'll feel real good at first, telling those people from corporate the truth. Right as you're talking shit about her and maybe for a little while after. For a couple of days, you'll be on top of the world, thinking about what a badass you are, how you've gotten Meredith back for the way she treats people, for the way she's treated you. Hmm?"

Diego bore into her with his eyes. Nicole almost couldn't help but nod in agreement.

"Yeah, so?" she said.

"Well, I want you to think about what happens next. What I think is you'll wake up a few days later and realize nothing is different. It won't matter how good it felt to speak your mind. She'll still be our boss, she'll still be in the warehouse every goddamn day, treating us like shit, driving us crazy, making us all miserable. Forever. Now, on the other hand, if you watch what you say—and that's all I'm asking you to do, to watch what you say, not lie, not to do anything you're not comfortable with—there's a real chance things could change around here. No matter who's promoted to group manager, having her off our backs will make things better—for all of us." He put down the candle and looked straight at her. "It's not just about you, you know."

Nicole was about to object—what right did he have to imply she was selfish?—but somehow the words got lost on the way to her mouth. She looked down, at the linoleum floor. Maybe she did feel a little guilty. Because she had a future—outside the store. Eventually Nicole would leave Town Square. She planned to get a "real" job, at UnitedHealthcare. Not everyone could do that. Diego couldn't, not with his accent. She doubted he could type well enough either. Where else could Diego go, except to Walmart or someplace similar?

"I'll think about it," she said. "I will. I promise."

"Okay."

He looked at her intently, with an imploring, hangdog expression that Nicole found nearly impossible to break away from. Finally, after what felt to her like a very long time, he nodded magisterially, as if to dismiss her. Almost automatically she complied.

During a brief period a couple of years ago, there had been a guy in Movement who threw parties at his place. Nicole had gone to enough of them to know that when he was drunk, Diego hit on any woman within a hundred feet. As she walked back from Domestics, she felt she finally understood why a surprisingly large number of those women—that is, not zero—went with Diego for the night, even ones who knew he had a girlfriend. Not that Nicole ever would—ew! she hated cheaters, and Diego was forty-two, old enough to be her father—but after that look, its effect on her, she got it a little better.

Back in Softlines, Callie was working on hanging clothes. Nicole walked past her without speaking.

When she reached her own spot, Nicole didn't immediately dip into her box. Instead she watched Ruby, who was humming to herself as she folded tiny pastel-colored T-shirts and shorts. Ruby's long, graceful hands moved with the speed and precision of a piano player's. Items of clothing, creased as precisely as origami, fell from her fingers, landing seamlessly in organized piles.

Ruby had once told her she'd learned to fold in Atlantic City, where she was born and where she'd worked for many years as a hotel maid.

No one else at the store appreciated—or even noticed—Ruby's skill. Meredith claimed to take an interest in Softlines—"I love clothes!" she'd say, as if you couldn't tell from a hundred feet away that Meredith was vain—but she was too self-absorbed to pay attention to anything that didn't directly affect her. And Little Will acted like he was too big and clumsy and dirty to be allowed anywhere near Softlines—he said he deferred to them entirely. He meant it as a compliment, a show of how much he trusted them, but the truth was, he didn't engage much with their work, the way he did with Diego's or Val's because they put together the big displays and broke out the sections he paid more attention to, like Paper and Chemical.

Ruby noticed Nicole watching her. She stopped humming. "You going to work or what?" she asked. "Not that I care. I just don't want Little Will to come by."

Even though they all knew he hated Town Square, Little Will cared about the work, about things being done right. It was one of his tics. If he saw any of them slacking off, he didn't get so much mad as sad, as if they had let him down, personally, as a friend. It was weird, yet they all respected him for it, too. At least it was better than Meredith, who cared only about making herself look good, not about the store itself.

"You know he'd make a face at you," Ruby continued, mimicking Little Will's disappointed expression. Her imitation of his sad eyes and deep frown was good enough that Nicole laughed aloud as she reached into her box.

If only Ruby could come with her to United, Nicole thought.

But she couldn't. Ruby didn't read very well. Nicole had figured that out soon after they started working together. Ruby kept referring to "Forever Vintage," Town Square's newly launched brand of junior girls' clothing, as "Foreign Vineyard." At first, Nicole didn't understand—she thought it was a joke she didn't get—but when Nicole finally asked Ruby why she called it that, Ruby had laughed a little too loudly. "I guess I didn't read the label carefully," she said, fiddling with her reading glasses. "I must need a new prescription." It wasn't long before Nicole understood. Once she did, a lot of other things began to make sense to Nicole, like why Ruby didn't have her driver's license. The written test, the road signs.

Nicole finally began working through her box, folding mechanically (and, compared to Ruby, poorly).

Click-click-swoosh, click-click-swoosh. The sound of Callie dropping hangers on metal racks, then sliding them over to make room for more, was hypnotic. Or maybe Nicole was just tired. She looked at her phone. Three o'clock. Five more hours to go.

Her mother kept asking why she was still at Town Square, doing this shit—retail, overnights, etc. She wanted to know when Nicole was going to grow up, apply to United. But Nicole wasn't in a hurry. In her mind, going to United would be the official beginning of her grown-up work life. She didn't want to go before she was ready. She didn't want to risk fucking up, the way Milo had, get her ass fired. Not that she'd fuck up in the same way. He'd had some sort of temper tantrum, threatened someone. It was so Milo.

Still, there were other ways to fuck up. Nicole didn't smoke much weed anymore, but she did sometimes. She was pretty sure United gave drug tests. What if she failed? That would be it. She'd be done, stuck in retail, possibly forever. She couldn't wait tables, she just couldn't. Not after listening to her mother complain all these years. Her mother had been at the diner for twenty-five years, ever since the company she'd worked for before Nicole was born, the one that made keyboards for IBM, moved to Mexico.

There were no other big companies like United in town. And it wasn't like she and Marcus could just up and move to a different place with more jobs. They relied on both her mom and his for babysitting. They couldn't afford day care. And Nicole didn't even have a car of her own. What would she do if she couldn't borrow the Dingmobile?

There was another reason she put off applying, although she didn't like to admit it, even to herself. Deep down, she was scared. What if she applied—and got rejected? What if they said her spelling and grammar weren't good enough? What if they were stuck up, like the women who worked in Sales at Town Square? What if they took one look at her and decided that she was trash, not office material? What if she didn't make it even as far as *Milo*? Then Nicole would not only be stuck in retail, she wouldn't even have what she had now—the belief, in the back of her mind, that she could leave for someplace better whenever she wanted, that being here was her choice.

It wasn't like there was any rush, no matter what her mom said. As Nicole had tried to explain to the union organizer who'd cornered her outside the store a few months ago—after her shift was over or she'd never have risked talking to him!—Town Square wasn't so bad. It was a lot better than the job Nicole had before, in fast food. Her boss was a dirtbag who hit on her all the time, promising to promote her to assistant manager if she'd sleep with him. It was gross—and more than a little bit scary when she was alone with him. One thing about Town Square was that it didn't tolerate that kind of shit. (Nicole appreciated Big Will's thing about keeping his office door open—it set the right tone.) Really, the worst thing about this job was Meredith, her micromanaging, the constant threat of being written up, her whole irritating energy, the way she ruined their goddamn fucking chill.

Maybe, Nicole thought suddenly, the others were right. Maybe it was worth lying to get Meredith off their backs? It was true—they would see much less of Meredith if she were store manager than they did now. For a moment, Nicole was almost persuaded.

Then she heard the jangling of keys. Val was walking past with a pallet of Seasonal. Aside from Little Will—who actually needed his, for the job—Val was the only person who carried her keys around with her while she worked. Nicole was sure it was so people who didn't know better would think she was a manager, think she had keys to the supply closet and to the heavy equipment in the back on that stupid key ring of hers.

With that, Nicole remembered why she disliked the pro-Mer plan.

It wasn't even that she disliked Val. She didn't, not really. Val was bossy and kind of ridiculous at times, but Nicole respected the force of her personality. She wasn't someone you could push around. Nicole appreciated that. No, what Nicole objected to was not Val personally but the idea of being a dupe. Nicole knew Val wanted the group manager job. It was obvious, even if Val seemed to think they were all too stupid to figure out that *she* was the one who planned to benefit the most from Meredith's promotion. If the others wanted to be Val's patsies, do her dirty work, that was their prerogative.

"YOU'RE TELLING ME you *want* Meredith to get promoted?" Joyce narrowed her eyes skeptically.

"Yup." Val grinned.

She had found Joyce breaking out makeup in Drug Store.

"I need a second to wrap my little old lady head around this," Joyce said.

She bent forward to reach into a box of eye shadows. Her long, thick brown hair—which she blow-dried and wore down most days—fell like a curtain over her face. (Her comment about being an old lady was ironic: Joyce knew she looked darn good for a grandmother of four.) She began inserting the eye shadows into slots on the display case, from darkest to lightest.

"You're probably right," she said finally. "They probably would promote Little Will this time. They probably won't give him the title officially, won't make him 'executive manager'"—she made air quotes around the words. "Not without a degree. It's a real point of pride with corporate. They don't like to let the riffraff into their little club."

Joyce snorted, Val smiled politely.

"So?" Val asked after a beat. "Will you help? We could really use you on our side. You're probably the most respected person on the whole team."

"Well, aren't you a sweetie for saying that."

Joyce was genuinely touched. She didn't get all that many compliments. When she got home later, she'd tell her husband what Val said.

"So, you're in?" Val asked.

"I didn't say that."

Joyce opened a box of lipsticks and began slotting them into clear nodules built just for them.

"For one thing," she said as she worked, "I don't think I can do what you what you want me to. Even if I went into that interview determined to say that Meredith was the best boss I ever had, you know me—I can't help running my mouth." She chuckled self-consciously. "Within five minutes I'd be telling them the truth about Meredith, and about a lot of things, too, no matter what I planned to say. But if I'm honest, it's more than that. It doesn't sit right with me, the idea of tricking corporate into making someone unqualified the manager."

"But—" Val tried to interject.

Joyce wouldn't let her. "Hold on," she said. "You know I worked at Caldor for almost ten years, right? Do you remember Caldor or are you too young? Well, I was an assistant manager, if you can believe it. And I never thought Caldor would go under. Then it did. That's how I learned the worst can happen, even at a big company that feels like it'll be around forever." Joyce tilted her head in the direction of the Catskills Mall. "I mean, look at the mall. It's dying, if it's not dead already. It's got, what, four, five stores left? I hear the developer is just waiting for the leases to run out on the stores that are left. Then they're going to turn it into a one-stop shop for medical services."

As a girl Val had gone to the Catskills Mall with her grandma every other Saturday, waiting while her grandma got her hair done at JCPenney. Then the two of them got lunch in the food court. JCPenney, like the other two anchor stores, had closed years ago. The food court was down to a single, locally owned pizza place. But Val didn't understand what this had to do with Meredith. Or Town Square.

"Corporate is already closing stores that aren't doing well," Joyce said, as if she had anticipated Val's objection. "And we're a low-volume store. If things here go south, how do we know they won't shut us down entirely?"

Val made a face. "They won't go south. Not because of Meredith. Store manager is more of a figurehead than anything else. It's really the executive managers that run the departments. All the store manager has to do is approve their requests and be a cheerleader for the store. Meredith would probably be better at that than her current job. She is . . . *enthusiastic*."

"Maybe," Joyce said, setting down her box and looking at Val. "Hell, you might be right. It might be fine, but it still doesn't sit right with me. Because of that, I can't do what you'd like me to. I'm sorry."

Val looked away, at a poster that hung above the makeup racks, a close-up photo of a model's face, the focus on her half-closed eyes and long eyelashes.

For an instant Joyce thought Val might cry. She felt a wave of tenderness for the young woman. There was a period in Joyce's life when she would have judged Val for being gay and having short hair and all the rest. But the world had changed and so had she. Working at Town Square had been good for her in that sense. The company was very modern. Besides, her oldest grandson was gay. Or so he said. (Joyce still thought there was a chance he might meet the right girl.)

"It's different for me, I know," Joyce said in a gentler voice. "I'm going to retire in a few years. You kids are in a different position. I get it. So you all do what you've got to do. I'll try not to get in your way. Okay?"

In spite of this concession, Val was disappointed. It wasn't just that she'd failed to enlist Joyce in the pro-Mer cause. What Joyce said had bothered her. She didn't think Joyce was right, that store #1512 would close because of Meredith, but she didn't like Joyce's implication that in helping Meredith she was doing something questionable or shady. Val wasn't a bad person. She tried as hard as she could to be ethical. But this might be her only shot at getting promoted *for years*.

Val was still feeling down at four, when it was time to unload the truck. To everyone's surprise, Meredith told them that Callie would be joining them on the line. She'd help Travis with his workload. It was a good idea. With Callie to help deal with his other boxes when he ran off to Bulk or Electronics, they never once had to stop the line and wait for Travis to catch up. See, Joyce, Val wanted to say—Meredith wasn't *that* stupid. While they worked, Val occasionally glanced at Nicole. Diego had said he'd made some headway with her, but Val saw no evidence of any change.

They'd elected to take their forty-five-minute lunch break (mandatory on all shifts longer than five hours) immediately after the unload. It was just past five when they got their coffee and stepped outside. The orange tips of their cigarettes glowed like fireflies against the still-dark sky.

Over the next forty-five minutes, the sky brightened slowly, turning navy, then azure, then, as the sun clambered up from behind the store, a pale baby blue. But there were still two more hours left on the overnight. To Val it felt less like the beginning of a new day than the ass end of a very old one.

13

IT WAS RAYMOND'S IDEA to organize all the Softlines boxes.

When they came in from break, he ran into Ruby and Nicole, pulling a full pallet back to the warehouse.

Some of the boxes on the pallet came from the factory and held new clothing styles. Ruby and Nicole hadn't noticed the small stamps on the sides that said HOLD UNTIL JULY 15 or HOLD UNTIL AUG. 1 until after they'd brought the boxes out. The rest of the boxes they were returning were packed at the distribution center and filled with whatever items the store was running low on. A single Softlines box might hold any combination of hanging clothes, folded clothes, packaged clothes—socks, tights, underwear, etc.—shoes and accessories, as well as (for reasons no one at store #1512 could fathom) baby products that weren't even Softlines at all: breast pumps, rattles, sleep monitors, bath toys, even baby food. Ruby and Nicole didn't even break out shoes—the store had a "shoe specialist" who came in during the day. Even among the categories they did break out, they couldn't do everything at once.

On a given day, they chose which categories to focus on and took the rest back to the warehouse.

"Having to take stuff out, only to drag it back in again, doesn't make sense," Raymond said. "It's redundant."

Disorganization and inefficiency bothered him viscerally. It always had. His mom said that when he was little, he was OCD about how his toys were arranged, insisting that the one he played with most should be the most accessible.

Raymond said he had an idea. Why didn't the three of them gather up all the Softlines boxes from all over the warehouse, sort their contents, and label the boxes. "That way, you'd know what's in each box," he said, "and what kind of boxes are on each pallet. You could take out only what you want to break out and not have to sift through all this other shit every time."

"It's not a bad idea," Ruby said. "But . . ." She looked skeptical.

Ruby's shift at ShopRite had ended at eleven the evening before. For half an hour after, she had waited on the bench outside for Nicole to pick her up for the overnight. It was now 6 a.m. She wasn't exactly in the mood to do extra. Besides, after thirty years in the service industry, Ruby didn't see why she should go out of her way for an employer that never went out of its way for her. Where was Town Square a few months ago when she'd begged for extra hours to hire a private lawyer for her son after the public defender dragged his heels on an appeal? "I wish I could help," Big Will had said, "but my hands are tied. You know how it is. The budget. Can you find someone who'll give you some of their shifts?" Ruby said she'd tried already. "What about your other job?" Big Will asked. "ShopRite? Can they help?" His response hadn't just disappointed her on a practical level, it had hurt Ruby's feelings, made her feel stupid. She considered Town Square her real job, ShopRite a temporary necessity to make ends meet. She thought that she and Big

Will were friends, that he would make an effort for her. If he wouldn't, why should she?

"I'm with Ruby," Nicole said. "It sounds like a hassle."

The prospect of putting her neck out to do something no one asked her to do ran counter to Nicole's deepest instincts.

"At least it'd be a break from what you've been doing all night," Raymond pointed out.

This was something. After a few more rounds of back-and-forth, Ruby and Nicole agreed. "Since it matters *so* much to you," Nicole said.

They began taking out all the Softlines pallets they could find—twenty-two of them, amounting to about three hundred and fifty boxes—and began going through their contents, putting like with like, labeling each box so they'd know what was inside. Soon they had filled fifteen boxes, i.e., a pallet's worth, with just Girls' and Boys' socks and underwear—writing on each one G s/u or B s/u, depending on the gender. Before they returned the newly organized pallet to the shelf, Raymond got the idea to draw a map of the warehouse, showing the type and location of all the pallets they'd organized, so they could refind them whenever they needed to.

While they worked, Raymond's thoughts drifted back to his fight with Cristina a couple of days earlier. They still hadn't made up. The house had been tense, full of silences and glares.

He was bothered by what she'd said the other night about his still being hung up on Steph, his ex. It complicated the narrative he wanted to hold on to: that he was the aggrieved party and she was wholly at fault. But he knew there was truth in what Cristina said, although Raymond would probably say what he wasn't over was the idea he'd long had of Steph, and about him and Steph as a couple and the life they were going to have together.

He and Steph had been neighborhood friends. When he was thirteen and she was twelve, she told him she liked him. Raymond couldn't believe it. Steph was pretty and fun. It had seemed impossible that such a girl would choose *him*. But Steph said he was sweet. And smart.

They stayed together all through middle school. And high school. They lost their virginity to each other. They planned to get married. Because Steph loved the beach, they would move someplace sunny, California or Florida, where she would go to beauty school. Raymond didn't much care what he did as long as he was with Steph. They'd even picked out names for their kids.

Raymond was a year ahead of her in school. When he graduated, he took a job doing maintenance at a hotel, saving money while he waited for her. But the following June, Steph said she wasn't yet ready to leave. A year and a half later, when Raymond was twenty and still waiting for Steph to "find herself," he learned she was cheating on him with a white wannabe rapper, a minor celebrity in Potterstown at the time, because it looked like he was going to get signed by a real label. He didn't, but Steph left Raymond for him anyway. She immediately got pregnant. She named their baby the very name she and Raymond had picked out for their future son. That was the second worst thing. The worst thing was when people started telling Raymond about the other times she had cheated on him over the years. Apparently he was the only person in Potterstown who didn't know.

He wasn't just angry. Nothing made sense anymore. They'd been together for seven years. He didn't know how to think about himself as other than half of a unit. She'd been the one stable thing in his life when his parents had gotten divorces and his dad had moved to Jersey. Raymond began to drink in a way he never had before. For many months, he courted disaster or annihilation—he didn't know what—starting fights with guys who were bigger than him, driving drunk, almost seeking an accident or arrest. If he hadn't met Cristina when he did, he had no doubt that he would have moved on to hard drugs. Or killed someone, maybe himself, while driving drunk.

Cristina was a housekeeper at the hotel where he worked. She was sweet and gentle and shy—so different from Steph. She was on her own, without family to fall back on. She needed him in a way Steph never had. She got pregnant soon after they got together. By giving him something to care about, Cristina—and the boy—very likely saved Raymond's life. But their life together hadn't been easy. In his dark period, Raymond had torn through everything he'd saved while waiting for Steph. Now there was a baby to take care of. By necessity, they lived with Raymond's mother, who also took care of their son when they were at work, but she and Cristina didn't get along. His mother wasn't very nice to Cristina, was the truth. Cristina had been unhappy before she started with the pills.

Raymond thought about something that had happened a few weeks ago. He had run into a guy named Kevin at QuickChek. Raymond and Kevin had been friends during his senior year of high school, when his mother had sent him to live with his grandparents in a small farm town on the other side of the river. He and Kevin had taken shop together at Pine Plains High School.

After they graduated, Kevin had gone on scholarship to an automotive college in Ohio. Raymond hadn't seen him since. When they ran into each other, Kevin told Raymond he was a mechanic for UPS. He made $35 an hour, plus overtime. Raymond asked if he had health insurance. Kevin said of course he did—UPS was a union shop. Raymond had colored, embarrassed of his ignorance. When they said goodbye, Raymond watched Kevin walk to a gleaming black Ram pickup, only a year or two old. The truck must have cost at least $45K. He waited until Kevin had pulled out of the lot to get into his car. It was the same Toyota Celica that Raymond had bought used in high school—it had been beat-up even then. Its model year, 1991, was the same year Raymond was born.

Back in high school, Raymond had been offered the same scholarship as Kevin. But he'd been with Steph. Their relationship had barely survived his forced nine-month stint in Pine Plains, and Pine Plains was only forty minutes from Potterstown. Ohio was too far. Raymond turned down the automotive college. He thought, at the time, that he might go the following year, with Steph, on their way to California or Florida.

Since running into Kevin, Raymond had wondered what his life would be like if he had gone to Ohio. Would he have a good job like Kevin's? Would he and Cristina live in a house of their own, like a real family? Would his relationship with Cristina be stronger if she didn't have to co-raise their son with his mother? If Cristina had been able to quit working at the hotel and gone to school to be a nurse like she'd wanted? If she hadn't hurt her back, lifting all those mattresses, making all those beds, she would never have started on those pills. Everything would be different. Or not.

Because Kevin had also told Raymond that he'd known someone at UPS, someone who got him in the door. And that's what people always said, wasn't it? That it's who you knew that mattered, that life came down to having the right connections. And Raymond didn't know anyone. Who's to say that college would have changed that? At least at Town Square he had a shot of getting the group manager job.

"Oh my god!"

Meredith's screech caught Raymond by surprise. He hadn't heard her enter the warehouse.

"What the hell is going on?" she asked angrily. She gestured with her arms at their surroundings.

Every single Softlines box had been taken from the shelves. A few had been repacked and put away, but most were still spread out on the ground, their contents spilling out like guts. The gaping boxes covered almost all of the warehouse's available floor space. Meredith turned to Ruby, as if, being the oldest of the three of them, she was most responsible.

Ruby refused, on principle, to be cowed. "Lordy! I didn't know you were here," she said to Meredith, her voice cheerful, as if she hadn't noticed that Meredith was upset. "I heard Little Will saying you went out for a while." Ruby nodded at the Starbucks cup Meredith was holding. "Did you just get a coffee? Oh, no you didn't. You must have gotten some breakfast because you've got a little something between your teeth." Ruby grinned and tapped her own front tooth with her pinky. "A seed, I think."

Meredith's cheeks reddened. "I had a health muffin," she mumbled. She pressed her lips closed and tried to extricate the seed with her tongue. Then she stopped. "Never mind. That's not important. What's important is what's been going on here."

As if she'd written Ruby off, Meredith looked from Nicole to Raymond and back to Nicole again.

Nicole was standing with her legs apart, her hands in her back pockets. Her face was as blank as a museum security guard's. Meredith turned back to Raymond.

Unfortunately for him, he could see how bad it looked from her eyes. One of his weaknesses was that he almost always saw things from the other person's point of view, whether or not he wanted to. In an argument, this made him wishy-washy, apt to lose fights to people like Cristina and his mother, who never entertained any doubt that they were entirely right and Raymond entirely wrong.

Meredith sensed his vulnerability. "I'm waiting," she said.

"We wanted to organize—" he began.

Meredith snorted at the word "organize," tilting her head at the disemboweled boxes surrounding them.

"—to, uh, organize the Softlines pallets," he continued.

The way Meredith was looking at him made Raymond even more nervous, and his voice came out clipped, staccato-like, as if he had to search his mind for each word. Meanwhile, his bad eye was flapping like a butterfly, as if it were trying to spell out a message in Morse code (SOS, presumably). To compensate for his anxiety, he thrust his chest forward and his shoulders back, to make himself bigger.

To Meredith, as he stood blinking, stuttering, his scruffy facial hair patchy on his cheeks, his posture simultaneously panicked and defiant, he looked like someone in one of those real-life cop shows, a lowlife caught in the glare of police flashlights as he was cuffed and led away. She curled her lips. "You're not drunk again, are you?" she asked.

"No!" Raymond said. "Not that—oh, never mind. I mean, they—the Softlines pallets—were all over the place. No one had any idea what was where. It's not smart—"

"What Raymond is saying is exactly right," Ruby cut in, her voice loud and confident. "Nicole and me, we came in here because we had a whole pallet with nothing but fall clothes. Fall clothes and shoes. What we supposed to do with them? Raymond was *helping* us, so next time when we come in, we can find what we need and not waste our time dragging out boxes that we're just going to have to put back."

Meredith was starting to get it.

"I hear what you're saying," she said. "I do. But there's just one problem. All these boxes are going to get broken out by Monday anyway. Remember? What's the point of organizing them right before we break them out. It's like rearranging the deck chairs on the *Titanic* when the boat is about to sink." She giggled at her own analogy. It was a mean giggle, the laugh of a popular girl after fake-complimenting an unpopular one.

"But this will *help* us break them—" Raymond started to say.

"How on earth does it help?" Meredith interrupted. "If they're all going to get emptied anyway?"

Before Raymond could explain how they'd be able to break out more efficiently, Meredith continued. "You have to factor in how many hours you're spending organizing," she said, "how many boxes you could actually break out if you weren't spending the time, you know, moving stuff from box to box, for no good reason. Besides"—and she smiled smugly, like a person about to pull out her trump card—"if it were helpful to organize the boxes before breaking them out, don't you think it would be part of our regular process?"

What she meant, Raymond knew, was that if this were a such good idea, someone smarter than Raymond—someone in corporate—would have thought of it. But she was wrong. Corporate could not instruct them to organize the backlog because corporate didn't know the backlog existed. Meredith and Big Will made damn sure of that.

But Raymond knew he'd only make her angrier if he argued.

"What's done is done," she said. "I get that you guys wanted to help. I do. And now that you started, you might as well finish. I mean, we can't leave the warehouse like this, can we?" She tittered again, the mean note creeping back into her laughter. "You've got to clean up this mess by the time you leave. If you aren't done by quarter of eight, just throw the boxes you haven't sorted yet back onto pallets and get them out of the way. And next time you get some big idea, ask me first. Okay? We can talk through it together."

They nodded.

When she was gone, Ruby excused herself to go to the ladies' room. Nicole turned to Raymond. "And that's who you want to be store manager?" she asked.

"Yup," Raymond said.

He tried to sound good-natured, like he too enjoyed the joke of it, but he couldn't quite pull it off. He was angry—and not just at Meredith. The way Nicole had just stood there, hadn't even tried to help him, pissed him off. Hadn't he stood up for Nicole when Meredith had given her a hard time, called her slow? Hadn't he gone to Big Will? Raymond was reminded of a side of Nicole he didn't like, a selfishness. It never occurred to her to exert herself for anyone else's sake, even though she always expected other people to come to her defense.

"Do you have any better ideas?" he said in a voice that was harsher than he'd ever used with Nicole. "Or do you just want to run down the only plan any of us has had in a long time to make our lives better?"

Nicole didn't know what his problem was. It hadn't been *her* idea to organize the stupid boxes, after all. She gave him a look meant to suggest that he was acting too big for his tighty-whities and should settle down.

But Raymond didn't back down. He stared right back at her. This pissed Nicole off even more.

"You do know that Val's going to get group manager, right?" she said. "I mean, I know you and Diego and the others are all in on her stupid plan. Which is sad because even if it works, she'll be the one to get the job. I just want to make sure you're okay with that, that you like being her errand boy."

Raymond had picked up a box of shoes (labeled SH, to distinguish it from Socks) with the intention of taking it to the shoe pallet, but he didn't walk away. "You're wrong," he said. "Val isn't a lock."

Nicole looked as if she felt sorry for him.

"There's stuff you don't know," he said.

"Yeah? Like what?"

Raymond barely hesitated before deciding to break Little Will's confidence. He put down the box of shoes. "Remember when Val flipped out about not being named Employee of the Month?"

"Duh."

Of course Nicole remembered. They'd given it to a guy in Plan-O, specifically citing his hard work in Seasonal. Val felt that Seasonal was her special domain, but because she came in early—before most of the store's executive managers got here—she didn't get the credit she deserved.

"Well," Raymond said, "Little Will told me that after the rest of us left, Val went into Big Will's office to complain. Val actually yelled at Big Will about how messed up it was that the people in Movement never get acknowledged. She was so loud that Svetlana from HR came in, told Val to calm down. That pissed Val off so much that she kicked Big Will's trash can so hard that it flew across the room and barely missed hitting Svetlana."

Nicole's eyes actually widened. Because of all the mass shootings, corporate had lately made a big thing about its zero-tolerance policy toward workplace violence.

"Little Will told me that if it had been up to Svetlana, Val would have been fired on the spot," Raymond continued. "But Val apologized immediately, told them she was so sorry and embarrassed. She said she'd acted like a toddler. Big Will convinced Svetlana that Val should be written up, not fired. Still. It sounds to me like the kind of thing that might interfere with getting a promotion."

Nicole had to agree.

When Raymond walked off with his box of shoes, she continued to turn it over. Nicole knew that even if Val didn't get the promotion, she—Nicole—was still unlikely to get it. It would probably go to Diego. But for some reason the thought of Diego getting group manager didn't bother Nicole as much as the thought of Val getting it. And "probably" wasn't the same as "definitely."

Or maybe she was looking for a reason to change her mind. During break, Nicole had once again sat by herself, pretending to be absorbed in her phone, but forty-five minutes was a long time to stare at a screen, especially when you had a limited data plan and didn't want to get charged for excessive use. (She had just scrolled through old texts, rereading them.) Moreover, listening to all the pro-Mer chatter these past couple of days—the others thought they were so sneaky, whispering all the time, but Nicole wasn't deaf—she had come up with some ideas of her own. She knew that they wanted to mess up Anita's T-shirt tables before corporate came on Monday. Nicole thought if they really wanted to mess with Anita, they should go even further—start a rumor about her, something that would turn her own team against her before the interviews.

After several minutes, Nicole told Raymond and Ruby she'd be right back. She found Diego in the front of the store, breaking out Paper. "You can tell Val I'm in. I'll join your little group."

Diego grinned. He still had it.

14

"HOW'S EVERYONE DOING?" In the glare of morning sunlight, Big Will squinted. "Good? Good."

He was speaking to twenty-seven front-of-the-store employees gathered in a large circle near Checkout.

"Today, I want to talk about the new Town Square app. I'd like to remind all of you that when you come across a customer who's looking for something we're out of, you should use the opportunity to tell them about our new, improved app—let them know they can access a wider range of items on the app and that we offer free shipping when they purchase through it. That way, we don't lose the sale to—uh . . . an online competitor."

An elderly couple entered the store. "'Morning!" Big Will called. "Welcome."

The man looked up from his walker, confused as to who was talking to him and why. His wife, a few feet behind him, hurried to his side. "The young man was just saying good morning," she explained. "He works here."

Her husband still looked suspicious.

Until a few years ago, the Huddle took place not at eight but at 7:45, before the store opened. Then management consultants had pointed out that it was wasteful to pay so many employees to be on hand before the store was even taking in revenue. Stores weren't exactly mobbed right at opening. If necessary, a salesperson or cashier could dart from the Huddle to assist a customer.

Big Will praised a member of Checkout for working a double shift on no notice the previous day—the store had been unexpectedly busy, pulling in just over $100K for the day, an excellent take for a weekday, before school had even let out for the year.

"Thank you, Kira!" he said. "We couldn't do this if you guys weren't so flexible, so willing to help out."

One of the primary purposes of the Huddle was to express appreciation for store employees. Cost-cutting notwithstanding, Town Square still sought to be an employer of choice, and indeed, internal surveys conducted by HR found that the majority of its employees appreciated the efforts it made to acknowledge them. That was why they preferred Town Square to their second jobs, the ones they worked because Town Square didn't give them enough hours or pay them enough to live on.

When the Huddle ended, Big Will got on his walkie-talkie. He paged Little Will, asked him to come to his office.

Little Will appeared in his doorway moments later. His khaki cargo pants sagged in the knee, and his navy flannel shirt was even more pilled and wrinkled than usual. Under his eyes, deep purple bags bled into his brown stubble, like war paint. He looked like he was playing a homeless person on TV.

Big Will felt bad for the guy. He'd been here since midnight. "Want to grab a drink before we talk?" Big Will asked. "Maybe one of those smoothies that Meredith likes? She claims they're better than coffee for energy. Vitamins or whatever. I'll write out a req slip."

Little Will shook his head no. "I'm okay."

Big Will smiled. "Okay then."

He was about to begin when a feeling of almost overpowering dread overtook him. He paused for a second, then pushed the strange feeling aside.

"I called you in because there's something I'd like to get ahead of," he forced himself to say. "You know, of course, that corporate is coming in on Monday. From what I gather, things will move fast. Some changes, some reshuffling may arise in your neck of the woods, changes that may, you know, lead to a change in your, uh, status—"

A flicker of emotion passed across Little Will's face. Noticing this, Big Will assumed that Little Will was scared he was in trouble. The store's group managers generally lived in fear of being fired or downsized. "Good changes," he clarified quickly. "I mean, if your position at the store were to, you know . . . evolve, in a . . . positive way."

Big Will smiled magnanimously.

But he had misread Little Will's reaction. Little Will wasn't scared of getting fired—the idea had never crossed his mind. He had winced at the thought of Meredith becoming store manager.

"Anyway," Big Will continued, "if there is such a reshuffling, decisions would need to be made about who would take on your current—"

Big Will stopped short. He suddenly understood the sense of dread that had come over him a moment ago. He knew what Little Will thought of Meredith. Hell, he probably agreed with most of it. The dread was fueled by embarrassment, shame: Little Will probably thought he was an idiot—or a coward—for going along with Meredith's promotion. But Little Will didn't understand the circumstances, how boxed in he was. And things might still work out. There was a good chance—a very good chance—that the interviews with her team would be so bad as to disqualify her, without his having to do a thing.

Big Will realized he'd stopped talking mid-sentence. He laughed self-consciously. "Uh, sorry. What was I saying? Oh, right. Corporate likes Meredith. They were impressed by her pitch to revitalize Logistics. They appreciate her ability to keep the department on budget. On the other hand, Meredith has certain, um, issues."

Big Will's eyes met Little Will's. In spite of himself, Big Will colored slightly. When he resumed speaking, he looked at first not at Little Will but a little bit above and to the right of his head, where a purple UConn pennant hung on the corkboard. "What happens will depend a lot on whether they think she's grown as a manager," he said to the pennant. Then he made himself look at Little Will. "They're going to listen carefully to what your team says about her in the interviews next week. If they do go with her—and just to reiterate, it won't be my call—but *if* they do, we'd likely ask you to step up in some capacity, to a bigger role in Logistics. If that happens, I'd like to get a sense of who you'd like to see take over for you as group manager for Movement."

"Oh," Little Will said. "Right."

"Any thoughts, right off the bat?" Big Will asked.

"I'm not really prepared, to be honest. I might need to think it ov—"

"Understood," Big Will said. "It's a hard decision. You've got some good people to consider." He smiled helpfully. "Let's see, there's Milo. He's been here a long time. What is it, seven, eight years? And he's got some college, which is good. No one doubts that he's a smart guy. But I have concerns about his temperament—maturity, that sort of thing."

From a slight nod that Little Will might not have been conscious of making, Big Will knew he agreed.

"And Joyce is too"—Big Will caught himself before he said "old," which would have been bad, illegal, etc.—"well, I'm not sure she's sufficiently motivated at this point in her career. I think she's looking forward to retiring in a few years, collecting Social Security. And she's rubbed Ryan"—the district manager, Big Will's boss—"wrong in the past."

Joyce's grumbling about how much better things used to be didn't go over well with everyone.

"Ruby, too, has been here a long time," Big Will continued, "but she doesn't have her GED." He made a sad face. "As we know, that's a deal-breaker as far as corporate is concerned. Then there's Nicole. She's definitely smart, no doubt about that. But she doesn't exactly radiate enthusiasm, motivation. And she's young."

Nicole was older than a lot of the recent graduates hired out of the management training program, who were brought on at the executive manager level as soon as they completed a three-month-long immersion course in store operations. But that was different. Everyone knew how the management training program worked. What Big Will meant wasn't that Nicole was too young to *do* the job of group manager—he meant she was too young to be angry if she were passed over.

"Plus, we have other strong contenders. Meredith has told me what a hard worker Travis is—but of course he hasn't been here long enough. I know you like Raymond—I haven't forgotten what you've told me about his work ethic—but I'd like you to think hard about Diego and Val. Diego's older than Val, of course, and he's been here a little longer, I believe—four years to her three—and he has, well, a certain gravitas that people respect. Everyone likes Raymond, but do they respect—?"

Big Will stopped himself. He felt guilty. He liked Raymond, too—Raymond was a nice guy, had a good sense of humor—but the fact was, his self-presentation could use work. The scraggly facial hair gave him a sort of shady, untrustworthy look, and the eye condition—the blinking—was the kind of thing that unnerved people in corporate. Why didn't Raymond see a doctor about getting it fixed? Then Big Will remembered that there had been an issue with the budget toward the end of last year—benefits costs were capped, and they had had no choice but to reduce the number of workers eligible for health insurance. Raymond had gotten the short end of the stick.

Big Will realized he'd lost his train of thought again. He began anew.

"There's also Val," he said. "It's my feeling that a one-off incident—I think you know which one I mean?—shouldn't disqualify her."

This was one of the things Big Will most wanted to get across to Little Will, why he'd asked him to come in this morning. He couldn't come right out and say what he meant, not without implicitly criticizing Svetlana from HR, and Big Will didn't like to run down his managers to one another. The truth was Big Will thought Svetlana had overreacted to the Employee of the Month incident. They all knew Val wasn't a mass shooter. She was a *vegan*, for Christ's sake. If Big Will had been alone, he wouldn't even have written her up.

On the other hand, Big Will did have one misgiving about Val. She was a rabble-rouser by temperament. A few months ago, she'd stormed into his office, banging on about how a T-shirt they carried was racist. And, okay, the shirt said MAKE CALIFORNIA GOLDEN AGAIN, and had a picture of several old-time, very glamorous, very blond, and very white movie stars. It wasn't as if Big Will didn't understand what Val meant. His name was Will *Flores*, after all. But what was he supposed to do? He didn't have veto power over the products the store sold.

Val was the type who'd have a hard time accepting that when you're a low- or even a mid-level manager at a large corporation like Town Square, you have to be flexible. Ordinarily that might be enough to tilt the scale toward Diego, but there were things that made Val an especially attractive candidate. Group manager of Movement was usually a guy. That Val was a woman was good, especially because this wouldn't be the kind of thing where she was getting the job *because* she was a woman, the way Meredith putting in for Logistics was kind of cute because it was so unexpected, given Meredith's girly, fashionista vibe. Val was far more suited to Movement than she was to more traditionally feminine areas of the store, like Customer Experience.

Val also had a good story. She had run away from home as a teenager—a homophobic father, something like that, maybe some animal cruelty, too (hence the veganism). She had lived in her car for a while, but had ultimately put together a nice, stable life for herself, with a wife and a baby. The fact that Val was married to a woman was also the kind of thing corporate liked. If Val were promoted, it'd be the kind of success story—"from homeless to management"—that, told carefully and cheerfully (no mention of the unpleasant father), corporate would want to highlight in its annual report, with a picture of Val and her wife holding their infant son.

Plus, Big Will had gotten a little carried away at Val's last performance review. In a moment of fear—unfounded, it turned out—that Val was looking around for other jobs, he'd all but promised her the next group manager position. If she didn't get the job, she'd no doubt feel as if he'd misled her. Big Will would prefer to avoid that. He didn't like the idea of being thought a liar. All in all, there was so much to recommend Val that Big Will had to remind himself that Diego would also be an excellent choice. He was a quick thinker and a very hard worker—Big Will was fairly sure that Diego hadn't been late to work once in four years. It was impressive. He also had natural leadership qualities. When something went wrong—the loading dock ramp got stuck in the wrong position or Movement got hit with a large shipment they weren't expecting and had no room for—the others turned to him to figure out what to do. Sure, Diego's oral and written communication skills weren't as good as Val's, but the middle-class vibe that was essential for executive managers could be waived for lower-level managers. Diego could make himself understood, and corporate didn't believe in discriminating against immigrants. Diego would also be grateful for the group manager job, see Town Square as his benefactor, behave accordingly—whereas Val would see it as merely her due.

Big Will was torn. But, really, Little Will should decide for himself who he'd like his deputy to be. Or at least have a significant voice in the decision. (Although Big Will continued to hope he wouldn't push for Raymond—Big Will would have a hell of a time convincing Ryan to sign off on Raymond.)

He smiled at Little Will. "Anyway, why don't you take a few days to think it over? Let's see, it's Thursday. You're off tonight, right? So maybe take the weekend? We'll talk Monday morning?"

Little Will agreed.

Only when Little Will was gone did Big Will realize that he hadn't asked a single question about his own possible promotion. It was puzzling. With his good looks and communication skills, Little Will could have a real future at Town Square—if only he'd play his cards right, project the right attitude, button his shirt properly (maybe even iron the damn thing every once in a while). Still, there was something appealing about the guy, something that made Big Will want Little Will's approval.

THE AIR IN that office had felt close, the atmosphere stifling to LIttle Will. Big Will wasn't a bad guy, but his way of thinking, the way he treated everything as a game, as if there were no real stakes, no actual people involved, depressed Little Will, made him wonder if he was the crazy one.

Because he'd come in at midnight instead of three, Little Will had only a few minutes left on his shift. He went to the part of the store he liked best: the warehouse. If he worked fast, he might be able to load the empty Town Square boxes into the truck before he left.

His mood improved as soon as he entered the warehouse. Raymond's organizational project had made a palpable difference: the space felt not only less crowded but cleaner, tighter, more like the efficient machine that it wanted to be. Whatever Little Will thought about Town Square, he felt real satisfaction in this. He liked to see things done well, and he felt proud of Raymond, who'd shown initiative.

As he began bundling stacks of Town Square boxes, Little Will thought that maybe he *should* put Raymond forward for the promotion.

Raymond might not come off as particularly impressive at first glance, but he was the kind of person Little Will's father would have championed. His father had prided himself on looking past résumés and outward appearances, and on not being conned by people who talked a big game but didn't deliver. He was good at seeing past all that, seeing people for who they really were, what they were capable of. There were more than a few former Saunders & Son employees who to this day remained passionately devoted to his dad, because he'd given them a chance when others hadn't—they credited him with changing their lives, putting them on a better path than they'd thought possible. (That's who Little Will liked to think of when he thought of his father, the person he'd been—not the cranky, sick shell of himself he'd become in recent years.)

As he worked, Little Will's glance fell on the tall, neat stack of empty pallets by the door. That was Diego's handiwork. He was the one who stayed in the warehouse after the unload to disassemble the line and tidy up. No one had asked him to—he'd just taken on that task, as he'd taken on so many others, as a matter of course, because someone had to.

Little Will sighed. The fact was, Diego deserved the job just as much as Raymond. And if Little Will were being fair, so did Val. Was it right for him to penalize Diego and Val just because he liked Raymond, because he had a thing for underdogs? Getting the job would make such a big difference to each of them.

Little Will didn't know what to do.

He glanced at his watch. He had to get out of here by 8:45. He had a biggish job to get to. A weekender with a large property had hired him to tear up an old stone patio and replace it with a bigger one in a spot with better light and a better view of the Hudson. He began working more quickly.

If only, he thought as he threw the last bundle of boxes into the truck, they could all be managers. But companies like Town Square needed a lot more worker bees than queens. Outside fast food—which had its own problems—management jobs were few and far between. This was why Little Will himself was still here, wasn't it? He'd won the lottery, been given a good, full-time job with benefits.

Little Will shut the truck's roll-down door so hard that he grunted. The door nearly slammed down on his fingers. He pulled his hand away just in time.

15

A VENDOR FROM a commercial bakery rang the bell on the delivery door. Because Little Will had left for the day, Meredith let him in. She scanned his invoice, then sent the vendor and his cart of bread to Harvest.

After that, she made a circuit of the store. Walking helped her think.

She wanted to fine-tune her pitch to corporate. Six months ago, when she'd put in for the transfer to Logistics, her argument—about being willing to embrace change—had been wildly successful. Corporate had praised her "energy" and "drive," said she was just the kind of manager they wanted more of. It had been the proudest moment of Meredith's professional life, better even than becoming an executive manager. That had been expected, the thing she had been working toward. In contrast, the lateral move to Logistics had been her own brainchild.

Even her parents had been impressed when she explained her thinking to them. "Smart," her dad said. Meredith couldn't believe it. All her life her parents had compared her—unfavorably—to her younger sister.

But her dad had also moved up through the ranks of a big corporation. He'd spent his whole career at IBM. By the time IBM left, he was near enough to retirement to be okay. At least he'd thought so, even though it meant Meredith and her sister would be largely on their own as far as college went. Meredith still hadn't finished paying off the $40,000 she wound up owing for the year and a half she'd spent to attend fashion school in the city.

She'd dropped out of FIT to pursue a singing career. At the time, it made sense. She had attracted the interest of a talent manager, was getting gigs. School seemed like a waste of her time when she ought to be practicing, out meeting people who might be important connections, focusing on her diet, sewing costumes, etc. But her singing career hadn't panned out. After a while, the gigs dried up, the manager took longer and longer to return her calls. Meanwhile, the relationship she'd been in ended badly. The low point of Meredith's life had been when she'd returned to her parents' house from the city at twenty-five, without a degree from FIT, without a record contract, with nothing to show for herself but a minor coke habit, a broken heart, and a slew of monthly loan payments. At the time, her sister had just finished her degree in elementary education and was starting as a second-grade teacher. When Meredith was broke and depressed, her sister was in the process of *buying* a house with the help of a program that helped teachers make down payments. Where was the program for starving artists who'd risked everything? Meredith wanted to know.

But Meredith had gotten herself back on track. She quit doing coke as soon as she left the city. For her, it had always been more of a lifestyle issue than an addiction. She started working at the boutique in Hudson. She kept regular hours, got serious about working out, began dating a guy she'd gone to high school with. Back then, Todd had been out of her league, but when they reconnected he was in recovery from a far more potent drug addiction than hers. He was grateful for Meredith's support. They married and—with help from Todd's parents—bought a house. Now their son was three, and Meredith was a successful businesswoman, on the cusp of making six figures.

It wasn't just an idle fixation, hitting that number. Todd only worked part-time, managing the office of a family friend's car dealership. He handled most of the child care. Meredith was the family's primary breadwinner. By now, she had paid off the credit card debt she'd racked up in the city, although she still wasn't done with FIT (or rather FIT still wasn't done with her). They also had a mortgage and the home equity loan they took out to do a much-needed reno. (Even with Todd's parents' help, anything they could afford in the current market had required serious work.) At least Todd did much of the work himself. Then there were her loans for her degree from SUNY Empire. While IBM had covered the full cost of her father's tuition, Town Square offered only modest assistance.

Meredith sighed as she walked past Office. The fact was, she and Todd still had a lot of debt. The vacation to Lake Placid the week before had been a splurge, but she had felt they needed to do something to celebrate the raise she'd gotten with her transfer, and they hadn't had a vacation since their son was born. Besides, when she got the promotion to store manager, their monthly payments wouldn't seem quite so crushing.

Near Sporting Goods, the air smelled of rubber. As she passed a row of bicycles, Meredith brushed the front wheel of each with her fingertips. Her thoughts turned to her upcoming interview. If only she could point to something concrete to demonstrate her success in revitalizing Movement. But it had only been two months. She wasn't yet past the egg-breaking phase of the omelet-making process. Probably it would be best if she didn't deny that, but leaned into it, emphasizing that she'd had just enough time to come to understand Logistics, if not quite enough time to remake it.

She could also remind the interviewers that Anita had never worked a day in the warehouse—Anita wouldn't know a pallet if one fell on her. This thought made Meredith smile.

From Sporting Goods, Meredith crossed the corridor into Women's Ready-to-Wear, the biggest subsection in Softlines. At the front of the section were several display tables showcasing T-shirts from Body & Mind, Town Square's proprietary line of clothes aimed at professional women. These were some of the company's best-selling and most popular items. But the tables were in terrible shape. Instead of being organized into neat stacks according to color or pattern and then arranged from smallest to biggest, the shirts on these tables were in a state of complete disarray. They looked as if they had fallen out of a dumpster, then been picked over by raccoons.

Meredith smiled again. Anita was responsible for the state of these tables.

"Excuse me?"

A thirty-something Asian man wearing scrubs—probably just off the night shift at the hospital—looked at Meredith apologetically, as if afraid of interrupting her.

Meredith put on her bright customer-service smile. "What can I do for you?"

The man wore trendy glasses and had the kind of expensive haircut that wasn't native to Potterstown but imported from coastal cities. Meredith was sure he was a doctor, not a nurse or a tech.

"I'm trying to find jumper cables?" He made a self-deprecating face. "Honestly, I don't even know where to look."

Meredith laughed warmly. "It's not you. Automotive is easy to miss. It's only one aisle, between Sporting Goods and Electronics. If you get to the TVs, you've gone too far. The jumper cables are on your left, about halfway down the aisle. But I'll take you over there."

When she left him in Automotive, the doctor thanked her profusely.

In surveys and focus groups, customers' number one complaint about Town Square was that they often had trouble finding either the items they were looking for or an employee to direct them. This was hardly surprising, given how much staffing levels had been reduced in the past several years. (To keep customers from recognizing that the lack of employees on the sales floor was a deliberate choice, corporate constantly posted large banners reading HELP WANTED—the implication being that any lack of staff on hand was a function of the tight labor market and/or a lazy populace's unwillingness to work service jobs.)

After her encounter with the doctor, Meredith felt a little peppier than she had before. She genuinely liked customer interface. She excelled at being what customers wanted—competent, friendly, upbeat. Now that she was in Logistics and had less contact with customers, she missed those kinds of interactions, missed the little highs they'd given her.

She made her way back to Softlines, but instead of returning to Women's, she wandered over to Kids. The back of the section was demarcated by a long metal rack that held socks and underwear. Boys were on one side, Girls on the other. The rack was very nearly empty.

Meredith felt her pulse rise. The sorry state of these racks was not a source of pleasure for her, the way the tables in Women's were. Anita's team was responsible for keeping merchandise tidy once it was on the sales floor, but Movement was responsible for getting the merchandise out in the first place. Meredith had no doubt that the socks and underwear that ought to be hanging on these racks were in the warehouse, in boxes, waiting to be broken out.

She reminded herself that they had three more overnights to get through the backlog. By Monday, these racks would be full if she had to break out every box herself.

Then it occurred to her that the people from corporate were likely to do spot checks. The store's newer scanners delivered up a lot of information—including an item's sales history, specifically the quantity sold in the past fourteen days and how that number compared to sales at other Town Square stores. Even if Movement restocked this section by Monday, one of the people from corporate could easily pick up a newly hung pair of Kids' socks, scan the bar code, and learn that the store hadn't sold a single pair for weeks. Kids' socks and underwear were some of the store's most popular categories—people buying up the inventory was how the section got depleted in the first place. A two-week period with no sales would be a red flag.

"Shit," Meredith thought, except instead of thinking it, she said the word aloud. For a moment, it hung in the air. Cursing was forbidden. She looked around nervously. Luckily she was alone.

She turned back to the empty racks.

Her mind began to race. It was Thursday morning. There was a whole weekend between now and Monday. And not just any weekend: a busy early-summer weekend, the kind in which weekenders and summer residents were apt to stock up on supplies for the whole family. If Movement could get Kids' socks and underwear on the shelves tonight, before the store opened on Friday morning, it might still be okay. A lot of merchandise would move in the next three days. By Monday, when corporate came, a spot check should look a lot better, a dip in sales followed by an uptick. That would be far less likely to raise uncomfortable questions than a flat line at zero. It would look like something that could be written off under the umbrella term "seasonality."

Yes, Meredith realized, this was the solution. The team simply had to get the sections that were in the worst shape stocked before the weekend.

The crazy, almost unbelievable thing was that they could. The two sections of the store that were in the worst shape were Men's socks and Kids' socks and underwear, both of which were part of Softlines. And in Meredith's pocket at this very moment was a folded-up piece of paper, a map of the warehouse that showed where every Softlines pallet was located and what type of merchandise the pallet held. Thanks to Raymond and his organizational project, they could easily target those two sections, bring out those pallets, and stock them first.

To think that only an hour earlier, she had been so sure that the diagram Raymond had drawn was useless that she had very nearly thrown it away.

16

AS A FULL-TIME hourly employee, Little Will could only work five eight-hour shifts in a week without incurring overtime, which was a no-go. This week, Friday was one of his two days off, which meant Meredith had to show up at midnight to cover the second overnight on her own. As it turned out, this suited her fine.

"We're going to do something different tonight," she told the group when they were clocking in. "A Smart Huddle."

Meredith loved to use terms not usually uttered outside corporate's training videos.

Ruby made a disdainful expression. "What in the world is a 'Smart Huddle'?"

Meredith laughed. She liked knowing things other people didn't. "A Smart Huddle is where a group of us work together on a single section, knock it out as a team, and then move on—together." Meredith pretended to pull on a rope, like a train conductor signaling ALL ABOARD. "First stop, Kids' socks and underwear."

The others looked at one another skeptically.

"It'll be fun," Meredith said.

Joyce snorted. "Real fun."

"Actually, you're not part of the Smart Huddle, Joyce," Meredith said. "You can stick with HBA. For the Smart Huddle, it'll be the ladies of Softlines, plus Travis, Raymond, Milo, and Diego."

Meredith had thought this through. She didn't need every single person on the Softlines backlog, and she liked the idea of having the smokers in one spot, where she could keep an eye on them. She didn't worry as much about Joyce or the old guys slacking off or getting into trouble.

They went back to punching in. Because the overnights had been added at the last minute, the shifts weren't in the system. When anyone tried to clock in, they got an error message. Meredith had to manually enter her own employee code, then issue a manager override for each of them individually.

When they were finished, Meredith pulled Raymond aside.

"We're going to use your map tonight," Meredith said. "To find the right pallets. I wanted to let you know."

Meredith didn't think anyone could blame her for reacting as she had to the mess in the warehouse the night before—it had been a shock to walk in and see that, especially considering how much she'd been counting on seeing progress on the backlog. Still, she felt a little bad about how dismissive she'd been.

"It's not that I changed my mind," she continued. "I do wish you'd talked to me before you spent all that time going through the Softlines boxes. But since you guys did, I figure we shouldn't let your hard work go to waste. We should take advantage of the time you put in and work section by section."

Raymond shrugged. His throat was killing him—the Advil he'd taken on the way to work hadn't yet kicked in—and as an apology, this one wasn't great, but it was something. Other than Little Will—

who apologized all the time, often for things that weren't his fault—Raymond had never had a boss who regularly admitted when they were wrong. Besides, he was relieved she wasn't mad anymore. In the warehouse the night before, he had been genuinely worried she was going to fire him. He'd felt real alarm. Not because he wouldn't be able to get another job—he would—but because this job, with these people, was what he had, maybe the best thing he had. Since things had gotten so rough with Cristina, work had become a happier, lighter place to be than home. And the people he worked with were some of his closest friends.

When he got to the section, the others had already used the map he'd made to find and then bring out all three pallets of Kids' socks and underwear. Raymond was getting a box down from one of the pallets when Joyce walked by.

"Smart Huddle, my ass," she said. "You all are sorting Kids' underpants in the middle of the night. Who does Meredith think she's kidding with that fancy name?"

"It's like people who call the can a 'lavatory,'" Raymond said. He began speaking in a pinched, faux-rich person accent. "Oh, let's go to the lavatory and have a Smart Huddle, shall we?"

"That's not a Smart Huddle, Raymond," Val said. "It's a Smart Shit."

Val was in excellent spirits, had been since the moment the night before when she'd learned that Nicole had agreed to join the pro-Mer group.

She began speaking in a lispy, almost panting, but still slightly whiny voice that rose with excitement at the end of each sentence. "See what it is, is that we all take a shit at the same time and then we wipe each other's asses. It's more efficient that way. Only one bathroom break. And you don't have to reach behind you to wipe. You can see your own work."

As an imitation of Meredith, Val's was much better than Raymond's rich person voice, which had been derived almost entirely from the Grey Poupon scene in the movie *Wayne's World*.

"At least the name 'Smart Huddle' makes sense," Milo said.

"What do you mean?" Ruby asked.

Milo sighed as if the answer should be obvious. "At the Huddle, everyone stands a few feet away from one another in a big circle. That's not what a huddle is. It's like no one from corporate has ever watched football. You're supposed to be close together. They should call the Huddle 'the Circle' or 'the Ring.' At least a Smart Huddle is more like an actual huddle."

Callie was next to Milo, hanging a package of days-of-the-week-themed girls' underwear. Her eyes met Milo's. She smiled politely at his joke or witticism or whatever it was.

Milo smiled back. Then he stood up and began to take off the blue-and-gray plaid cardigan he was wearing over his Town Square T-shirt. He carefully folded the sweater in half and laid it on top of one of the nearby tables. "I don't want it to get dirty," he said. "It cost a hundred and fifty dollars."

Callie turned over a set of two pastel-colored training bras on a double hanger, looking for the bar code.

Milo began talking louder. "I probably shouldn't wear it to work."

Callie sensed that Milo was talking to her.

She looked up from the bras. "I get it. I hate when nice clothes get dirty."

This was all the encouragement Milo needed. He began to talk. And talk, thought Nicole, who was working on Milo's other side. (She had forgotten her headphones and had nothing else to do but listen to Milo and Callie's conversation.)

Milo told Callie that he had a lot of clothes from Banana Republic. (An ex of his had worked at the one at the mall before it closed.) These clothes, he told Callie, were of far better quality than anything they sold here, at Town Square. And he ought to know, since he'd worked here for eight years. Before that, he'd worked at UnitedHealthcare, he said. Callie started to say that she was in school for a "job in health ca—" Milo didn't let her finish before saying that he, too, had been to college.

It wasn't that Milo wasn't interested in what Callie had to say or what she did outside Town Square. Milo cut her off because he took for granted that *she* was accomplished and desirable. He instinctively felt it was incumbent upon him to prove himself to her, show her that he was worth her time. Which meant regaling her with his accomplishments.

Milo told Callie he was only one semester short of getting his degree. Nicole noticed that Callie *did* look a little impressed by that. "It's great you're finishing so soon," she said. "You must be psyched." Milo laughed and said no, he'd gone to college a long time ago and had no immediate plans to finish. Callie asked why not, "seeing as how you're so close." Milo launched into a long story—which Nicole had heard before—about how he'd started at Ulster County Community College early, through a program at Potterstown High that let some kids do their senior year there. The first year had been great, but in the middle of his second year, with just a semester left before he got his associate degree, his girlfriend had broken up with him. She'd been his ride. "I didn't have a car at the time," he said, then quickly added, "I do now." With no way of getting to campus, he stopped going to class. He figured he'd go back later, but at the end of the semester Milo found out his professors, instead of simply dropping him, had given him incompletes. He was charged full tuition for the semester, even though the breakup had occurred the first week of school and he'd only attended the first couple of classes. "What I think," Milo told Callie confidentially, "is that the professors are paid for every person enrolled in their classes. They pretended that I was there so they could make more money. But now I'm screwed. If I want to go back, I have to pay for the semester I missed, plus interest, before they'd let me."

"Can't you get a loan?" Callie asked. "I mean, wouldn't it be worth it? For one more semester? That's what I'm doing for my sleep—"

"It's the principle," Milo interrupted again. (Dumbass, Nicole thought.) "They cared more about making money off me than about the fact that I stopped coming."

"Hmm..."

Callie sounded skeptical, Nicole thought.

But Callie had finished her box. She got up to get a new one. The box she picked up was Boys' underwear. It took her to the other side of the section, which meant Milo wasn't able to explain that he was less interested in college than he had been. When he was in school, he'd wanted to work as a counselor to troubled kids, but in the years since, he had watched a lot of inspirational YouTube videos and TED Talks. They all made the same point: the key to success is to follow your passion, not do what was safe. His passion was to become an entertainer.

For several minutes, they worked in a silence broken only by yawns. It was only the second overnight, but they were all feeling the lack of sleep.

Nicole thought over what she'd heard. Clearly Callie thought Milo should go back to school, that he was stupid not to. Nicole, too, had always thought Milo's story didn't add up, but she'd assumed that the real truth was that the school wouldn't let his ass back in after he flunked out. She figured Milo just pretended he didn't want to go back to save face. But what did Nicole know about college? Nicole's own line on the subject had long been: Of course she wasn't going—she'd barely gone to high school, and that had been free. Why would she *pay* to go to more school? Still, she was starting to think that joke had been funnier a few years ago than it was now, five years after she'd finished high school.

Meredith came to check on their progress. She liked what she saw. In two hours, the section had been transformed. Row after row of metal shelving unit was now filled with different-colored packages of socks and underwear.

"You guys rock!" Meredith said. "You're almost halfway done."

Then Meredith looked at their faces. She made an overly empathetic expression of concern, the kind of exaggerated look a kindergarten teacher puts on to teach her pupils about emotions.

"I know," she said. "You guys are tired. Overnights are rough."

She reached into a little woven purse she was wearing crossways over her blue V-neck and she pulled out a small bottle. "Caffeine pills," she said. "They're good. Anyone want one?"

No one responded, but Callie happened to yawn just then. Meredith turned to her. "Callie?"

Callie had slept for exactly two hours and forty-five minutes before coming in, her second night in a row of less than three hours' sleep. She had tried to get her two-year-old down early so she could get a little more rest before the overnight, but her daughter had refused to go along. Still, Callie didn't want to take a pill from Meredith if no one else was going to. She shook her head no.

"Okey-dokey," said Meredith. "Let me know if you change your mind, if any of you do."

Seeing that Ruby was about to finish her box, Meredith walked to the nearest pallet to bring her a fresh one. She got up on her tippy-toes and reached for the top of the pile. Travis was working next to the pallet. He lunged to help her. "Here, let me," he said.

Meredith laughed. "I can do it, you know. I'm stronger than I look. Before I started in Logistics, people didn't think I could handle it. You know, because I'm"—she gestured at her body as if what she really wanted to say was "sexy"—"*because* I'm small. They had no idea that I've been taking kickboxing and strength training classes for years."

She grinned at Travis almost flirtatiously.

"No, it shows," he said.

Travis's voice, Nicole thought, managed to be respectful—not leering or gross—but still convey flattery. He had game.

It was a funny thing, game. Travis and Diego both had it. Raymond didn't. And Milo? Listening to him flirt had been painful. He hadn't asked Callie one question about herself. Milo had the opposite of game: negative game. He was a black hole where game went to die.

AT 2:30, HALFWAY between their start time and their 5 a.m. lunch, they were entitled to a short smoke break. When they got outside, Val offered to hold Nicole's phone so Nicole could light her cigarette more easily. When Nicole thanked her, Val gave her an affectionate punch on the bicep.

All night, Val had been treating her the way a small-town football coach treats his star player. Nicole liked it. She wasn't sure she'd ever felt so wanted. And she hadn't even told them her idea to start a rumor about Anita yet. She did now.

"We can say Anita plans to get rid of free meals on Thanksgiving and Christmas," Nicole explained.

Diego whistled. "That's good, girl. We could also say she also don't want to grill on the Fourth of July or the other holidays."

"But why would anyone believe us?" Raymond asked. "I mean, how would we know what Anita is planning?"

Nicole had thought of this. "We'll say Val overheard Anita talking to Big Will. Everyone would believe that." With the exception of Big Will himself, there was hardly a person at the store who didn't know about Val's habit of eavesdropping outside his office. "We can say Val heard her tell Big Will that if she's promoted, her goal will be to make this location the most profitable one in the district, and this is part of her plan to cut costs."

Raymond nodded. "That tracks."

Nicole waited for Val to weigh in. But Val seemed distracted. She was looking past Nicole, past all of them, her gaze fixed on the large blue-and-yellow Best Buy sign glowing in the distance, the brightest light in the dark expanse.

Val had remembered something that had happened a year or two earlier. A trainer from corporate had come to the store to give updated instructions for the handling of hanging clothes. At the time, Val worked Softlines, so she was part of it. The trainer, a perky blond woman, told them to "edge" pants on the hanger—fold the sides over so that the waistband appeared to line up exactly with the hanger clips. "It looks neater that way," she explained, looking right at Val. As she went on, she kept asking Val what she thought. Meanwhile, she ignored Anita and the other two women. Val figured that the trainer had gotten confused as to who was who and assumed that Val, not Anita, was the boss. At first, Val thought it was funny. Then she thought about it. Anita was black. The two other women were Hispanic. Val was white. It was no longer funny. It was racism—a microaggression against Anita. When the trainer started talking about how hanging clothes should be zoned on racks, not just from lightest to darkest and smallest to biggest but also from lightweight fabrics to heavyweight fabrics ("Linen-Cotton-Denim—LCD," she said chirpily, grinning at Val)—Val and Anita exchanged a glance of recognition, a subtle eye roll. At that moment, Val had genuinely liked Anita. She appreciated Anita's willingness to share a moment of insubordination with a mere rank-and-file employee.

Since she'd come up with her plan to get Meredith promoted, Val had thought of Anita not as a person, but only as a game piece to be moved out of the way. But when Nicole laid out her idea, something had shifted in Val's mind. And now Val couldn't unsee it. Was Val really going to out-and-out lie about Anita—expressly to keep her from getting a promotion she probably really wanted and certainly deserved more than Meredith?

Val felt a little nauseated.

Diego waved a hand in front of her face. "Earth to V."

Val tore her gaze from the Best Buy sign. She looked around. She realized they were all staring at her, waiting for her to say something. And what was she going to do—tell them she didn't want to lie? Who was she, George Washington? Besides, she was the one who had put this thing in motion. They were counting on her.

"It's a terrific idea, Nicole," Val forced herself to say.

Anita didn't need her sympathy, Val told herself as they put out their cigarettes and returned inside. As an executive manager, Anita made at least $75K, and probably $80K or $85K, like Meredith. Last year, Val made $17K.

17

THEIR NEXT BREAK was at five, when they'd finished the unload and were due their lunch. They'd just gotten outside when the employee door swung open. Instinctively, they all braced themselves for Meredith, with some complaint or criticism. But it was Callie.

"What you doing out here?" Ruby asked. "You forget something in your car?" With her hand, Ruby imitated the clicking motion Callie made to unlock the car with the remote control on her key chain.

Callie looked puzzled. It seemed to her that Ruby talked about her car a lot. "I was hoping to bum a cigarette," Callie said.

"What!" Ruby looked shocked, as if she'd known Callie for years, not days. "You ain't a smoker."

"I have one every now and then."

Callie didn't say that if she was going to do these overnights, she needed something, some sort of treat to look forward to when she dragged herself out of bed and into the shower in what felt like—what was—the middle of the night.

Callie turned to Nicole, the person she knew second best, after Ruby.

"You don't want one of mine," Nicole said. She held up her cigarette case. "I roll my own. No one but me likes them. All these guys think they're too strong." Nicole grinned. "Pussies."

Milo held out his pack of Camels. Gratefully, Callie took one.

"Thanks."

"It's okay. I don't mind."

The way he said it, it was as if Callie were the one doing him a favor. Nicole looked at Ruby pointedly. She had told Ruby that Milo was falling all over Callie.

But Ruby had turned to Val. "So when we going to start spreading this rumor about Anita?" she asked. Ruby was going to be central to any rumor-spreading operation. The rest of them tended to become nervous and defensive around strangers.

"Who's Anita?" Callie asked.

Milo started to answer, then wound up explaining the whole pro-Mer plan to her.

Callie nodded. "I think I get it."

But Milo's explanation had gotten him thinking. "I wonder if there's a pro-Anita group," he mused.

"What?" Val turned to him. In the two and a half hours that had passed since their last smoke break, she had talked herself out of whatever misgivings she'd felt earlier; she once again felt protective of her plan. "Why would you think that?"

"It stands to reason," Milo said. He turned to Callie as if she were a natural arbiter—as if she hadn't just been told about the plan two minutes earlier. "I mean, if we're working to get Meredith promoted, people on Anita's team are probably doing the same thing."

"That's ridiculous," Val said.

The idea that a pro-Anita faction would have naturally come into being implied that the formation of the pro-Mer group was inevitable, what anyone would have come up with under the circumstances. But it wasn't inevitable. It was the opposite of inevitable. Val had willed this plan into existence. If Milo wanted proof, all he needed to do was think back to the last time the position of executive manager of Logistics became vacant, when the position wound up going to Meredith. Back then, no one had gotten together to try to throw the job to Little Will so one of them could get group manager. Why not? Because Val hadn't been here to think of it, to organize them. At the time, she had been on her six-week maternity leave.

"There is no pro-Anita faction," she told Milo. "For one thing, her team isn't as much of a team as we are. I don't think they're planning *anything*. Remember, they don't get to take break together the way we do."

This was one of the best things about Movement. At most retail jobs—including at Town Square—breaks were staggered to ensure that there were enough workers on the floor to help customers. It was only because Movement's shift took place before the store opened that they got to go out together.

"Second," Val continued, "I think Anita's people are pretty indifferent. They don't hate her the way we hate Meredith."

Milo wasn't entirely satisfied, but he sensed he'd be better off avoiding a direct confrontation with Val. Especially in front of Callie. Val was aggressive. She wouldn't let it go. He nodded. Meanwhile, Travis looked up at the video camera installed above the employee door. It was aimed at pretty much the exact spot where they were standing. He'd noticed the camera on his very first day at the store, but since he himself had been careful not to talk about Meredith or say anything he didn't want overheard, he had stopped thinking about it. Now he realized that he too was implicated in their plan.

"Are they filming us?" he asked.

The others followed his gaze. The small camera was so silent and unobtrusive that they tended to forget it was there, but in the murky light of the gathering dawn, its blinking red light and dark, cylindrical scope looked ominous, almost military in nature.

"Don't worry," Val assured Travis. "No one ever watches the footage, not unless something happens, a fight breaks out or something. Then they go back and watch, to see whose fault it was, or whatever." She turned to Raymond. "Right?"

Raymond was friendly with the store's head of Asset Protection, the man in charge of all the cameras. "Val's right," he said. "They almost never watch the tape."

WHEN HE ARRIVED at work a couple hours later, Big Will found Meredith waiting in the hall outside his office. "Last night's Smart Huddle was a huge success," she told him as he unlocked his door.

"Glad to hear it."

He sat down at his desk and tapped at his keyboard to wake up his computer. After several seconds, the Town Square logo, an image of the earth with an urban skyline on top and a tractor on what would be the Southern Hemisphere, appeared on the screen.

"Check out Kids' socks and underwear," Meredith said as she plunked down in the love seat. "It looks amazing. We're going to do another one tonight, in Men's socks. We'll have both sections stocked for the weekend."

"That's great, Mer."

So she'd come in solely to be complimented on the Smart Huddle? Big Will found this irritating. He was her boss, not one of her girlfriends. It was unprofessional, disrespectful of his time.

"Have you given thought to what we talked about?" he asked.

"Hmm?" she said distractedly.

"Who you think should take over for Little Will. In the event he moves into your current role. Like we discussed yesterday?" He'd called Meredith in the day before, same as he had Little Will.

Meredith sighed. If she'd known Big Will was going to get on her case about this, she wouldn't have come, not now, when she was in such a good mood about the Smart Huddle, when she finally felt confident that everything necessary for her success was in place—that all she had to do was coast along for another few days, see to it that the store got cleaned up and the team was in the right frame of mind for their interviews.

"So?" he asked.

"Well . . ." She knew he wasn't going to like her answer. "I know he hasn't been here long, but Travis is high-energy. He has the right attitude. I think he'd be terrific."

Big Will's eyes widened. Travis had been at the store for, what, two and a half months?

"How do you think the rest of the team would respond?" he asked, trying to keep his voice calm. "Do you think they might resent it if someone who hasn't even been here six months gets promoted over them?"

"I think it should inspire them," Meredith said. "Show them what's possible with a positive attitude and a willingness to work hard."

Big Will waited until the desire to bang his head against his desk had passed. "Are you even sure Travis is eligible?" he asked. "Does he have his GED?"

"Of course he does," Meredith said. "I mean, why wouldn't he? He's smart."

On Big Will's computer, the Town Square logo bobbed up and down and from side to side, ricocheting like a pinball off the sides of the screen.

It was Friday. After work, he would drive to Connecticut. He and Caitlin had an appointment to look at houses with a real estate agent over the weekend. He didn't want to get into a fight with Meredith, not right then.

"Okay," he said. "I'll take it under advisement."

18

THAT NIGHT, TRAVIS failed to show. It was the second to last overnight, Friday evening into Saturday morning.

"Maybe he's sick," Joyce said as they were clocking in.

"I don't think so," Nicole said. "He seemed perfectly healthy a few hours ago."

She'd run into Travis earlier that afternoon at the food pantry. He'd shown her where to go—not to the main church but to a smaller building in the back. They'd left together, too, chatting as they walked back to the parking lot about how it sucked that the pantry didn't stock baby formula. Then Travis rode his bike home, his groceries bungee'd to its rear rack.

"He's never been late before," Meredith shot back querulously. It was Little Will's second day off for the week, which meant she was once again Leader on Duty—or as Val liked to say, Loser on Duty.

Nicole shrugged.

Ruby pointed upward. Sheets of water were pummeling the store's roof. "It'd be hard for him to get here on his bike," she said. "In this rain."

As a fellow carless person, this was obvious to Ruby.

The others realized she was right. "Poor guy," said Joyce.

Meredith didn't seem as put out as the others would have expected, based on her usual tendencies. "Well," she said, "we'll just have to make do. I'll take his place in tonight's Smart Huddle. We're doing Men's socks." Seeing the looks on their faces, Meredith laughed. "Why do you guys look so shocked? You know I want to work with you more than I do—it's just that I usually have too many other things I have to do. But I'm excited. It'll be fun."

Convinced after the Smart Huddle that the store would be in good shape by Monday, Meredith had turned to a new goal for the final two overnights. She wanted to shore up her relationships with the team before their interviews with corporate.

At first, her presence had a chilling effect on the group in Men's socks. For ten or fifteen minutes they worked in near silence. Then Milo and Raymond started talking about Ultimate Fighting, tentatively at first. When Meredith didn't tell them to stop, their voices became more animated. There was a fight coming up that they were looking forward to. It was on pay-per-view.

Listening to them, Diego wondered where they got the money. He was just glad they'd gotten paid that morning. He'd gone straight from Town Square to the Verizon store to get his phone turned back on. Meanwhile, Milo and Raymond could afford pay-per-view.

Diego thought of a conversation he'd had with a guy named Isaac who used to work with them. Isaac had said that even at a store like Town Square, where they're all paid shit, white people were still better off than black people. It was part of a bigger, historical picture, Isaac said. Isaac was a smart guy, a college student, studying American history down in New Paltz and only working at the store for the summer. He told Diego that right as black people finally got their civil rights in this country, the good jobs started to go away. "It used to be that most people could get a job and live decently. If they were white. After World War Two, the only people who were excluded, who couldn't get these good jobs that paid middle-class wages, were black people, who were used as scabs if they were men. If they were women, they were maids and cooks. Then the civil rights movement happened, and the good jobs should have opened up. But wouldn't you know?"—Isaac had paused dramatically—"Right then, the manufacturing jobs started to disappear, leave for other countries. Unions lost power, and pay for all but the professional classes started to decline. Everyone who didn't have a college degree was screwed, whether they were black or white. But the thing is"—here Isaac took a hit from the joint he was smoking (not Diego: Diego didn't do drugs)—"it didn't play out the same for everyone. The white people already had stuff, passed down from their families, who'd had access to the good jobs for a couple of generations. They'd already bought cars and houses—while the government had gone out of its way to make it almost impossible for black people to get mortgages. When the jobs started to go away and wages started to fall, it was like a game of musical chairs. The people who already had stuff—white people—got a chair. Black people were left standing, with nothing but our civil rights." Isaac had made a wry face. "The ones in a position to go to college did okay, but the rest were screwed. And the fucked-up thing is that now liberals be like, 'Oh, the poor people should all just go to college, then they wouldn't be poor.'" Isaac snorted. "What a joke. Can you imagine if the left had said that about steelworkers and coal miners back when the labor movement was heating up—'They don't need a union; if they want better pay, they should just go back to school and get another job'? 'Get a career—go to med school'?"

Maybe Diego had absorbed some amount of racism from society, because until that conversation he had tended to blame black people themselves, at least in part. But what Isaac said made sense. It went a long way toward explaining things, even in Movement. After all, both Raymond and Milo were white—never mind about Raymond's claim to be a "person of color" because his father was Filipino. Raymond's mother was white, wasn't she? And he lived rent-free in her house, just like Milo lived in *his* mother's house, which had previously belonged to Milo's grandparents. And Nicole—white—had lived with her mom until recently and still borrowed her mom's car to get to work. Val—white—lived in her grandmother's house and drove her grandmother's car. Even Little Will, who made more money than any of them, lived with his fiancée in his parents' basement. Whereas Diego and Ruby had no inherited assets, no family properties or cars to fall back on. They had to pay rent. No wonder they couldn't afford cars.

A gust of wind outside made the sound of the water pounding on the roof above grow momentarily louder. Diego thought of Travis, presumably out there somewhere on his bike. Travis might be the exception to the rule. White or not, Diego got the feeling Travis had had it rough.

Raymond and Milo started laughing—something about a UFC fighter who had flamed out. Diego remembered something Raymond had told him the other day. He'd said the reason he'd gone to live with his grandparents for his last year of high school was there had been a KKK rally in downtown Potterstown. After that, Raymond said he'd started getting harassed on the way to and from school. "But you ain't even black," Diego had pointed out incredulously. "The kids in my neighborhood knew my dad was Filipino," Raymond said. "They knew my name was Santos."

Now Diego got an idea. He stood up and darted off, returning to Men's socks a minute later, with a small black box. He dropped it on Raymond's lap.

It was a game, called "The Race Card."

"I saw it the other day when I was breaking out Toys," Diego said. "I thought of you. I know how much being a person of color means to you."

Before Raymond could reply, Val reached for the box. "Let me see that."

She began to read aloud from the description printed on the box. "'Race Cards for Race Hustlers. This is not a game. It's a common-sense statement. When someone interjects race into a discussion, it is often done gratuitously. Hand out these Race Cards to race hustlers who accuse other people of racism when they have nothing better to contribute.'" Val looked up from the box. "You guys, this is some seriously messed-up shit. This is what actual racists say. Like, for real. We shouldn't be selling this. It's not even funny."

The others just smiled. It was like with the shirts that said MAKE CALIFORNIA GOLDEN AGAIN. They all made fun of Val for getting so mad—not because they thought she was wrong, but because it was funny how worked up she got. But they kind of respected it, too. At least Val cared about things.

Val set the card game aside—she'd show it to Big Will later, see if she could get him to finally grow a backbone.

A phone pinged. Meredith's, obviously. Everybody else had theirs on vibrate. Most managers wouldn't enforce the no phones rule during an overnight, but with Meredith, you couldn't be sure.

"It's Travis," Meredith said when she'd read the text. "He's outside, but the door's locked." She was about to ask Raymond, who was sitting nearest to her, to go let Travis in when she remembered that Travis needed a manager override to get punched in. She sighed. "I guess I have to go let him in."

When she was gone, Ruby shook her head in sympathy for Travis. "I hope she's not too hard on him," Ruby said.

Meredith and Travis reappeared a few minutes later. Travis's dark, spiky hair was wet, and the hems of his pants were soaked.

"Look who the cat dragged in," Meredith said.

But she was smiling pleasantly. Nor did Travis give the impression of having just been chewed out. His lopsided grin was only a little sheepish.

When she'd let him in, Travis had explained to Meredith that he'd called a cab company at ten thirty, when he realized it was raining too hard for him to get to the store on his bike. He told the dispatcher he absolutely needed to be here by midnight. But the cab didn't come at eleven thirty as promised. Travis called back, and the dispatcher said they were backed up because of the rain. The driver didn't show up until twelve thirty. And still charged Travis twenty bucks for the ride. Travis said he'd called Meredith to let her know, but she hadn't picked up. Meredith had looked at her phone. It was true. The missed calls were in her log. "I turned off the ringer when I was sleeping," she said. Then she told him it was okay. "Just try not to let it happen again."

Diego recovered from his surprise first. "Hey man," he said, tossing Travis a plastic package of tube socks. "Why don't you try doing some work for a change?"

It was a bad throw, but Travis leapt for the socks. He caught them, then fell to the carpet with his arm outstretched, socks held high.

While they worked, Travis said that a coach from Virginia Tech once tried to recruit him to play football.

"Really?" Meredith asked.

"He's shitting us," Diego said. "Obviously."

Travis said he wasn't. He told them that back when he lived in Virginia, he was friends with a guy whose girlfriend went to Virginia Tech. One night Travis had gone with the two of them to a house party. Some guys from the football team were there—including Michael Vick, who was already a big deal, although not as famous as he would become when he played in the NFL. Late in the evening, Travis ended up in a park behind the house, playing ball with some guys from the team.

They thought he was good and asked him to join them again. He did. A couple of weeks later, one of the assistant coaches saw Travis and talked to him about his potential, said he wanted to get one of the other coaches to watch him too. He gave Travis his card, told him to stay in touch.

The others were trying to figure out how much of this story was true when Meredith asked Travis what position he'd played in high school. "Wide receiver? Cornerback?"

Travis raised his eyebrows in surprise. Then he said he didn't actually play in high school. "I mean, not officially. On a team."

"How come?" Meredith asked. "You were clearly talented."

Travis laughed self-consciously. "You have to pay for your uniforms and shoes and travel. We didn't exactly have that sort of cash lying around."

Travis and his mother and sister had lived on his mother's disability checks, which tended not to last the whole month as it was. They often ran out of food. He could imagine his mother's reaction if he'd asked her for money to play sports.

"I can't believe you hung out with Michael Vick," Nicole said. "My fiancé will flip when I tell him."

"What were you doing in Virginia?" Raymond asked. "I thought you were from here."

"My mom met a guy who lived down there," Travis said. "When I was sixteen."

Not that his mother wanted to take Travis with her. She'd sent him to live with his dad and stepmother, while his sister—who had already turned eighteen—moved in with her boyfriend. Within a few weeks, Travis and his dad got into a fight. The cops were called, Social Services got involved. Since his mother officially had custody of Travis, they called her in Virginia and told her she'd be charged with child abandonment unless she let Travis live with her. So he went.

Travis had been in Blacksburg for two years when he was spotted by the coach from Virginia Tech. By then he had a good job, doing HVAC, even though you were supposed to have a high school diploma or GED to get a license. (Travis's mother and her boyfriend hadn't exactly been the generous types. Needing money more than a piece of paper with his name on it, Travis had dropped out.) But the owner of the HVAC company let him work on the down-low. Plus, with the encouragement of his mother's boyfriend—who took a cut—Travis was dealing a little. He was making good money when he met the football players. And then, for a very brief period, it seemed like the coach might try to get him enrolled and on the team. It seemed like his whole life might change.

Then he got arrested. Not for dealing; for armed robbery. A former friend who wanted to get Travis back for something with a girl gave the cops a fake tip. But Travis hadn't done it—and he could prove it, if only they'd let him. They didn't. Bail was set at $100,000. As if anyone in his family had that kind of money—as if they would have put it on the line for him if they did. Travis was locked up for months before his public defender unearthed the security camera footage that showed he was at a strip club at the time of the robbery. The charges were dropped.

When he was in jail, he'd broken up with the girl he'd been dating. He should have handled it better because, though she'd originally told him she was sixteen, she was—as even he knew by then—actually fifteen. Travis was eighteen. Virginia had strict age-of-consent laws. After he broke up with her, she reported him. He was only sentenced to three months—and thankfully, due to a more zealous public defender than he'd had the last time, he wasn't put on the sex offenders' registry—but it was his second time locked up in less than a year. By the time he was released, he'd lost his HVAC job, lost touch with the friend whose girlfriend went to Virginia Tech and with the guys on the football team. (Not that they'd have wanted to play with someone convicted of "inappropriate sexual contact with a minor," even if he wasn't on the registry.) He had lost everything.

A week after his release, he got into a fight outside a bar. He slammed the other guy's head into the hood of a car. It got him another eighteen months. His final stint was for a parole violation. By then Travis had soured on the Commonwealth of Virginia. As soon as he was free to leave, he moved back to Potterstown, the city of his birth. Now his only real tie to Virginia was the money he still owed in court fees—almost ten grand with interest. He couldn't get a driver's license, even here in New York, until he paid them off.

Despite everything that had gone wrong afterward, Travis had never stopped thinking about what that coach had said about his potential. It was too late for football, obviously, but the coach's interest felt to Travis like proof that there was something in him, that in spite of his record, in spite of who his family was, he could be something—a manager at Town Square, for example. Then he could make enough to pay the ten grand over the course of a year or two, if he lived cheaply enough—he could finally be free of his past.

The others began telling stories about their own encounters with famous people. Meredith named some of the people who'd come into the bar she used to work at in the city—music producers, reality show stars. No one had heard of them.

Nicole, who had no stories of her own to tell, volunteered that Ruby had met the president.

"The president of what?" Milo asked. "Town Square?"

"No, dumbass," Nicole said. "The actual president."

Ruby said it was true, although he wasn't president at the time. She'd worked as a housekeeper at one of his hotels in Atlantic City.

It wasn't a famous person, but Diego told them that he was in the World Trade Center on 9/11. He was twenty-three and working as a dishwasher in a corporate dining room on the fifty-first floor of the first tower. He made it down and walked all the way back home to the Bronx.

Diego didn't tell them that one of the chefs at the dining room had been teaching him how to cook. The chef made good money, and Diego thought there was a future in it for him. But after the towers went down, months passed before the dining room was reconfigured, in midtown. By then his dad and his stepmother had decided it was better for Diego to stay close to home. His dad was the superintendent of an apartment building in Manhattan; his stepmother was a home health aide who worked nights. They were gone a lot, and Diego had three much younger half brothers to consider. Diego went back to his old job, at the McDonald's in their neighborhood, so he could be there in an emergency. After his father had gone to the trouble of bringing him to the United States, it was the least he could do. And it had worked out. His manager at McDonald's encouraged Diego to take the GED test. Which he did. Passed on his first try, too. Of course he took it in Spanish.

After Diego's story, no one said anything for a minute. Then Raymond threw a bag of ankle socks at Diego's chest. "Nice job bringing everybody down."

Before Diego could respond, Val poked his arm.

"Look!"

Diego turned. Milo had fallen asleep sitting up. His head was leaning on his shoulder and he was clutching a pair of wool hiking socks. Nicole chortled.

Milo woke with a start. "Wha—what?"

By now, everyone was looking at him, grinning.

"Oh man," Diego said to Milo, "you should have seen your face while you were sleeping. You looked so sweet, so innocent, like a little baby. You were holding those brown socks like a teddy bear."

Milo's cheeks turned red.

Meredith took the bottle of caffeine pills out of her little purse. "Take one," she said to Milo.

Almost automatically Milo took the pill from her hand.

"You should get some water," Meredith suggested. "They're pretty big—"

"I don't need it," Milo said, swallowing the pill. It was a mistake. The pill scratched his throat on the way down. For several hours, he felt as if it were still lodged there.

"I HEARD YOU TOOK a cab here," Joyce said to Travis at the beginning of their lunch break. He and the other smokers were getting ready to go outside.

"True thing," he said, grinning. He liked Joyce, who reminded him of his grandma. She'd died when he was ten, but she had been the best person he'd ever known.

"It cost what, fifteen dollars?" Joyce asked. "Twenty? It's a shame to waste that kind of money. You live downtown, right? Take my number. Next time it rains, or if you're just too tired to ride your bike, call me. I'll pick you up on my way."

Travis stared in disbelief.

"And you probably need a ride home today?" she continued. "I mean, it's still raining, and you don't have your bike with you."

Travis nodded. "Thank you," he said. For once there wasn't a hint of irony either in his expression or in his voice. "Thank you," he repeated. "That's very kind of you."

When Joyce turned into the break room, Travis headed with the smokers for the door.

Instead of standing in their usual spot, they made a run for the customer entrance, where a concrete overhang blocked the rain. As he smoked, Travis thought about how glad he was to be here, at Town Square. His girlfriend Jeanie didn't understand. She thought the job was stupid, beneath him. She constantly reminded him that he had made more money when he was dealing. But Travis knew being here was about so much more than that. It was about the future and about getting to know people like Joyce—good, decent people.

Travis put Jeanie and her complaints out of his mind. He began paying attention to the others' conversation. "Have you guys noticed how the shit that's labeled 'green' and 'sustainable' comes wrapped in just as much plastic as the regular stuff?" Raymond was saying. "They print the label on brown cardboard instead of white, and people are like, 'Oh, it must be good for the earth.' They have no clue that they're shipped to the store wrapped in six layers of plastic packaging, same as all the other crap."

"That's why we break out when the store is closed," Val said. "Corporate doesn't want shoppers seeing stuff like that."

"Green. Organic. Sustainable—it's all bullshit," Diego said. "The other day I was breaking out organic peanut butter cups. You know how much they cost? $3.99! For a pack of two! At that price you ain't supposed to eat them—you supposed to shrink-wrap them and hang them on your wall."

Callie said she hated to think about organic food because she couldn't afford to get it for her daughter. It made her feel guilty, like she was poisoning her.

"Has anyone told you about the Healthy Employee Program?" Milo asked Callie.

She said no, and he explained that the program gave employees an extra 20 percent off, on top of their standard 10 percent employee discount, on items that "promote a healthy lifestyle," such as certain high-end brands of athletic clothing. It was mostly a joke, as he told Callie now—"Thirty percent off expensive-as-fuck is still fucking expensive,"

Val cut in, by way of explanation, prompting Milo to glare at Val (he hated to be interrupted). *There were*, Milo continued, deals to be had on organic produce. Because its grocery business was struggling, Town Square priced its produce competitively. "At thirty percent off, the organic bananas are a good deal," he said. "And the berries wind up costing less than regular berries at ShopRite."

Callie was looking at Milo with big, grateful eyes, apparently very interested in what Milo was saying. Nicole was surprised. Maybe Callie did like Milo, at least a little? Maybe she was one of those really mature women who don't care about things like game—or looks.

"I buy fruit for my daughters here," Milo continued. "Especially for my toddler." Then he realized Callie might not have heard about his complicated situation. "I have her during the day while my ex is at work," he explained. "I'm always trying to get her to eat healthy because her mother feeds her junk. She just wants to keep her quiet. If she has to put Lily in front of the TV all night and give her M&M's, that's what she'll do."

Callie smiled sympathetically. "You sound like a really good dad," she said. "I wish—"

"I owe my daughters everything," Milo interrupted. "I've got two. I don't know if you knew that either. My sixteen-year-old lives with me, has since she was little. Knowing that they needed me kept me going through some dark times." Milo laughed, as he tended to do after delivering what he viewed as a profound truth, as if to punctuate his words.

"Depression runs in my family," he continued, caught up in an overwhelming compulsion to tell Callie who he was and what he'd been through. (He'd hoped to do this ever since their conversation about college the day before, but hadn't found an opportunity until now.) "My grandfather killed himself," he said. "Broken heart. So did my little brother. Well, technically he died of an overdose, but it was because of a girl. He fell for a girl who was sixteen. He was twenty-one. They were together for a year, with her parents' consent, but he was charged with statutory rape anyway. He was never the same after that. He couldn't even live at our house after he got out of prison because my daughter lived there, and he was on the registry. That's when he started using."

"Oh god," Callie said. "That's horrible."

Milo was quiet as he thought about the morning it happened. He had been here, at the store, unloading the truck. His sister had called the store line. Little Will came and got him from the back.

"I wish my ex were half as good a dad as you sound like," Callie said after a moment, to change the subject. "How did you get to be that way? Did you, like, have a good role model growing up? My dad never—"

"My dad is great," Milo broke in, but his voice was different from usual—tight, clipped. "Unfortunately, my mother drove him away. She partied all the time, cheated. What choice did he have? My brother was still a baby. That's probably why he was so messed up—he didn't have that time with our dad that my sister and I did."

Veins on Milo's neck that Callie had never noticed before had become pronounced.

Behind Milo, Callie saw that Ruby was shaking her head at her, pointing with her forehead toward Milo and running a finger across her neck, to indicate Callie should quit talking.

Callie understood. Break was just about over anyway.

They left the protection of the overhang and ran together to the employee door. When they filed into the break room for the morning meeting, Callie—not wanting to seem rude in the wake of Milo's disclosures and apparently unaware of the de facto rule that men and women sat separately—took a seat next to him.

It was as if a dam had broken. Val joined Raymond and Diego at the adjacent table, while Travis approached the table Nicole was sitting at with Ruby. He came upon them quietly—he had a stealthy way about him, moving lightly, as if he were weightless. He would have made a good cat burglar, Nicole thought.

At the front of the room, Meredith began talking. Nicole glanced at Travis, then wondered why it hadn't occurred to her to offer him a ride, not even after she'd seen him pedaling away from the food pantry with all those groceries strapped to his bike. But the thought hadn't once entered her head, not until she heard Joyce doing it earlier.

Travis turned to her. He gave her one of his small, closemouthed, lopsided grins. That was when Nicole realized it was better she hadn't offered. Marcus wouldn't have liked it—her giving a ride to a guy. A guy with game.

MEREDITH FELT SHE'D made real inroads in the course of the night. She had seen the looks that passed between the guys when she had suggested that Travis might have been a wide receiver or cornerback. (She'd watched football with her dad growing up, initially because her sister didn't, but she'd come to enjoy it.) And she'd been chill about Travis's lateness. But this was only the half of it. She had something planned for tomorrow night—the last overnight—that would, she felt sure, seal the deal.

At the morning meeting, she told them there'd be no Smart Huddle tomorrow. For the last overnight, they were going to spread out, get through whatever odds and ends were still left to be broken out. Then she dismissed them. "Let's kick some ass for the last part of the shift," she called as they began to file out.

Something tugged at her as she watched them go. It had to do with their smokers. She couldn't quite put her finger on it, but something seemed different, something in their affect. Had they sat in different places in the break room? In any case, they seemed to her more cohesive, like a unit.

She tried to shrug off this strange feeling. She told herself whatever she sensed was probably attributable to the Smart Huddle, which corporate intended in part to foster team spirit. But a few minutes later, when she was walking through Bath, Meredith noticed Ruby and Callie talking intently in Women's Ready-to-Wear.

Meredith was too far to hear what they were saying, but she could tell from their body language that they were both absorbed in whatever they were discussing. The feeling that something was afoot returned, and the more she thought about it, the more she felt sure that there had been a lot of whispering, a lot of clandestine looks, these past few days. Was it possible they were up to something?

With only forty-eight hours until the interviews, Meredith couldn't be too careful. She thought of the camera above the employee door. If they were up to something, they'd have discussed it outside. Maybe, just to be safe, she should check out the video from the past few days, see what they were doing out there.

19

"WHAT?" RUBY SNAPPED at Meredith, who was staring at her.

They were clocking in for the next and final overnight. Ruby's patience was at a low ebb, in part because she was exhausted. She had put in her notice at ShopRite the day Little Will told them about the overnights, but her manager had asked her to stay for the full two weeks. For the past several days, she'd been at ShopRite from six to eleven and then at Town Square from twelve to eight. Moreover, her days had been too busy for her to get much rest. On Friday, she took the bus to Social Services to certify that she still required food stamps. This morning, she'd gone to her doctor for a note attesting to her asthma.

Meredith reddened. "Sorry!"

She hadn't yet had a chance to watch the footage from the security camera. She was trying to glean from the group's behavior if they were up to something. Ruby, she thought, would be central to any scheme. Meredith told herself she'd watch the video as soon as she had a moment.

Meanwhile, Ruby and Nicole and Callie made their way out to the sales floor. Ruby yawned. "At least we ain't getting a truck," she said.

The only times the store got a truck on Sunday mornings were during the holiday and back-to-school rushes.

"Yeah, but you know what we have left," said Nicole.

Ruby sighed. "Don't I know."

"What is it?" Callie asked.

"Lingerie," Ruby said.

"What's so bad about—?"

"Just wait," Ruby said. "You'll see."

When they brought the Lingerie pallet to the sales floor, they found Meredith waiting for them. "I came to help you guys!" she said cheerfully. She would watch the video later.

"Suit yourself," said Ruby.

Underwear wasn't so bad. Except for packaged sets, which were hung on racks, they were laid out on display tables or tossed in baskets that customers could root through themselves. Bras were a different story. They came off the truck already on hangers, but in transit their straps were always getting tangled with the hangers of other bras. They had to be unspooled carefully—if you yanked too hard, their delicate, birdlike hangers snapped in two. Moreover, there were a million types: strapless bras, bras with demi cups, push-up bras, padded bras, underwire, wire-free bras, sports bras, nursing bras—to say nothing of the different brands and colors. Each bra type had its own tiny rack, above which Plan-O had printed out and posted a label, but even when you had found the right rack, you weren't done. The bras were supposed to be zoned on the racks: arranged from smallest to biggest by bust measurement, then within that by cup size. Bras made swimsuits—including those two-pieces in which tops and bottoms were sold separately—seem like a breeze.

"And summer only lasts a couple of months," said Nicole. "It's always bra season."

"Bra season!" Meredith laughed. "I love it. You crack me up, Nicole."

Nicole made no reply. She refused, on principle, to countenance lameness.

At first, Meredith worked enthusiastically. Then she grew frustrated. "Why are some Maidenform nursing bras over here while others are on the endcap?" she asked. "There's no logic in the way these are organized."

As if she were the first person to have noticed this.

After twenty minutes, Meredith said she was going to go check on the others. "I'll come back to help more later. If I have time."

"Finally," Nicole said. She turned to Ruby. "Should we—?" Nicole tilted her head toward the back of the store.

Ruby nodded. "C'mon," she said to Callie. "Do what we do."

They grabbed boxes from the pallet and then took out all the underwear so that only bras were left. Then they carried the bra boxes to the fitting room. There, Callie watched as Ruby and Nicole dumped the contents of their boxes into the shopping carts the changing room attendants used for clothes that had been tried on and needed to be returned to the sales floor.

Ruby grinned at Callie. "See? Two boxes of bras broken out just like that. Only took a minute. Dump yours, and we'll be up to three."

Laughing, Callie did as she was told.

"Why do we have to take out the underwear?" she asked.

"Customers aren't allowed to try them on," Ruby said. "If the fitting room people saw lots of underwear in their carts, they'd know something wasn't right."

"The women who work fitting room are so fucking lazy," said Nicole. "It serves them right. They sit around and gossip instead of doing their damn jobs. That's why there're so many carts of clothes back there."

On their way back to Lingerie, they spotted Val, tucked away in a nook in Women's Ready-to-Wear.

"I know what you're doing!" Ruby called.

Since she'd been unable to get Big Will to stop selling the MAKE CALIFORNIA GOLDEN AGAIN T-shirt, Val made a point of stopping by the Graphic Tee section every few days. She'd put the shirts with camouflage backgrounds and images of guns or pointed references to "liberty" and "freedom" at the back of the racks, behind ones that were more to her liking, the ones that said things like BE KIND; OUR VOICES, OUR VOTE; and WINE MOM.

Ruby, Nicole, and Callie dumped another round of boxes into the fitting room carts. Then Ruby said they had to stop. Any more bras in the carts would raise too much suspicion. They went back to Lingerie and began breaking out the normal way.

When Ruby got up with an armful of sports bras, Nicole tried to work up the courage to ask Callie something.

The conversation she'd overhead the other night between Callie and Milo had made Nicole realize she didn't know as much as she thought about how college worked. Just in case it didn't work out with UnitedHealthcare, Nicole wanted to know if college was even an option for her. She wondered if anyone could get a loan, even people with bad credit. And what if your grades in high school hadn't been exactly stellar? What if you'd, say, gone to summer school twice?

Callie was rehanging a bra that had fallen off its hanger in the box.

"I was wondering . . ." Nicole began.

When Callie looked up, Nicole noticed for the first time how straight her teeth were. She had probably had braces growing up. She was one of those people. Suddenly Nicole wondered if Callie would think she was stupid for thinking she was the kind of person who belonged at college. And maybe she *was* stupid. Certainly no one in Nicole's life had ever indicated to her that she had college potential— not her teachers (especially not the math teacher who said the only reason he passed her—with a D—senior year was that he was sick of seeing her face at summer school), and not her parents.

Not that Nicole's parents knew anything about college either.

Callie was looking at her, waiting for her to ask her question.

Before Nicole could make up her mind whether to risk spitting it out, she saw Ruby from the corner of her eye, returning from the rack of sports bras.

"I was wondering if you're sick of bras yet," Nicole finished. She didn't want Ruby to feel left out or embarrassed. She'd talk to Callie about college another time.

Ruby started talking about how stupid Meredith was for revealing she had no idea how to break out Lingerie. Ruby said when she was an assistant manager at LOL Burger, she made damn sure she knew the ins and outs of every job in the restaurant so no one could catch her looking clueless. Callie giggled. In the past day or so, she had noticed that Ruby was being nicer to her. After break yesterday, she'd pulled Callie aside, said she wanted to explain about Milo, the way he'd reacted when Callie had asked about his dad. "There are some things you should know," Ruby'd told her. "Milo's . . . a sweetheart—he's got one of the best hearts of anyone in this store, if you need something, a little bit of help—but he isn't—well, I don't want to say that he isn't right in the head. He's fine most of the time. But certain things set him off. He's sensitive about his father."

"I didn't mean to upset—" Callie had started to say.

"I know you didn't," Ruby had cut in. "You didn't know."

Now Ruby told Callie about being put up in a hotel for a month to help open a new LOL Burger. She was still smiling at the thought when Callie asked her why she'd left that job, since she'd seemed to like it so much.

Ruby's expression changed. "It was a lot of stress, being in management. All the paperwork, the extra time you had to put in. At a certain point, I was ready to retire. Now I just come in here, and when my shift is over, I'm done. I go home, have my drinky-drink. No hassle."

Ruby turned back to her box, no longer in the mood to talk.

The real reason she'd quit was that LOL Burger put in a new head manager, a racist prick who wanted to get all three black assistant managers out so he could get his buddies in. Ruby quit before he could make up a reason to fire her. (One thing Ruby would say about Town Square was that, unlike LOL Burger, it didn't tolerate that racist shit. At Town Square, an employee used a certain word, and that was it—they were out. It was as bad as getting caught talking to a union rep.)

Leaving LOL Burger had nearly broken Ruby's heart. But she had resolved that something good would come of it. She signed up for a free GED class offered by the county employment office. If she had that damn piece of paper, Ruby knew she'd be able to get another management job. She vowed this time would be different from the other times she'd tried. Her kids were grown. She could devote herself to her studies.

The class was held at a fancy new employment office the county had opened. On Ruby's first day, the teacher, a middle-aged white lady, gave her a test, which she said wasn't really a test: it was just to assess where Ruby was so she could gear the material to her properly. "We do mostly independent study," she explained. "Since everyone is at a different level." When Ruby handed the packet of papers back to her, the teacher indicated that Ruby should wait as she went through her answers. After a minute, Ruby could tell from the teacher's expression that something was wrong. Finally, she looked up from Ruby's test-that-was-not-a-test. She told Ruby that her reading and writing was at a third-grade level. Ruby tried not to flinch as the teacher continued. Unfortunately, the teacher continued, she was only trained to teach people who were already at a high school level—"or at least eighth grade." She looked at Ruby apologetically. "This isn't a literacy class," she said. "We cover subject material. You know, literature and history and math? But if this is the class that works best for your schedule, I can ask around, drum up some early literacy material?" Since this was the only class within walking distance of Ruby's apartment, Ruby said she'd appreciate that. But the next week, it snowed. Ruby told herself that was why she didn't go to class. But she didn't go the week after, either. Ruby felt bad that the teacher had taken the trouble to find "early literacy" materials for her—but she'd just started at Town Square, was still getting used to the early hours. It wasn't the right time. Besides, deep down, Ruby suspected she'd never be able to learn, no matter how hard she tried. When she was a girl, she got lead poisoning. A lawyer who'd filed a suit on behalf of the residents of a building Ruby had lived in when she was little said this was likely the reason some things were hard for her.

What did it even matter? Even without her GED, she'd made a success of herself, hadn't she? She had always worked—she had been a good role model for her kids. They looked at her as a source of stability in their lives, someone they could turn to for help. So what if she had been on welfare at times? Who wasn't when you were in the service industry and trying to raise kids? Her kids always had what they needed, and except for a very short period in a shelter—when Ruby left her abusive ex-husband, the father of her younger boy and girl—they always had a roof over their heads, although none of their apartments were as nice as Ruby's current one, a sunny one-bedroom on the second floor of a Victorian house in a part of Potterstown that hadn't yet gentrified but was walking distance to downtown. She loved the apartment and took excellent care of it. Aside from her kids and grandkids, she rarely invited anyone over, for fear that the place would get messed up. She was particularly careful about her couch, which looked and felt like real leather, and her glass table. She'd bought them with the settlement money from the lead poisoning lawsuit.

WHEN MEREDITH WAS starting out as executive manager of Hardlines Sales, she had made the mistake of eavesdropping on a conversation between some members of her team. Hoping to gain insight into who the troublemakers were, she had instead heard one of them refer to her as "Butterface." Another, a non-native English speaker, had been confused. "It means she'd be good-looking—but for her face," the first one explained. Meredith had been mortified.

This, she realized on Sunday morning, was why she hadn't been able to bring herself to watch the security footage of the smokers outside. She couldn't risk a repeat of such a painful experience, not now, when she needed to stay in a positive frame of mind. She decided that she'd be better off trusting them. And trusting to the success of her own careful planning.

She waited until four to drop her big surprise. To thank them for the overnights, she was going to buy all of Movement breakfast from McDonald's. And not just sandwiches, she said when Milo asked. They could upgrade to meals, therefore getting coffee and hash browns as well. None of them could believe it—this was better, much better, than the time she got talked into buying them treats from the in-store Starbucks.

It was almost too good to be true. From Val's perspective, the timing was also perfect. On Sunday mornings, about a third of the Plan-O team came in at four, to remove the signs and posters detailing the previous week's specials and replace them with the new ones for the upcoming week. The pro-Mer group had long intended to use this time to seed the rumor about Anita's intention to get rid of all free meals.

Who could have anticipated that while they were busy striking up "casual" conversations with Plan-O people about killjoy Anita's plans to get rid of free holiday meals, news of Meredith's unprecedented generosity would be spreading through the store?

Meredith delivered the food at the beginning of break. Out of habit, the smokers took their meals outside, rather than eat in the antiseptic break room with Joyce and the old guys.

"Oh man," Travis said when he opened his Styrofoam container. He actually beamed at the Sausage and Egg McMuffin and hash browns. Since he'd started at Town Square, Travis had lived almost entirely on ramen and beans—and cigarettes. He saved the eggs and pasta and mac and cheese from the food pantry for Jeanie and the kids.

"I haven't had a restaurant meal in ages," he said. "I didn't even know how much I needed this."

"Same here," Nicole agreed. She felt almost giddy from the warm, sweet smell of fried meat and butter and syrup rising from her lap.

While they ate, Val laid out her plan for messing up Anita's display tables the following morning. They'd do it just after their shift ended the next morning, right when corporate was scheduled to arrive, she said. Raymond would go into the server room and make sure none of the security cameras were trained on the tables Val was going to target. The store's head of Asset Protection knew Raymond was interested in technology and had shown him how the cameras worked.

"What if the server room is locked?" Raymond asked.

"I'll get the key," Val said. "I'll tell Little Will or Meredith I need to use the forklift to get something in the warehouse." Val and Diego were the only people in Movement authorized to operate the forklift. "They'll give me their whole key ring—they always do."

Raymond nodded. Val turned to Diego. "Your job will be to distract Anita. It shouldn't be a problem. We all know how charming you are with the ladies. Anita's a single mom—she probably doesn't get enough love."

Diego grinned. "I can do that."

"Nicole and Ruby, you guys will be lookouts," Val continued. "You'll hang around Women's Ready-to-Wear, keep the rest of Anita's team busy, and warn me if anyone is coming. I'll mess up the tables. It's only fair that I take the biggest risk since it's my plan." She looked at Travis. "See, I didn't forget. I left you out of it. Nothing for you to worry about."

"What about me?" Milo asked.

"Oh, right." Val had forgotten about Milo. She thought quickly. "You're Raymond's lookout. You'll hang out by the server room and let him know if anyone's coming."

Milo nodded.

Then Val explained the code she'd worked out so they could communicate with each other on their walkies without being understood by other employees.

By the time she finished, they were done eating. The sun was just starting to rise up from behind the store. The rain of the previous evening had dispelled the heat from earlier in the week—the air was crisp and pleasant. Travis got up and walked toward the parking lot, to smoke and look at the view that was coming into focus. Nicole followed him.

"I finally figured it out," she said.

"Figured what out?"

"I knew I'd seen you somewhere before here, but for the longest time I couldn't figure out where. Tonight it came to me. At least I think so." As Nicole spoke, she thought she detected something uneasy in Travis's expression, but it was too late to stop now. "Don't take this the wrong way," she continued, "but did you—did you used to deal weed? I think you brought a bag to my cousin's house once."

Travis's face went pale.

He had trust issues. Of course he did: one of his supposed friends had gotten him arrested on a bogus robbery charge when he was eighteen, and an ex-girlfriend had gotten him rearrested soon after. Because he'd trusted the wrong people, he'd lost years of his life, maybe even—in the squandered interest of the Virginia Tech coach—the best opportunity he'd ever have.

Nicole realized Travis was genuinely afraid. "Don't worry," she assured him. "I won't tell anyone. And *I* don't care." She grinned. "It's not like I don't smoke."

Travis's panic began to subside. Of course *Nicole* wasn't going to rat him out. She was cool.

"Can I ask you something?" she continued. "Why are you working here? I mean, you must have made good money dealing? And without having to do much work?"

Travis laughed.

"I wouldn't say that I didn't have to work. I mean, the money *was* pretty good, a lot of the time, you're right about that. But I was always on call, twenty-four seven—middle of the night, et cetera. It was stressful like you wouldn't believe. I was always worried my stash was going to be stolen or confiscated by the cops. I was always one bad night away from being totally fucked. It was no way to live. I hated it, honestly. I was depressed, like, clinically."

While speaking, Travis noticed how intently Nicole was looking at him, how interested she seemed to be in what he was saying. It had been a while since Jeanie had been interested in hearing what he had to say about anything other than when his next paycheck was coming and if he could take the kids to her mother's for a while so she could have some peace.

He became more expansive.

"Let me explain it this way. When I was a kid, my grandma—R.I.P."—he stopped and made the symbol of the cross—"had one of those tiny little yappy dogs. One time, when I was maybe nine, I was sleeping at her apartment, and she gave the dog a treat. A pig's ear. You know what those are like? They're big and tough—chewy. He went wild over it. But it was too much for him to eat all at once. He went at it for as long as he could, but his jaw must have gotten tired. After a while, you could tell he wanted to go to sleep. He hid the rest of the pig's ear under the couch cushions and climbed onto his pillow. But he couldn't sleep. I sat there and watched him. He would try to sleep, but every few minutes he would get up and go back and check to make sure the pig's ear was still under the cushion where he left it, as if he thought *I* might steal it. As if I'd want to touch that disgusting, slobbery thing." Travis's expression of disgust made Nicole laugh aloud. "Anyway, after a while, he moved the pig's ear from the living room. He put it behind the toilet in the bathroom. But he still couldn't sleep. He kept getting up and checking. Finally, he started to whine and cry from sheer exhaustion—he couldn't sleep, but he was too tired to do anything else. Honestly, that's how I felt for years, like I was living on a knife edge between the cops and my suppliers. I could never relax. That's why I was so happy when I got the call from Town Square that I was hired."

Ruby had heard Nicole laughing and wanted in on whatever was so funny.

As she walked toward them, Nicole grew nervous on Travis's behalf. Even though she didn't go to church much, Ruby was just religious enough that she had a very low opinion of drugs, and, like Diego, she didn't distinguish between weed and hard drugs. She was apt to get a little moralistic about a dealer, even a former dealer.

But Travis was quick on his feet. Before Ruby could ask what they were talking about, he started telling them about how he got on his walkie the other day only to hear Big Will saying into line two, "Meredith, what kind of naked do you want? I repeat, what kind of naked do you want? Do you read me?"

"I was, like, 'What the fuck? He's doing her?'" Travis recounted. "Then *she* gets on the line and says, 'Mighty Mango, please, over and out.' I was like, 'Is *Mighty Mango* what she calls his dick? That is some weird-ass shit.' Then Big Will said he'd write out a req form. I thought for a second he wanted to get, you know, *paid* for his services. Then I realized they were talking about smoothies. Those ones she likes? They're called Naked. It's the brand. He was getting her one."

As he told this story, Travis had projected his voice so the others could hear too. By the time he finished, they were all laughing, even Milo.

"The only kind of naked I'd like from Meredith is the kind where she has a bag over her head," Val said. When Nicole looked at her in horror, Val said, "What? She has a good body, okay? She does—I can admit that. All that kickboxing and whatnot."

By now, the sun had risen completely. The sky was radiant. A single cloud, shaped like a lobster but lit from below so that it was the color of cotton candy, floated above the mountains. Nicole felt giggly and happy. Maybe it was the hot food in her stomach, combined with exhaustion from all the overnights, but she felt strangely as if she were not at work at all but in the midst of one of those magical nights from when she'd been a teenager, when she'd been with friends and friends of friends and everything had clicked and they had stayed up all night, getting fucked up but not too fucked up, one of those nights when the world had briefly seemed both funny and full of possibility.

The good mood was widespread. They were all giggly, even when it was time to file in for the morning meeting, which was led by Little Will. During his two days off, Little Will had gone to the barber. His new buzz cut muted his good looks. His head appeared oddly small above his wide chest and shoulders—he looked like a stubby pencil sharpened to too fine a point. This added to the smokers' general sense of hilarity.

"Where's Meredith, Will?" Val asked.

Little Will said that after bringing theirs, Meredith had gone out to get her own breakfast.

"I guess she don't like McDonald's," Ruby said.

"She probably wanted a smoothie—Mighty Mango," said Val, and the smokers cracked up, for no reason that Little Will could fathom.

He waited until they stopped laughing to hold up a sign-up sheet he'd been instructed to pass around. Corporate wanted them to sign up to be interviewed in fifteen-minute time slots between 9 a.m. and noon the following day. Anita's team, he said, would be interviewed in the afternoon.

Little Will expected pushback. Being asked to come back to work after their shift was the kind of minor hassle they were apt to get huffy about, even though they'd punch back in for the interviews and get paid for their time and even if the interviews were, technically, optional (participation encouraged but not required), and even though they rarely complained about things that seemed much worse to Little Will—like when the store cut people's hours at the end of the year to prevent them from being eligible for benefits the following year—maybe because those things didn't happen to everybody all at once, or maybe because they were suspected but impossible to prove.

After setting the sign-up sheet on a table, Little Will left the room so they could attempt to work it out among themselves, but he fully expected a lengthy, grievance-heavy conversation to ensue when he returned. He couldn't have been more surprised when he reentered the break room five minutes later. The old guys were watching the news on the TV—there'd been another mass shooting, this time at a club in Los Angeles; Joyce was on her phone, checking Facebook. And the smokers were sitting quietly, hands folded on the table, like obedient children, like the goddamn von Trapps. The sign-up sheet was sitting right back where he left it, with everyone's name printed neatly in each of the time slots. Little Will shook his head in disbelief.

FOR THE LAST PART of the shift—the last two hours of the last overnight—Travis and Raymond were breaking out Office.

Travis asked Raymond how he thought the pro-Mer plan was going.

"Honestly, it's working better than I thought," Raymond said. "The store looks good, really good. Between that and all of us all saying nice things about Meredith tomorrow, it's hard to see why they wouldn't give her the job. I mean, Val said Meredith was marked 'fast track' for promotion even before this job came up, and Val is pretty reliable."

"And you think one of us has a shot at getting group manager?"

By now it was full-on morning. Office was at the front of the store, next to Women's, and Travis was facing the wide entrance. When he looked at Raymond, he angled his head to avoid the glare of the sun through the automatic glass doors.

Raymond nodded. "It always goes to someone already in Movement. I don't know if it's an official rule or just a tradition, but that's the way it works. Anyone in Movement could get it." Raymond thought for a second of Ruby. "I mean, anyone with a GED or a diploma."

Travis almost dropped the box he was holding. "What?"

Sunlight or not, Travis stared directly into Raymond's face, searching for some indication that Raymond was shitting him.

"You didn't know about the GED requirement?" Raymond asked.

"Not a clue."

Raymond could see from Travis's expression that he was upset, but he was confused as to why. Travis had only been at Town Square a couple of months. Regardless of whether he had a GED, he wouldn't have gotten the promotion.

Raymond went back to shelving packages of pens.

Stupid, Travis thought. How could he have been so fucking stupid?

Of course the group manager job was always a long shot. But he'd thought that even if he didn't get the promotion this time, he'd have a good shot at the next available management position, with Meredith running the place. She clearly liked him.

It had never occurred to him that he wasn't eligible for promotion, period.

Travis had considered lying when he applied to Town Square the last time, checking the box that said he had a high school diploma. After all, he'd applied so many times before and never gotten so much as an interview. But he knew from a buddy that the store ran background checks on people they were close to hiring. He worried they'd find out he lied, so he didn't do it. Then, once he was hired, he hadn't given it another thought. In all the years Travis had applied to legit jobs, he'd always thought the hard part was getting in. He'd taken it for granted that once they saw how good a worker he was, how smart and energetic and helpful, he'd be set.

Suddenly Travis felt very, very tired, more tired than he'd been in ages, as if all the exhaustion he'd been holding at bay, not only for the past few days—during the overnights—but for the past few months, had caught up with him all at once. He lived in a one-bedroom apartment with a toddler and a newborn and a girlfriend who was always mad at him, who thought he was a fucking tool for working retail. Yet he'd been coming in here every day chipper as shit and working like the fucking Energizer Bunny, doing the job of three people on the line most days. To get here, he rode his bike down a pitch-black highway in the middle of the night. Several times he'd nearly been hit by a car.

He thought about the other night, when it had rained, how worried he'd been about being late. He'd spent twenty dollars that he and Jeanie needed on a cab, just because he hadn't wanted to call out, to risk being thought unreliable. He thought of how he'd put up with Meredith's weird-ass shit, the way she'd laughed at his needing to "feed his baby," how she'd waved her tits at him ("Ha-ha, I'm so small and sexy!"), not because she was flirting, but because she wanted to feel hot. (He wasn't stupid.) But he had gone along, done his best to give her whatever she wanted. And for what? A fucking Egg McMuffin? The fact was, he'd need to be scheduled for at least thirty or thirty-five hours a week to match what he made dealing—and from what he was learning about how this place operated, how likely was that?

Travis kicked the box that was sitting on the floor in front of him. It was tightly packed with reams of printer paper and harder than he expected. "Fuck!" he howled.

Meredith happened to be walking by. She wagged her finger at him. "No cursing!" she said playfully before continuing on her way.

Travis looked at his phone. It was just after seven. There was almost an hour left on the shift. But he just couldn't, not for another minute. Maybe Jeanie was right. This job wasn't worth it.

"I'm out of here," Travis told Raymond. He was still hanging packages of pens.

"Are you okay?" Raymond asked. "Should I tell Little Will you got sick?"

But Travis was halfway to the door that led to the employee area and the time clocks. He had already started taking off his oversized blue Town Square T-shirt, leaving just a black T-shirt underneath. He turned to Raymond. "Whatever."

20

AT 3:53 ON Monday morning—the day of corporate's visit—Movement was preparing to start a regular 4 a.m. shift. It was the first time in almost a week that they hadn't worked an overnight. "I feel positively peppy," Raymond said while they waited to clock in. "Like I slept in."

Meredith looked around anxiously. "Where's Travis? Has anyone seen him? Will?"

She was wearing a light blue blazer over her snug-fitting blue shirt. It was her lucky blazer, the one she wore when she was interviewed for her promotion to executive manager.

When Little Will shook his head, Meredith turned to Ruby as if she might once again have the answer.

"No idea."

Ruby thought light blue was a strange color for a blazer. She thought Meredith looked like a groomsman in a spring wedding.

Meredith began to pace. Why on earth would Travis pick today of all days to be late? He knew how important he was on the line. It wasn't even raining.

"Where could he be?" she said aloud.

"He was sick yesterday," Raymond said. "Remember? He had to leave early. Maybe he's not feeling well?"

"Well, he should have called, then," Meredith said. She'd checked her phone twice already—no texts or calls from him.

She turned to Callie, looked at her in a way that suggested it was Callie's fault Travis wasn't here. "Well, Callie," she said, "you'll just have to manage the best you can in Travis's spot."

Raymond and Diego glanced at each other. How was Callie, who was about five foot two and maybe a hundred and ten pounds, supposed to handle Bulk?

But she managed—or rather they did. Callie was able to get the bigger items off the line and set them at her feet. When Raymond or Diego had a break in terms of their own boxes, or when Little Will wasn't running a full pallet out to the floor, one of them would carry those items to the Bulk area for her. It worked—at least until Meredith got on the line. In her keyed-up state, she started pushing even faster and more erratically than usual.

Within a minute, a box of cat food tins fell off the line. A sulfurous, fishy smell filled the warehouse.

Meredith swiveled her head, trying to decide who should clean it up—who would be missed the least on the line? The answer was obvious to everyone but her: her. She was the least essential person.

Before Meredith had made up her mind, a voice rang out from the doorway.

"What the hell is that smell?" Travis said. "I have a sewer pipe running behind my house that smells better than this place."

Above her groomsman's suit, Meredith's face brightened—from the neck up, she was a bride who'd until that instant thought she was being left at the altar. "You're here!" she called happily. "Thank goodness."

Raymond, too, was relieved to see Travis. After the way he left yesterday, Raymond had thought maybe Travis wasn't coming back.

Raymond wasn't wrong to have wondered. Travis had been pretty set on quitting when he walked out. Jeanie had been trying to convince him to quit for weeks. She had pointed out that they were behind on rent, dependent on her food stamps, the food bank, and her mother to get by. "It wasn't that bad before, and you know it," she said. In the past, Travis had held firm. He'd been so much happier these past months at Town Square than he'd been for years, maybe since he was locked up the first time, when he was eighteen. But yesterday he started to think maybe Jeanie had been right all along.

He bought a six-pack on his way home. He drank it, then slept a few hours, then went out and bought another. Alcohol was Travis's thing, always had been—his lack of interest in the product was part of what had made him a good weed dealer. A couple of cans into the second six-pack, he'd grown sentimental. He started thinking about his grandmother, as he often did when he drank alone. But yesterday those thoughts had eventually led him to Joyce. It had been a long time since a person like her—decent, classy—had taken an interest in him. The idea of Joyce being disappointed in him bothered him. Then he started thinking about the others—Nicole and Raymond and even Val. It had been nice of Val to include him in her plan, even though she didn't know him well, nice of her to leave him out of the shadier elements—messing up tables, spreading rumors. Raymond had offered to cover for him when he left work, to say he was sick. And he liked Nicole. She'd made him feel good when she'd asked him questions, laughed at his jokes. He felt like they had a connection.

When he'd started this job, Travis had intended to do whatever it took to succeed. He thought he'd be like one of the bad contestants on a reality show, the ones who said they were there to win, not to make friends. But yesterday, as he drank, he realized that something had changed. He'd come to like those guys. He realized that he didn't want to let them down, not when their plan was so close to succeeding. Even if he couldn't get the promotion, he wanted one of them to get it. When he finally went to bed, Travis set an alarm for 3:15—but he was hungover and didn't wake up right away, which was why he was late.

After Travis's arrival, the unload proceeded smoothly. They finished at 4:58.

ANITA AND A FEW of her minions in Softlines Sales were already out on the sales floor, tidying tables, when the people from the line emerged from the warehouse.

The people of Movement kept an eye on them as they broke out their boxes. Then it was six, breaktime. There was much to discuss. The day before, when Little Will passed out the sign-up sheet for the interviews, Diego had taken the earliest slot, at nine. Val figured he could set the tone, start the interviews off on the right note. Val thought it wisest to preserve Nicole and herself for later. They were the best talkers, the best equipped to "close the deal," ensure that the interviewers left with the best possible impression of Meredith's managerial skills.

To make it work, they'd had to figure out rides for everyone. Nicole normally had to get the Dingmobile back to her mother by ten, so her mother could get to the diner for the lunch shift. But Nicole's interview wasn't until eleven. So Raymond had given Ruby and Nicole a ride this morning and would also take them home—this way, Nicole could stay as long as she needed. Meanwhile, Milo normally left Town Square by eight thirty to pick up his two-year-old so her mother could get to her job at Walgreens at nine. With Ruby's help—Ruby was good at organizing things—he and Callie, whose daughter was also two, had come up with a plan: they would both leave work at the regular time and get their daughters, bring them to the store. The girls would play in Rich

Kid Toys, watched by Callie when Milo was being interviewed and by Milo when it was Callie's turn.

To Milo, it sounded almost like a date. Almost as soon as the plan was conceived, he'd planned to build on it.

At break, he turned to Callie. She was looking toward the part of the parking lot that was for the mall. (It was empty, as usual.) He cleared his throat. She turned to him.

Milo suggested that they take their daughters to a playground after their interviews, maybe even grab lunch. Callie was about to say sure, maybe, if it wasn't too hot and her mom didn't need her for anything. Then she looked at Milo's face.

Sweat had flattened his dark hair against his head, making his long, pink-tipped nose even more prominent. But it was the look in his eyes and the set of his mouth that jolted Callie—she saw something pleading, almost adoring. Callie realized then that he thought there was something between the two of them.

She'd noticed that Milo was friendly to her and seemed to like talking to her. It had been a relief. Nicole and Ruby had been kind of cold, especially at first. She had been so glad that someone at her new job was being nice to her that, honestly, she hadn't really stopped to think about *why* Milo might have been so friendly. Besides, he was so peculiar, so unlike any guy she could imagine being interested in, that it never occurred to her that he might see her romantically. And she was also in a relationship already, her first since her marriage had imploded—she had sort of assumed everybody knew she wasn't in the market. But, she realized now, in all the conversations she'd had with Milo, he really hadn't asked much about her.

She knew she had to clear it up.

"Zoe's going to be in heaven," she said, tilting her head upward because Milo was so tall that she had to, to meet his eye. "Most days she doesn't see anyone but me and my mom and the people at my mom's doctor's offices. But yesterday she went with my boyfriend and his five-year-old son to Twin Lakes, so I could take a nap and finish a project for my class. And now she'll hang out with you and Lily—it'll be the most exciting few days she's had in a while."

Milo seemed to hear her on a time delay. Several seconds passed before the word "boyfriend" sunk in. Then something began to change in his expression. His smile remained, but the animating force behind it slowly died until it looked as if it were painted on, like a doll's smile. He managed to say, "Right. Yeah."

He turned away from her. In his mind, the word "boyfriend" continued to repeat, as if on a loop.

It didn't make sense, didn't compute. Callie had been so nice, so sympathetic and gentle and interested in what he had to say. She'd laughed at his jokes, she'd asked him questions about his life, his childhood, his parents, his education, had gone out of her way to sit next to him at the morning meeting. He'd told her about his brother. They had, it seemed to him, bonded. Had he been living in a dream these past few days?

Yes. He had. He saw that now. And like every single dream he'd ever had, this one had blown up in his face.

Over the years, Milo had gotten so much advice about women. Diego, for example, said not to worry so much, that if you didn't care too much or try too hard, they'd find you attractive—but what did Diego know about being Milo? Milo had tried every single approach—acting aloof, acting nice, negging, complimenting—and he still had been dumped and cheated on and rejected more times than he cared to count. He had thought Callie was different—almost a reward for his patience, for everything he'd been through. But he had been wrong, again. After a few days' reprieve, a few days of happiness and hope—he was back in a landscape both familiar and bleak. In his head, he heard, *Hello darkness, my old friend.* (His dad's Christian rock band covered that song, except they altered the lyrics to make it about Satan.) Milo knew people thought he was a happy-go-lucky sort of guy because he did comedy, but as he tried to remind them, people had probably thought that about Robin Williams too.

As break finally drew to a close, Milo filed inside with the others, feeling as if he might cry.

In the break room, Nicole took a seat next to him. She'd been standing next to Milo during his conversation with Callie. She'd heard everything. She'd been as surprised as Milo to learn of Callie's mystery boyfriend.

While Little Will did his thing—thanking them yet again for their hard work on the overnights, for getting the store in such good shape ("It looks like 2005 in here," Joyce said)—Nicole wondered what Callie had been thinking, keeping this boyfriend of hers a secret. Callie had to have seen that Milo was into her. It had been obvious to Nicole, hadn't it? The strange thing to Nicole had been how receptive—or at least not unreceptive—Callie had been. Even Nicole had started to think he had a chance.

Nicole glanced at Milo now, and for perhaps the first time in three years of working with him, she didn't see the goofy, often annoying, occasionally funny, but incredibly self-involved man-child who believed that all the sympathy in the world ought to flow in his direction. She saw a little boy who'd sat on his stoop with his sister and baby brother as they watched their father drive off for the last time, a boy who was slightly strange-looking, whose mother was neglectful, whose awkwardness and neediness had surely made him easy to pick on at school.

For a moment, Nicole thought *she* might cry. Which was weird because she was not a crier. She'd always been tough. She reminded herself that whatever Callie had done or not done, it *had* been stupid of Milo not to ask her if she had a boyfriend. Nicole would never be so dumb as to get attached to someone when she had no idea if they were even single, let alone interested in her.

FROM GRAPHIC TEES, Val had a clear view of the front of the store. Big Will was standing by the main entrance, talking to Ryan, the district manager.

Ryan was two years older and four inches shorter than Big Will. Diego once said Ryan looked like a baby who'd been squashed in the birth canal. His head was narrow and cone-like on top, something he tried to compensate for by using product to make his sparse, light brown hair as puffy and voluminous as possible. Underneath its pointy top, Ryan's head seemed to spread out, as if his cheeks were being stretched sideways from the sides of his mouth. This funhouse-like alternation between narrow and wide continued throughout his body. He had broad shoulders that tapered abruptly to a narrow, almost delicate waist. Below that, his hips flared out like a woman's, while his feet looked almost dainty, in his tiny brown loafers.

While Val watched Big Will and Ryan—she assumed they were waiting for the other two representatives from corporate to arrive—she picked up a shirt that said BORN IN THE USA. She considered. She liked Springsteen, but she suspected most of the people who bought the T-shirt thought it meant something very different from what he'd intended. She silently apologized to the Boss as she tucked the shirt behind one that said A WOMAN'S PLACE IS IN THE HOUSE AND SENATE.

Two women approached the entrance. Because the store wasn't yet open, Big Will manually unlocked and held open a regular glass door next to the automatic ones that customers were encouraged to use. Val could tell that the women were serious bigwigs because they weren't wearing blue and khaki. One was wearing a real business suit, with a pencil skirt that made her not-insubstantial bottom half look a bit like a sausage. The other was thin and pretty. She looked like a fancy lawyer on a TV show, in high heels, skinny pants, and a blouse with a sweater on top.

Hoping to get close enough to listen to their conversation, Val moved to Discount Zone, a cluster of tables at the front of the store that featured a revolving selection of low-priced, seasonally appropriate items. She tried to look focused on tidying stacks of pineapple- and watermelon-themed reusable outdoor plates. But before she heard much of anything, the overhead lights flickered.

It was eight o'clock. Time to get started.

Raymond was already in the employee area when Val entered. He nodded at Val, then slipped into the server room.

The store's head of Asset Protection had already arrived; the door was unlocked. Raymond sat in the big chair, facing several computer screens. He typed in a username and password that were for general use, then used the mouse to move the cameras. Even though Milo hadn't shown up to act as lookout like he was supposed to, Raymond wasn't worried. There was nothing suspicious about a longtime employee like Raymond checking out what was going on in the store or even fiddling with the cameras, reorienting a camera a little to the left so that a particular T-shirt table happened to no longer be visible. The Asset Protection team moved the cameras all the time. They had to. Shoplifters were good at figuring out the store's blind spots—they made little messes to see how long it took for anyone to notice. If nothing happened for a while, they figured that the area wasn't being watched, that it was a good spot to steal from. To keep them guessing, you had to keep the cameras moving.

When Raymond had adjusted the cameras so that none were aimed at the tables Val planned to target, he got on his walkie. "Diego, your ride is confirmed," he said.

Using the walkies for "personal business" was frowned on, but Val had figured out that no one would begrudge Movement using them to arrange rides today, when they'd had to rearrange their schedules for the interviews with corporate.

When he heard Raymond's message, Diego jumped up from his chair in the break room. He pretty much swaggered down the narrow hallway to the sales floor and all the way to Softlines.

He was looking forward to chatting up Anita. She was an attractive woman, with short hair that she straightened and wore in a hip, slightly asymmetrical but flattering cut that emphasized her big eyes and round cheeks. He didn't know why he'd never thought to flirt with her before, except maybe that he had been intimidated by her job title.

But when he got to Softlines, he found Anita talking to Big Will and Ryan and the women from corporate. She was smiling and asking the women how their "journey" was, as if they'd come on horseback, climbing mountains and fording rivers, instead of via a major airline, and whether their hotel was "satisfactory." (That was the thing with Anita, Diego realized—she overcompensated, tried too hard to conceal the fact that she hadn't grown up rich like most of the other executive managers.)

In any case, there was nothing for Diego to do but wait, in case the others moved on and Anita became unoccupied. He got onto his walkie and said, "Ruby and Nicole, your ride is confirmed."

Ruby approached one of Anita's minions, a young woman named Yanique. Yanique was in Baby, touching up a table of onesies and tiny T-shirts that already looked good.

"How you doin'?" Ruby asked. "You're going to be interviewed today, right? Me too. I'm just waiting for mine to start. Hey, that reminds me—what's up with Anita wanting to get rid of the free meals? You heard that? Crazy, ain't it?"

Meanwhile, Nicole kept an eye on the other minion, who was straightening the tables in Men's. Nicole didn't bother to talk to her.

Better to keep herself free to give Val the cue to go, which she did when she was sure neither woman was looking in Val's direction. "Val, your ride is confirmed," she said into her walkie.

The first table Val planned to target was in the front of Women's Ready-to-Wear and was single-handedly responsible for thousands of dollars' worth of revenue each week. Because of its importance, Anita had fixed it up herself. Val had seen her bent over it for hours this morning.

Val rotated her right arm, as if in preparation for a major exertion.

As she came within a few feet of the table, Val saw that Anita had done an excellent job. Stacks of different-colored shirts were folded into perfect rectangles, their corners at exact ninety-degree angles. The tidy patches of color and pattern suddenly reminded Val of the neat, geometric swatches of farmland she'd seen out the window on the first and only trip she'd taken in an airplane, when her middle school science team had unexpectedly made it to the finals in Chicago. Val thought about what those T-shirt tables had looked like only a few hours ago, the mess Anita had tamed. Val had spent enough time in Softlines to know how much effort it had taken Anita to transform them to such a degree.

Then another memory came to Val.

A few years ago, not long after she had started at the store, Val had found Anita crying in the ladies' room. Val asked what was wrong. Anita must have been eager to talk to someone, because instead of blowing Val off, she asked if Val knew a certain gymnastics studio for little kids, over in the next strip mall from the store. Val did. The place had a big wall of windows out front. It was impossible to miss. Everyone passing by saw the kids somersaulting on the red mat and jumping on trampolines. Anita told Val that she'd been running errands with her daughters the day before and had walked by the gymnastics studio. A class was in session. Her girls were riveted—they'd pressed their faces to the glass and stared as one by one the kids jumped off the balance beam into a ball pit. On the way home, Anita's older girl begged to take gymnastics there. Anita figured why not. Then the little one started to cry and said she wanted to take gymnastics, too. Anita said she'd look into it, see how much it cost. The girls had cheered, they were so excited.

Well. Anita had just gotten off the phone with the studio. She learned it would cost more than $1,500 for both girls to take an hour-long class once a week, not including summer. More if she paid by the month, instead of up front. Anita was a single mom, she could barely keep up with rent and car payments and student loan payments and Internet and clothes and food and child care. And she was supposed to be saving for their college. She couldn't justify $1,500 for a class like that, a class that wasn't even a real gymnastics class—it wasn't even about the acquisition of skill or future competition, but was billed as "enrichment," whatever that meant.

Anita had told Val all this quickly. Then she'd looked up at Val, as if embarrassed. She apologized and said it was a stupid reason to cry. But she'd seen the looks on her girls' faces as they watched the class. And now she'd have to tell them no. She'd always known that sooner or later, they'd figure out that they couldn't have what richer kids had, but she had wanted them to go a little bit longer without finding it out. "Also," she told Val, "every kid in that class they watched was white. Every single one."

Val had tried to make Anita feel better—"I'll bet they won't even remember about the class by the time you get home today," she assured her—but Val was just being nice. The truth was that Val thought it *was* a dumb thing to cry about. The gymnastics studio was stupid. What's the point of jumping off a balance beam into a ball pit? How will kids learn if they never have to manage real risk? And she thought it was a good thing for Anita's daughters to learn early that life isn't fair. Why shield kids from the truth?

But now, with her arm poised to mess up Anita's perfect table, it struck her differently. Maybe because Val now had a kid of her own. She recognized the unexpectedly powerful desire to make her son's childhood as nice as she could, to give him things she herself hadn't had—and to protect him from realities that she herself was glad to have been exposed to because they'd made her tougher. For the second time since Val had come up with the pro-Mer plan, she saw Anita as a person—this time as a single mother, trying to give her kids a decent childhood.

Suddenly Val didn't want to mess up Anita's table. It was in fact the very last thing she wanted to do.

Val looked around—as if searching for an escape route. Instead she saw Nicole. Nicole was watching her, looking a little puzzled as to why Val had stopped a few feet from the table. She nodded encouragingly, trying to assure Val that it was safe for her to go.

Val couldn't bail now.

She stepped forward and swept her arm across the table, running it like a propeller through a sea of cotton, upending those perfect geometric stacks and leaving in their wake messy piles of unfolded shirts.

The second table was easier. This time, Val didn't think about what she was doing. She just did it.

21

DIEGO WAS FIRST to be interviewed. The others waited for him outside.

After what felt like ages, the employee door opened. Diego stepped out. The others gathered around him eagerly, but he was determined to milk the moment. He gestured that they should back off, give him some space. He asked Raymond for a cigarette. Only after he'd taken a long drag did he start talking.

The interview took place on the far side of the break room, on the other side of the accordion curtain, in the part of the room used for corporate-mandated training sessions about exercising caution when operating heavy equipment or not sexually harassing your coworkers. Today, Diego said, the desks were not arranged in classroom-like rows, but in a semicircle with a single desk in the middle, for the person being interviewed. "It feels like you're onstage," Diego said, not unappreciatively. The setup had made him feel important, as if they really cared about what he had to say. "They took notes," he said, then nodded at the Poland Spring water bottle in his hand. "They put out water, too."

Nicole was getting impatient. "What'd they ask?"

"*Girl.* I'm getting to that."

He said they wanted to know what working with Meredith was like. He told them working with Meredith was excellent. "I wasn't sure they'd understand me because of my accent, so I kept it simple. I kept repeating the word 'excellent.'" Diego looked up at the others and grinned. "I said that I was impressed with how fast she picked up logistics. 'Excellent understanding,' I said. They asked me what team morale was like, and I said it was 'excellent.' When I wasn't sure what to say, I just thought about the truth and said the opposite. One of them asked if Meredith 'empowered' me. I almost cracked up. I wanted to tell her how Meredith is always watching me like she thinks I might steal something—but I just said, 'Yeah, yeah, she empowers me big-time. I've never felt so empowered in my life. It's excellent to be so empowered.'"

Even Val laughed. She was finally shaking off the bad feeling she'd had since messing up Anita's tables.

Callie pulled into the parking lot in her little red car. She hoisted her little girl out of the backseat. "Don't forget to lock it," Ruby called out to her. With her hand, Ruby imitated the clicking gesture in case Callie hadn't heard her properly.

Ruby wasn't even mocking her. In the past couple of days, Ruby had started to come around on Callie. And Potterstown had its share of junkies who'd grab anything that wasn't locked down—she didn't want anyone to steal the little girl's car seat.

Minutes passed before Milo returned with his daughter. He'd cut it close, timewise. He and Callie went to large-scale toys to get the kids set up.

In the brief time he was outside, the others noticed that Milo was acting weird, barely speaking except when spoken to, and then in a curt, clipped voice. But then Milo was an emotional and erratic person, prone to sudden mood swings. No one, aside from Nicole, gave his behavior a thought.

MILO TOOK A SEAT in the break room. On the other side of the curtain, one of the old guys was being interviewed. The interview was apparently running long.

As he waited, Milo thought how even the old guys were married, even the grumpy one. Even the one with a hunchback. Meanwhile, Milo couldn't even get a date.

Finally, Ryan pulled back the accordion curtain. The old guy who had just been interviewed—not the one with the hunchback—exited. "We're ready for you, Milo," Ryan said.

When Milo stood up, Ryan placed a hand on his shoulder, then immediately seemed to regret it, think the gesture too familiar for a person of his station. He pulled his hand away as if Milo's shoulder had burned him.

In the classroom, Ryan introduced Janine, Town Square's regional operations manager for the Northeast. She was on the squat side, had short, dyed blond hair, and wore a business suit. Then he introduced Katherine, an executive vice president from corporate HQ. Katherine had silky-looking, shoulder-length brown hair and a neat top—the kind that looks like two shirts layered on top of each other, a sweater over a blouse, but which Milo knew (from the ex who had worked at Banana Republic) was really one piece.

Katherine smiled at him. "It's nice to meet you, Milo. I see that you've been at the store for eight years. Wow. You must know this place better than almost anyone."

Despite his mood, Milo smiled slightly. So few people appreciated his experience.

"Well, I've been the store's primary thrower for years now, so yeah—I do know the store pretty well," he said. "Technically, stores are supposed to rotate, as you probably know, but I guess Will—Store Manager Will, I mean, not Little Will, our group manager, who's also named Will—anyway, I guess Will thinks I do a good job, and that it's better for the store if I do the whole truck every day. I'm glad to do it—but it does take a lot out of me." Milo laughed. "My back—" he started to say when Katherine stopped him.

"The store is lucky to have you," she said.

That was when Milo realized that Katherine's voice, even her manner, reminded him of someone. He began trying to think of who.

"You must have worked with a number of executive managers in Logistics," she continued. "Do you think you could help us out by giving us a sense of how Meredith fits in? How does she compare to the others, and how effective is she, in your expert opinion?"

Milo wasn't sure if anyone had ever called him an expert in his life, though god knew he was expert in many things, including but in no ways limited to Town Square store #1512.

"Feel free to take your time, think about it for a minute," she said when he didn't respond immediately..

Milo had realized who Katherine reminded him of.

At several points in his life, he had been forced to see a therapist for anger management: once when he was in high school and got into a fight, then when he was fired from UnitedHealthcare—wrongly, as far as he was concerned—and finally when he'd shoved his ex-girlfriend's brother, who'd come with her to clear her stuff from the apartment she and Milo had shared and had tried to take things that were indisputably Milo's. In Milo's experience, therapy primarily consisted of judgy, frowning, late-middle-aged women asking him what he was doing to work on his temper, how he planned to control it.

Robin, at the family therapy clinic, was different. The first time he saw her, she noted that he was raising his older daughter on his own, after her mother had cheated on him, left, and then wound up in jail for forging prescriptions. Milo told Robin how even after his ex got out of prison, she didn't want custody of their daughter, which was fine because Milo was better equipped to take care of her. Robin connected this to Milo's own childhood, when he'd taken care of his younger brother and sister because his dad had left and his mother was usually drunk or high or in thrall to some new man. A session or two later, Robin had pointed out that even in his other relationships with women, the ones that didn't involve kids, Milo had been caretaker and breadwinner—for most of his adult life, he'd worked two or three jobs at a time; whenever he was dating someone, he was the one who paid rent, bought groceries, even made car payments for his girlfriends. Ms. Banana Republic, for example, had quit that job soon after they moved in together to focus on her (nonexistent) modeling career, while Milo worked at Town Square and Walgreens and paid for everything.

Robin said that it sounded like Milo had spent most of his life taking care of other people. She wondered if anyone had ever really taken care of him, if he even knew what that felt like. The moment she said that, Milo had felt seen, understood in a way that he'd never felt before in his life. He had never articulated it exactly the way Robin had, but she had put into words an injustice—*the* injustice—he'd spent his life trying to bring to the attention of others. He'd very nearly cried in Robin's office, but in a good way—with relief.

From then on, Milo had looked forward to his sessions with Robin—even though she did, in a gentle way, push him to see a situation from a different point of view. Every once in a while, he even made a small concession—admitted that maybe "evil" wasn't the right word to describe his daughter's mother, maybe "addicted" and "irresponsible" were more like it. And maybe he had ignored signs that Ms. Banana Republic was a narcissist who was using him, maybe he could have paid attention to these clues earlier, before she dumped him for someone with deeper pockets.

The last time he saw Robin was a regular therapy session—or so Milo had thought. But she told him it was her last week at the clinic. She was just an intern, and her internship was coming to an end. She told him he shouldn't worry because she'd give her notes about their sessions to her replacement, who she said was a very good, very experienced therapist. This was not true, at least not in Milo's opinion. Robin's replacement was an uptight older woman with very short hair, bug eyes, and a disapproving expression. Practically her first words to Milo were, "What steps are you taking to work on your anger?" Milo never saw Robin again.

"Milo?" Ryan said. "Are you still thinking?"

"Oh, uh, sorry."

Milo realized he had forgotten the question. He looked at Katherine for help. "Uh?"

"We were talking about how Meredith compares to the other executive managers of Logistics you've worked with," Katherine said gently.

"Right," Milo said. "Meredith is fine. I *guess*."

At that moment, he hardly remembered what he was supposed to say or that he was supposed to say anything at all. What he wanted right then—the only thing he wanted—was sympathy, understanding.

"I've seen better, and I've seen worse," he said. "I mean, I wish Meredith appreciated what I do more, but at this point I don't expect her to—I mean, I don't expect it from any boss. But, well, it *is* frustrating. I mean, the line literally couldn't run without me, so when Meredith comes back from vacation and calls Nicole 'love' and greets every single other person on the line but doesn't even say hello to me, it's a little much"—he laughed—"but I'm also used to it. As I said, at this point I try not expect that much, you know?"

When he looked up at Katherine, Milo saw, to his disappointment, that she looked more confused than indignant on his behalf. He wanted so much to connect with her, make her see who he was and what he'd been through, the way Robin had.

Ryan emitted a shrill, squeaky titter. "Thanks, Milo," he said. "What can you tell us about team morale under Meredith?"

Milo had an inspiration. "Morale is all right," he said. "Although I'm not sure an executive manager ought to be pressuring her team to take drugs."

The pen dropped from Ryan's pudgy pink hand. "Did you say *drugs*?"

"Yup," Milo said. "I'm not sure she ought to be making people feel bad because they won't take her pills. Which I did—because what choice did I have, really? I mean, she's my boss—but the pill she gave me made me feel really sick."

"You're saying Meredith pressured you to take illegal drugs?" said the other woman, the one with the short, dyed blond hair. Her eyes darted accusingly to Ryan, as if he would be held to account for whatever had happened here, then back to Milo. "While you were on the job?" she asked.

Milo laughed, pleased to have finally gotten a reaction.

"Not an illegal drug," he explained. "Prescription, maybe. Or maybe they were over-the-counter. I'm not sure. But you can ask anyone. She pressured Callie too, I think." Milo's expression became thoughtful. "I think Callie said no . . . Or maybe she took one? I don't remember."

Katherine cocked her head. "Maybe you could back up and tell us the whole story, Milo?"

Milo sighed as if put out. "So, we did a few overnights in a row. You know, to get the store ready for you guys? By the third night, we were all tired. I barely got any sleep at all because I've got two daughters. I take care of the toddler during the day. The other one is sixteen, and I have to pick her up from her job in the evenings—she works at the rest stop on the interstate, at the Starbucks, and I don't want her getting a ride with sketchy older guys, you know? So I was barely getting any sleep before coming in here. I was tired, I admit, and Meredith kept pulling out this bottle of caffeine pills, or what she said were caffeine pills. Maybe they were Adderall, for all I know? All I know is that she was popping them like candy and offering them around. At first I didn't take any, but one time after she told me I should"—he didn't see any reason to mention that he'd fallen asleep in Men's socks—"I did. And it hurt my throat. Plus, I felt nauseous and jittery—for hours. You know?"

Milo also didn't see any reason to mention the two or three energy drinks he'd consumed that night in addition to the pill Meredith had given him.

"I'm very sorry to hear this, Milo," Ryan said. "Obviously, it's unacceptable. We'll look into the matter further. It's concerning—extremely concerning."

This should have been gratifying—even jerky Ryan was taking his side—but Milo's initial high at having gotten a rise out of them was beginning to dissipate. Besides, to him the pills were far less important than his other, more substantive, emotional grievances. But life was often like this—people reacted with horror to minor technical violations of the rules while not saying anything about the things that really mattered, the things that hurt. It was like when you go to the store and the cashier acts so concerned about whether you want a bag and a receipt with your purchase, like it's the most important thing in the world to them—but if they really cared so much about your happiness, wouldn't they also care that you had really wanted to buy deli meat but couldn't afford it so had to get peanut butter instead? Milo had recorded a monologue about this on his YouTube channel.

"Honestly, I've experienced a lot worse," he said. "This was nothing. I've been through a lot, you know? I mean, not just in general, but here, at the store. You know that Little Will and I started at the same time?

We were both seasonal hires—the only two who were offered permanent jobs after the holidays. And then a few years later, he gets promoted, and I don't, even though I'm older than he is, and I have more experience, and I've been to college. And I know everyone *loves* Little Will, says he's so nice, but no one's ever going to convince me he didn't scheme to make me look bad so he could get promoted over me." Milo noticed Ryan and the woman named Janine looking sideways at one another. From long experience of trying to make himself heard, Milo had a premonition of what would happen next. To prevent them from cutting him off, he began speaking faster. "And that's not all. Not even close. Before that, when I was at UnitedHealthcare, I was fired for being late—even though I was only late because I had a dentist appointment, and I could show my boss the bill to prove it, and even though I had the highest numbers for customer satisfaction out of anyone on our floor of the call cen—"

"I'm sorry that you had a bad experience in your previous job," Katherine broke in, "and also that you're frustrated with your experience at Town Square, which is certainly something I suggest you bring up with your store's HR rep—uh, Irina?"

"Svetlana," Ryan said.

"Svetlana," Katherine continued. "But for now, would it be all right if we stayed on topic? Our time is so limited, and as you can imagine we're very concerned by the allegation that Meredith pressured you to take drugs that were possibly prescription or even illicit."

Only then did Milo realize that he might have started something he couldn't contain. If they made a stink about the pills, Val and the others might find out. They'd get mad at Milo for telling them.

"Did I say 'pressure'?" Milo laughed. "I didn't mean it like that—I just meant that she offered them, but I didn't feel actual pressure. I could have said no."

But it was too late. Milo could tell from their faces that they were not going to be pacified so easily. The unpleasant one with the short hair looked at Ryan pointedly.

Ryan took the hint. "You know, Milo," Ryan said, "we probably shouldn't keep you any longer."

Before Milo knew what was happening, he had been escorted out.

22

RYAN POKED HIS HEAD out from behind the accordion curtain. "Hi, uh, Callie," he said. "Something's come up, and we're going to need a few minutes to confer. Can you please hold tight?" Without waiting for her answer, he pulled the curtain shut.

About ten minutes later, they finally called her in. The short-haired woman—Janine, Callie thought—began talking as soon as Callie sat down. "We can see that you're very new," she said. "Less than a week—"

"Welcome," Katherine interjected.

"Yes, of course, welcome," Janine continued. "What I was going to say, though, is that it was an error on the part of your group manager to sign you up for an interview of this sort. Ordinarily, because you're so new, we wouldn't take up your time—"

"Oh!" Embarrassed, Callie started to get up. "I thought I was supposed to—"

Janine cut her off. "No, no, please sit," she said. "It turns out, we're glad you're here because an issue has come to our attention, and your name has come up."

"Oh," Callie said again, blushing. This whole setup, being in the middle of a semicircle, with three people facing her, made her feel self-conscious.

"Has Meredith ever pressured you to do anything you didn't want to do?" Janine asked.

Callie looked confused.

"You know, to do anything you weren't comfortable with?" Janine clarified. "Something that wasn't part of the job?"

Callie gasped. "Has she assaulted me? Sexually? Is that what you're asking?"

Janine's face turned red. "Excuse me. I may not have spoken clearly. I mean, has Meredith ever encouraged you to take drugs?"

"*Drugs?*"

Janine nodded.

"Illegal drugs?" Callie asked.

"Or any sort of drugs? You know, pills? Prescription, perhaps?"

"Oh . . ."

Finally, Callie understood. They were talking about the caffeine pills.

For her own sake, Callie didn't much care whether Meredith was promoted or not, but she wanted to help Val and the others. Unfortunately, she'd never been good at thinking on her feet. She lied in the most unimaginative way possible. She just shook her head and said, "I don't remember anything like that."

They asked her again in different ways. Each time, Callie said that she couldn't remember Meredith ever offering pills to anyone and that she certainly never took any or felt pressured to. "She may have taken some caffeine pills herself—over-the-counter ones, I'm sure she said they were over-the-counter," Callie said. "That's not illegal, is it?"

Janine looked at her in a way that suggested that such a question was too high-level for someone like Callie to venture an opinion on.

Katherine led her out. "Thank you again for your help, Callie."

"SHIT, SHIT, SHIT," Val said.

"Who the fuck told her?" Nicole asked.

Upon exiting, Callie had immediately told Val and Nicole what happened in there.

"Why'd they make it sound like she was pressuring people to take the pills, or as if the pills were prescription?" Nicole wanted to know. "They were clearly the same crap we sell at the store. They probably had less caffeine than a Red Bull. Who the fuck would do that?"

"One of the old guys?" Callie ventured.

"Maybe," Nicole said. "Or maybe it was Joyce." She turned to Val. "You know how she is. No filter. Always running her mouth."

Val looked unsure. Joyce had explicitly promised Val that even if she wasn't willing to help, she wouldn't do anything to get in their way. But Nicole was right—Joyce had no filter. Joyce herself had admitted as much.

While this conversation was taking place, Travis was in the classroom, being interviewed. They asked him about the pills, too. He reflexively took the same approach as Callie ("I don't know anything about any drugs, ma'am—as far as I am concerned, Meredith is the best manager I've ever had"). The interview setup—including the offer of bottled water—reminded Travis of being interrogated by police officers who pretended to be friendly. Though he had nothing to hide, Travis felt tense, nervous. The interviewers sensed this. Janine glanced at Travis's file and wasn't surprised to see he was an ex-con. That mix of caginess and overformality, the sirs and ma'ams, were a tell. She made a mental note to remind whoever became the store's next manager to keep an eye on him.

Then it was Nicole's turn. Thanks to Callie's warning, Nicole had had time to prepare before she was called in. They didn't lead with the drugs, which meant Nicole had a chance to tell the interviewers about the interest Meredith had taken in her. "I feel like she really cares about me—you know, as a person," Nicole said. "In a lot of ways, Meredith has been a role model to me, a mentor."

Nicole's hair was in a French braid. Her hands were clasped together and placed neatly in her lap. She smiled dreamily, as if remembering Meredith's benevolence all over again.

She could tell that the women especially were eating it up—smiling and nodding happily. The sense that she was doing well gave Nicole a jolt of pleasure.

Ryan glanced at the women before turning to Nicole. He spoke in a more careful tone. "I know it seems odd, Nicole, but did Meredith ever pressure you—or anyone else—to take drugs? We're hearing some conflicting reports. They're a little disconcerting."

Ryan's voice tended to veer up and down in pitch. In professional situations, he made a concerted effort to keep it as low as possible. The focus required to do this was considerable. When he spoke at any length, a wrinkle of concentration formed between his eyebrows, like an OCCUPIED sign on a restroom door.

"Oh, you mean the caffeine pills!" Nicole said. She smiled as if this were a delightful joke. "The ones she got from here—from Town Square? No, she never pressured me. She never pressured anyone. She would never do that! To be honest, she's just *extremely* considerate. She knows some people like to drink Red Bull for caffeine when we do an overnight, and she knew we were tired. She wanted to help people out, so they didn't spend so much money on those energy drinks. She's so thoughtful, isn't she? Did anyone tell you how she bought us breakfast from McDonald's the other day, when we were doing an overnight?"

"And you're sure they were just caffeine pills? The kind of thing you can buy here? Or at any convenience store?" Janine asked.

"Absolutely," Nicole said. "I looked at the bottle myself. I read the label. They were the Love & Wellness brand we sell at the store. Aquamarine bottle."

The three interviewers looked at one another. Nicole could see that they were relieved. Still, Katherine asked again if there was a chance anyone else might have felt pressured to take the pills.

Nicole laughed merrily. "Of course not. No more than they felt pressured to say yes to breakfast from McDonald's."

"Thank you, Nicole," Katherine said. Then she walked Nicole to the door.

It was Val's turn next. The last interviewee, she not only had to finish the patch-up job Nicole had started—she also wanted to wow them, ensure they left blown away. But she had to be careful. She didn't want to go too far, risk making them suspicious.

Taking a page from Diego, Val considered everything she had ever thought about Meredith and said the opposite. She thought of Meredith calling Nicole slow and pretending to imitate her by making jerking movements with her body while her mouth hung open. Then she told the interviewers how sensitive Meredith was, how even if she had something critical to say, she did it in the nicest possible way. "Oh, and she is always so compassionate when it comes to disadvantaged people—you know, minorities, the handicapped, gay people." Val smiled and gestured to indicate that she herself was included in the latter group. The interviewers looked very pleased, and Val grew emboldened. "You might describe her as a beacon of kindness in a cold world," she said.

"That's truly lovely," Katherine said. "Touching."

"Agreed," Janine said. "But if I may, what is she like as a manager?"

"Oh, terrific," Val said. "She's a natural leader—inspiring, you know? Very energetic. But she's also the kind of person who, you know, if she doesn't know something, she isn't afraid to ask questions. And if she makes a mistake, she apologizes. She doesn't need to be right all the time."

All three were nodding along, smiling happily.

Encouraged, Val thought of how Meredith was obsessed with staying on budget and ignored the backlog when she thought that corporate wouldn't notice. "Meredith genuinely cares about the well-being of the store," she said. "She isn't one of those managers who tries to cover her own a—uh, butt."

She thought of Meredith's myopic obsession with the unload time, with having a "failure" on her record, no matter how little difference it made to the store: "And she's too smart to sweat the small stuff. She always has her eye on the big picture, the greater good, not just her own self-interest."

At this, Ryan turned to the other two interviewers and grinned, almost proudly, as if he were personally responsible for all the stellar leadership qualities Meredith exhibited.

Finally, they asked about the drugs. Val threw her head back and laughed breezily, the way she imagined people do at fancy cocktail parties. "Meredith is sometimes a little too caring for her own good," she said. "She always wants to help people. If she sees that someone is tired, her impulse is to do something. As I said, a beacon of kindness. But pressure?" Val laughed. "Of course not. I mean, why would she? If anyone felt pressured, it probably says more about their mental health than anything else."

The way the interviewers looked at one another when Val said this was telling. Val realized that this was not only the answer they wanted to hear but that it sounded right to them. They were clearly inclined to believe that the person who said the thing about the drugs, whoever it was, was of dubious mental health. This was surprising. It was hard to imagine anyone coming away from a conversation with Joyce and feeling that she was mentally unstable. Overly chatty, sure. But the content of Joyce's chatter was a window into her inner life that left no room for doubt that she was anything but deeply, thoroughly, even boringly sane. Could it have been someone else? But who? The old guys were so disengaged, and it was hard to imagine Meredith offering them pills—or them even hearing her if she did, given their penchant for turning off their hearing aids whenever she approached.

But Val didn't have any more time to pursue this line of thought. Suddenly they were all standing up and thanking her. Katherine patted her on the back and walked her out.

"You've been a tremendous help, Valerie," Katherine said on their way to the door.

"It's Va—" Val started to say. Even Meredith knew better than to call her Valerie. But she stopped herself and smiled back.

As the door closed behind her, a feeling of elation came over Val. Last-minute crisis or no, they'd done it. No, *she* had done it. She had brought together a bunch of people who bickered constantly and gotten them to work together for a common purpose. Together they had not only cleaned up the store in a few days, they'd made the store's worst manager look like a genius. As Val headed outside, her keys jiggled like wind chimes, as if they were clamoring to be joined by more keys, by the keys to the store.

23

AT LUNCHTIME, RYAN found Big Will in his office. "With one exception," he said to Big Will, "what we learned about Meredith this morning was very positive. The warehouse looks terrific, very well organized, and the store is well stocked. We did some spot checking and what we found was fine—no irregularities that couldn't be chalked up to seasonal fluctuations. Meanwhile, the one concern we had, we ultimately attributed to an exaggeration or misconstrual by a group member who may not be the most stable . . ."

Ryan leaned in to speak more confidentially. The wrinkle of vigilance appeared between his eyebrows.

"Otherwise, the team interviews were remarkably good. Surprisingly good, I have to say. I know about the complaints in Meredith's file. But it sounds as if she's really learned from her past missteps, as a manager. Which reflects well on you—I know you've been guiding her and that she's been learning from the example you set here. So kudos. Her current team loves her. It was actually touching to hear some of the things they say about her as a mentor and role model, a sort of beacon of kindness. They've really taken to her."

Big Will stared at Ryan in disbelief.

The first part—about the store looking good—he had followed, but *Meredith's interviews were remarkably good? She had learned from past mistakes? Mentor and role model? Beacon of kindness?* What the fuck? Had Ryan gotten confused? It was possible. Ryan's success in climbing the ranks at Town Square was not generally attributed to any particular quickness or skill, but rather to his having graduated from a more prestigious university than most people in the management training program. (For all its talk of egalitarianism, corporate had a fetish for people with Ivy League degrees, no matter how unexceptional many of them proved to be in practice.)

But even plodding, yes-man Ryan was unlikely to be so very mixed up.

Big Will's next thought was that Meredith had bribed the team. Either that or she had threatened to retaliate if they badmouthed her. He couldn't think of any other explanation.

"Of course, nothing will be decided until after we interview Anita's team this afternoon and speak to both Meredith and Anita individually," Ryan continued, "but between us, given what our predisposition was when we came in today and what we've learned so far, it looks to me like the writing is on the wall. If I were you, I'd make sure to have my ducks in a row, in terms of how to handle Logistics going forward, who you want to be Movement's group manager, et cetera. We'd like to approve all promotions at once, so as not to leave gaps in the chain of command during the summer rush."

Big Will couldn't manage more than a nod.

Ryan got up to go. "Oh, and we have something else to discuss over dinner." He had paused in the doorway. "The automation study has wrapped up. There is some news. But we'll get you up to date on that tonight."

Great, Big Will thought. Just great. He made himself smile as convincingly as he could.

When Ryan was gone, Big Will stood in front of the one-way mirror overlooking the sales floor. He hadn't expected this. He had, he realized now, been on some level counting on the interviews to derail Meredith's promotion.

It was with a heavy feeling that he picked up his walkie and called Little Will to his office. When Little Will appeared, Big Will asked if he'd thought over what they'd discussed the week before, about the group manager job.

Little Will was cagey. "I, uh, I'm having a hard time choosing," he said without meeting Big Will's eye. "I'd be fine with Raymond or Diego or Val—any of them are more than capable of doing the job, probably more capable than I am."

Little Will was the only manager at the store who went in for self-deprecation. The others were too afraid of being taken at face value. But Big Will was too annoyed to find this amusing. Meredith and Little Will had one task: pick a new group manager. And what do they do? First Meredith suggests they promote Travis, someone who'd only been at the store for a couple of *months*. Not only that, but who was actually ineligible for the job. (After his conversation with Meredith, Big Will had double-checked Travis's file. The guy didn't have his GED!) Meanwhile, Big Will had given Little Will the whole weekend to think about it. And the guy still couldn't make up his mind. It suddenly struck Big Will that the whole Logistics operation was mired in unprofessionalism. He had no doubt that Anita and her deputy were more than capable of suggesting appropriate replacements in a timely manner—he was sure he could call the two of them in this minute and have a name nailed down within half an hour, no problem.

Before he let Little Will go, he asked if Little Will had noticed anything odd about his team recently. What Ryan had said about the interviews made no sense—there had to be an explanation.

"Odd?" Little Will thought about the sign-up sheet the other morning, the way they'd all just gone along so agreeably. But that wasn't something he could ding them for, was it? He didn't want to go throwing suspicion on the members of his team when he had no real cause. "No," he said. "I haven't noticed anything."

Big Will dismissed him.

What difference did it make to him who they promoted here? Big Will thought when he was alone again. He would be gone in a few weeks. Over the weekend, he and Caitlin had seen almost a dozen houses. It was a bit demoralizing. They'd have to set modest expectations. At least until he got the next promotion. *If* he got the next promotion—if he didn't screw it up by doing something stupid now.

If only he'd spoken up about Meredith a week ago when they were making plans for today. There had still been time then. Now corporate had practically signed the store over to her. Big Will sighed.

Caitlin would tell him that the fact that Meredith's team said nice things about her in the interviews should come as a relief to him, an indication that he'd mentally overstated her unfitness for the top job. Caitlin would say to let it be, to avoid creating more stress for himself. She'd call it "self-care."

But it wasn't so simple. Big Will hated Potterstown, but he couldn't help caring about the store and the people who worked here. And if store #1512 *were* to fall apart under Meredith's management, that would reflect poorly on him, too, since he had championed her. And if Meredith *had* threatened her team to get them to say nice things about her? If that came out later, he'd look like an idiot, totally clueless as to what was going on right under his nose. It could come back to bite him.

AT SIX THAT EVENING, Big Will, Ryan, and the two women from corporate drove to the southernmost of the five major strip malls that lined this strip of 11W. Their destination: Alamo Prime. It was, regrettably, the nicest chain restaurant in town. As far as Big Will was concerned, Potterstown's inability to support an actually good chain restaurant, an Outback Steakhouse or a P.F. Chang's, told you everything you needed to know about the place.

Since it was Monday and early and—Big Will thought to himself—*Potterstown*, they were seated immediately. While they looked over their menus, they ate peanuts out of their shells. That was part of the restaurant's shtick, serving big vats of nuts and encouraging customers to throw the shells on the ground, for "ambience."

The conversation quickly turned to the events of the day. The visitors had conducted one-on-one interviews with Meredith and Anita after the rank-and-file interviews.

"I really liked what I heard from Meredith," Janine said. "She seemed to have put real thought into it. She made the case that she was in Logistics just long enough to soak up the knowledge she'll need to be extremely effective as store manager. I was also impressed by her ability to keep her department on budget. That's always something I look for—as long as it doesn't come at the expense of performance. I was a little concerned when I picked up several pairs of girls' socks and saw that they'd only started selling again this past weekend after a surprisingly long drought. But Meredith assured me that that's normal for the store. Increasing seasonal fluctuation, et cetera. The funny thing is that when we opened Potterstown in 2003, we saw it as more of a traditional suburban market, rather than a seasonal destination. We didn't realize at the time that the loss of IBM would be quite so persistent in its impact. But thank goodness Potterstown has taken off as a summer spot." She smiled. "All's well that ends well, I suppose."

Big Will wasn't sure that most citizens of Potterstown would agree that IBM's departure had "ended well," but he smiled politely.

Katherine turned to Big Will. "I second everything Janine said. Props to you for bringing her to our attention as a rising talent."

"That's just what I was about to say," Ryan said. He raised his glass toward Big Will. "Hear, hear."

Big Will looked down at the table, at the phony grains on the phony wood.

"How were the interviews with Anita's team?" he asked.

The way the three of them smirked at each other told Big Will that they were on the same page. Katherine said that the interviews were fine—"not disqualifying, but not nearly as enthusiastic as Meredith's. People seemed to be afraid she'd take away their fringe benefits—holiday meals and the like." She laughed. "What a strange notion to have gotten into their heads."

Big Will looked genuinely puzzled.

"To be honest," Katherine continued, "what we heard today largely confirmed what we thought coming in. It affirms why you were right to push for Meredith's promotion to executive manager and why Meredith was marked for fast track. I think I speak for all three of us when I say that what she lacks in experience, she makes up for in enthusiasm and vision, and I think her team responds to that, for the most part. She may make the occasional error in judgment"—she smiled at Ryan and Janine—"but I think that stems from an excess of enthusiasm more than anything else."

Before Big Will could respond, a ponytailed waitress arrived to take their orders.

Janine asked the waitress if a side of Brussels sprouts was gluten-free. The waitress said she thought so. "I mean, Brussels sprouts are a vegetable?"

For an instant, Janine could only stare at the waitress open-mouthed. Then anger overtook shock. "They're often prepared with bread crumbs," she sputtered. "Please check."

When the waitress left, Big Will looked around the table. Ryan's lips were pursed and his face had a pinched look. He was probably tense from all the effort he'd expended today keeping his voice low with Janine and Katherine. Janine's expression still bore traces of the glower elicited by her close brush with calamity. ("I mean, really," she'd said when the waitress was scurrying off. "For all she knows, I could have celiac disease. She could have *killed* me.") Only Katherine was smiling pleasantly, as if every sight on which her eye fell—the drooling toddler crawling in the peanut shells on the floor, the wheezing man in a nearby booth who'd brought an oxygen tank into the restaurant—delighted her.

Big Will cleared his throat. "There's something I need to say."

Ryan picked up a roll from the bread basket. "Oh?"

"I, uh, have some concerns. About Meredith, about her fitness for the position of store manager."

Ryan's eyes widened. He set his roll on his bread plate.

"To be perfectly honest," Big Will continued, "I've come to the conclusion that I made a mistake when I recommended Meredith for promotion to executive manager."

Now it wasn't just Ryan. They all looked stunned. For a moment, no one spoke. The toddler at the next table started to cry.

"Is this about the drugs?" Janine asked when the child's wailing abated.

"What?" Big Will asked.

"*The drugs*," Janine said again, more loudly, as if the problem was that Big Will hadn't heard her the first time.

"Did someone say Meredith is on drugs?" Big Will asked. "That's ridiculous."

But even as he spoke, the thought flit across his mind that he could take advantage of whatever baseless idea they'd gotten about Meredith and drugs—he could pretend that he had recently come to suspect that Meredith did currently have a drug problem. That might be the smartest way for him to get out of this mess. But, no. He couldn't do that, he couldn't lie. He was Catholic.

"I mean," he said, "she told me she once had a—I mean, she may have previously—but that was a long time ago, when she lived in the city. No, it's nothing like that."

"So, what is it you're concerned about, Will?" Ryan asked. The words came out squeaky and high-pitched, as if he were too unhappy to modulate his voice. "Can you please *elucidate* for the rest of us?"

In spite of himself, Big Will started to smile. *Elucidate* was today's word-of-the-day on the "Vocabulary Builder for Business Executives" email that Big Will subscribed to. Ryan probably subscribed to the same list.

"Are you *smiling*, Will?" Ryan asked. "Is this a joke to you?"

"Sorry." Big Will made himself look appropriately penitent. "No, it's not a joke."

Under the table, he crossed, then uncrossed his legs. His foot brushed against a layer of broken peanut shells. Disgusting, he thought. What were they, elephants?

"When I recommended Meredith for executive manager," he said finally, "I thought her drive and determination would be enough. I thought she'd grow as a manager, smooth out her rough edges. I'm starting to think I misjudged. I can't speak to what you heard today—clearly you were told something different—but I can tell you what I think. She lacks tact—her interpersonal skills are poor. She alienates people needlessly. She has poor judgment. She's too self-involved to evaluate other people's concerns in any sort of reasonable or even-handed way. She judges people based on whether or not they flatter her. She yells at them for inconsequential things, creating an atmosphere of terror. She's insecure about her authority. I'm afraid that if she were promoted, conditions at the store would deteriorate. You know what that means in a tight labor market—people would quit. And, as you know, for the past several years our store has had one of the lowest rates of turnover in the district. It's been one of our greatest strengths."

Big Will hoped that this reference to one of his undeniable successes as store manager would redeem him in the eyes of the others.

But Ryan rocked forward in his chair with something bordering on ferocity. "I don't even know what to say, Will," he squeaked. "I've talked to you almost every day for the past week. When did you come to these extreme conclusions? Was it after you recommended her for promotion a year and a half ago? Or in the past week, since we planned this visit? Or since you and I spoke on Friday?"

Big Will felt his cheeks grow warm.

"Your timing is really something," Ryan went on. "Do I need to remind you that schedules were rearranged on short notice, that Janine flew in from Boston and Katherine came all the way from St. Louis? You might have thought about giving us a heads-up about your feelings before now."

"It is extremely irregular," Janine agreed. "On the plane this morning, I read the recommendation you wrote for Meredith when she was first up for the executive manager position. I believe you called her one of the smartest and most motivated managers you'd ever worked with?"

Big Will tried not to flinch.

At that moment, he would have given anything to have kept his mouth shut, been politic. For all his hand-wringing, he hadn't expected them to be quite as angry as they seemed to be. He had always had good instincts about people, a way of bringing them to his side. But what if he had judged incorrectly this time? What if this were the end of what had just been a run of good luck? What if they canceled his transfer as punishment for his poor handling of this situation? What if he was stuck here, in a town where the nicest restaurant had a floor coated in peanut shells?

"Did something happen that caused you to change your mind about Meredith?" Katherine asked.

Her tone and expression suggested that she was actually interested in hearing his answer, and not just biding her time before deciding whether firing squad or guillotine would be most appropriate for him. Big Will felt a stirring of hope.

Katherine's hazel eyes were big and round. Big Will looked directly into them.

"It wasn't anything specific," he said. "At least, not any one thing I could point to. I think maybe Logistics was too much for her. I really believe Meredith was better before, when she was in Sales, because she felt more confident. With a better grasp of the overall operation, she wasn't so easily threatened. If she had stayed in Sales . . . Well, who knows? But you see what a person is like when they're challenged. I think this transfer revealed certain limitations on her part. Unfortunately, I don't think she can handle managing a hundred fifty people and seven departments. To do this job, you've got to be even-keeled and fair to people—you can't hold grudges. You've got to acknowledge that you don't understand everything, and to listen to other people, to trust them."

Katherine nodded thoughtfully.

"I still don't get—" Ryan started to say, but Katherine raised a hand ever so slightly.

Katherine was the highest-ranking person at the table. She had a master's degree in psychology from an even more prestigious university than the one Ryan had attended as an undergrad. A retail trade magazine had recently profiled her, calling her a rising star and bright new talent. She'd made her reputation at Town Square by designing policies that were worker-friendly but cost-neutral, and she spent a great deal of time traveling to stores around the country, talking to managers about the importance of praise in worker retention—how much it means to employees to be complimented, how it's often as valuable, if not more valuable, than raises when it comes to keeping workers happy. She called her approach the "well-crafted carrot." The idea was not to puff employees up so much that they up and quit, but to "make store-level workers feel that Town Square is a place where they are seen and valued." She had also formalized the policy of throwing storewide pizza parties at stores where union organizers were afoot and personally approved the language used in the flyers that were distributed at these parties, in which corporate's case against unionization was laid out in friendly, upbeat terms, with only the subtlest insinuation that any union agitation would force corporate to curtail some of the generous benefits it currently gave to employees voluntarily. She was active, too, in arguing for the company to be a leader in terms of issues around inclusivity and equal treatment. "Especially for our team members who are people of color or LGBTQ+, or for women who've dealt with sexual harassment," she explained to store managers, "working for a company that operates according to progressive values is its own kind of nonmaterial employee benefit." Then she'd smile. "Of course, these policies also reflect what we believe is right."

While he waited for Katherine to utter a verdict, Big Will directed his eyes to the table. A beam of predusk sunlight had made its way through a window and into the restaurant's dark, (faux) wood-paneled interior, creating a golden parallelogram on its surface.

"I think perhaps I'm starting to understand," she said finally. "Since she moved to Logistics, your estimation of Meredith's abilities has been gradually falling, but you didn't know what to do about it. You didn't want to be precipitous, you wanted to give her time to adjust to a new position. So you were trying to manage the situation as best you could. And then this position came up and forced these issues to the surface?"

She'd said it so much better than Big Will could have. Like a child, he nodded eagerly, gratefully.

"You thought you'd see how things went today with the interviews and the walk-through?" she continued. "But when it all went well, you felt like you had to speak up? To stop us from making what you think would be a mistake for the store?"

"Exactly!" Big Will had never felt so relieved to be understood. "I, uh, waited because I thought I'd let it play out, not interfere, trust the process. And I didn't want to blackball her. She's not a bad person, exactly. She's just—well, she's just—" He didn't know how to finish. He let the thread drop and started again. "But it's all gone differently than I expected. I thought the interviews would be more . . . equivocal. And to be honest, I'm suspicious. The first thing that went through my head when Ryan said the team raved about her was that Meredith bribed them. Or threatened them. What does that say, that that's where my mind went? That either of those things seemed more likely than that they actually said good things about her of their own free will?"

Janine picked up a breadstick and made a thoughtful face. "Maybe they just wanted to get her out of Logistics?" Her voice was different now, almost chummy. She turned to Big Will. "Maybe they thought if she got promoted, they'd get a new executive manager of Logistics that they liked better?" Her eyes narrowed. "Are they capable of thinking that far ahead?"

From her expression, Janine clearly didn't think so. But suddenly Big Will wasn't so sure. Because Janine had made a good point. If Meredith got promoted, Little Will would get her job, or some *simulacrum*—

yesterday's word-of-the-day—of her job with a different title, since, without a college degree, he couldn't truly be an executive manager. But everyone in Movement—except Milo—loved Little Will. Was it possible that they would all act in concert in this way?

Before Big Will could fully consider the possibility, Janine went on.

"To tell you the truth, the drug thing made me extremely uncomfortable," she said. "From a liability perspective. This might not be a bad thing. It's not as if we don't have another strong candidate in Anita."

Big Will, though still confused by the references to drugs, didn't want to ask, not now, when he could feel the tenor of the conversation changing so dramatically in his favor. Instead, he assured them that Anita was a solid candidate. "The thing with her tables this morning was not at all characteristic."

There had been an unfortunate moment when they toured the store in the morning—to the horror of Ryan and the women, two of the frontmost Women's T-shirt tables had been absolute wrecks.

"I saw those tables when I got to the store this morning," Big Will continued. "They were in perfect order. A customer must have messed them up after the store opened. Probably a mother who wasn't watching her kid. Kids are drawn like magnets to those tables. The neater they are, the more they want to destroy them."

"There was a certain . . . less than enthusiastic quality to the majority of the interviews with Anita's team," Katherine said slowly. "Not bad, just a little, well, indifferent."

"I'm a little surprised," Big Will said. "I mean, I wouldn't have expected people to fawn over Anita, but I would have thought people would say that she's fair. She may not go out of her way to win them over, do things like buy them all breakfast the way Meredith did for her team, but in another sense, she doesn't have to—because she rarely makes them angry."

To everyone's surprise, Katherine laughed—a real, throaty laugh.

"I once had a boyfriend who was always failing to show up at key moments. That or he'd show up drunk. I'd be ready to break up with him, but the next day he'd send the most beautiful flowers and the most abject apology, and I'd be won over. My brother told me he wished I had a boyfriend who sent me fewer flowers—who didn't have so many things to apologize for. Maybe that's what we're talking about here." She turned to Ryan. "What do you think, Ryan?"

Ryan touched his hands to his hair, pulling the puffy tufts out even farther from his head than they were already. The tightness in his expression made clear that he was unhappy—he really didn't want to let Big Will off the hook so easily. But if this was the line Katherine was taking, what choice did he have? She could very well become chief operating officer for the entire Town Square Corp. in a few years.

"I've always thought highly of Anita," he said finally.

It pained him. He couldn't for the life of him understand Katherine's motives.

In fact, Katherine had made a calculation earlier that had colored her reaction tonight. Big Will, she had realized over the course of the day, was an excellent manager. It wasn't just that he was capable, organized, and well spoken; it was his personability and natural charisma. He was more valuable to the store than Ryan or even Big Will himself realized. Katherine had, in fact, been so impressed with Big Will that she had briefly wondered why he'd gone into retail management at all, and not into a sector with more cachet, like banking or insurance. He had, after all, gone to UConn, a decent school. Then she did the math. He'd graduated during the financial crisis. Many banks—the ones that didn't actually go under—suspended their internship programs and rescinded the job offers they'd made to recent grads, especially ones who weren't from the Ivies or Ivy equivalents. Retail might have been Big Will's best option.

By the time their entrées arrived, it had been agreed that they wouldn't conclusively settle the question of who would become the store's manager over dinner. The question would be discussed further over the next few days—other voices from corporate would be brought in. Nevertheless, Big Will felt pretty confident as to who would be chosen.

Once they'd eaten, Janine turned to Big Will. "There was something else as well. We wanted to update you on the automation study for Movement. The consultants have run the numbers every which way, and while a machine could of course unload the truck and sort boxes faster than a team of people, the technology would have to be custom built to our specifications. Even so, we'd have to change our processes to accommodate its limitations. Moreover, we'd still need roughly the same number of employees to unpack the boxes and get them onto the store shelves—the breakout process is too complicated a job for a non-human right now. All in all, it turns out that automating the unload simply isn't cost-efficient at this point. Especially since the technology is only going to improve with time, and we know how costly it is to act too soon." She looked at the others wryly. She was referring to the company's massively stupid (in retrospect) decision to invest hundreds of millions of dollars in brand-new scanners for all stores nationwide—just months before smartphone technology took a major leap forward. Their "new" $700-a-pop scanners quickly came to feel as slow and clunky as 1980s video games to a modern gamer. "In any event, the management consultants recommended that the thing to do right now is hold tight, wait for capabilities to increase and costs to decrease. Which, if we're honest, is likely to be a very long time."

Big Will was delighted to learn that automation was off the table, at least for now. But Janine had more to say.

"The consultants did, however, come up with an alternative, one that should yield some very significant cost advantages." She smiled. "We're going to be implementing a schedule change that will affect Logistics operations all across the country."

The consultants, she explained, had pointed out that one reason customers liked the online retailer was that they could use the search function to instantly pull up whatever item they wanted, no matter how particular, instead of spending large amounts of time searching the aisles of a physical store with no guarantee of success and very few employees on hand to help them. Meanwhile, the people of Movement, responsible for stocking the store, had a very thorough knowledge of its contents. But since Movement did its work while the store was closed, that knowledge was of no use to the store's customers. At least until now.

The consultants proposed that Movement unload the truck and break out boxes when the store was open, from eight until noon, during which hours they could, while they worked, answer questions from shoppers. This would be the equivalent of having an additional eight to fourteen customer service employees on hand for the first four hours of the day—and it wouldn't cost Town Square a dime, as it only entailed moving preexisting labor hours from one time slot to another. Stores could even, if they wanted, bring in fewer Sales staff for those hours—in which case the plan would actually reduce labor costs.

Corporate loved the idea.

But the consultants had studied at selective universities; they hadn't worked retail. Nor had most people in corporate HQ. Thus it had fallen to store managers involved in a pilot program to explain, with only minimal hyperbole, that unloading a truck big enough to move several McMansions and getting the merchandise onto a sales floor the size of a couple of football fields could be dangerous—it wasn't something you wanted to undertake while customers were underfoot. The people of Movement zipped up and down corridors, moving pallets piled high with boxes. Boxes fell all the time. What if one fell on a customer? Think of all the moms pushing baby strollers around the store while they shopped.

Then there was the PR issue. The store had made a big show of "going green," touting reusable bags at checkout and printing receipts in the most compact and efficient way possible, to minimize the use of unnecessary paper. If the volume of garbage the company generated each day—to say nothing of its continued reliance on Styrofoam packaging in the transit process (although not in the packaging that customers saw)—were more widely known, bad press might ensue, leading to pressure to make deeper changes to Town Square's internal distribution system, such as banning Styrofoam. Such changes would wind up costing more than the company would gain from the new schedule.

In the end, a compromise had been settled on. Movement would start at 6 a.m. From six to eight, before the store opened, Movement would do the messiest and most dangerous work. Then, just before the store opened, they would clean up—remove all packaging from the items they had left to break out and dump the items from boxes into shopping carts. All pallets and jacks would be returned to the warehouse. For the second half of their shift, the members of Movement would work neatly out of carts, the way Softlines did already. Meanwhile, for those two hours, they would be available to answer customers' questions, just as if they were members of the Sales staff.

When Janine finished, Big Will laughed nervously. "It might not go over so well," he said. "At least at our store, most of the people in Movement like the early hours."

"It's better than losing their jobs to robots," Ryan pointed out.

"True," Big Will said, "but they didn't know that was on the table, so . . ."

Ryan smiled as if this were a joke, but Janine, sensing that Big Will was genuinely nervous, sought to assure him. "It's worth remembering," she said, "that the people who work these jobs aren't like you and me. We're people who value stability, who worked hard to achieve it for ourselves. But our store-level employees often react better to change than you or I would. They're accustomed to it."

"I think what Janine means," Katherine cut in, "is that our store-level employees are remarkably resilient. That's one of the things I admire most about them."

Big Will nodded.

After dinner, Ryan was returning to Newburgh, where he was based. Big Will drove the women back to the Hampton Inn. It was just after eight, still twilight. On their way up 11W, they passed a store employee, a guy from Plan-O named Johnny Cruz (for some reason he was always called by both his first and last name), walking along the side of the road. Big Will automatically averted his eyes, as he did whenever he passed a store employee walking on this dismal road.

When he pulled up to the Hampton Inn, Katherine remained in the passenger seat. She waved Janine on. "I'll be just a minute," she said.

She turned to Big Will.

"I want you to know that I respect what you did tonight. It took courage to admit you made a mistake, especially when there was nothing in it for you personally. I know Ryan and Janine were, uh, *surprised* initially. But I don't want you to worry that this will be held against you going forward, even if the timing was a little . . . irregular. The fact that you spoke up about your concerns more than makes up for a well-meaning desire to believe a person could grow as a manager. I want you to know that I'm going to put a note in your file that your willingness to speak up is a credit to your character. To be honest, I see district and regional in your near-term future." She smiled. "I mean, if that's what you want."

Big Will gaped. "I do want that," he said. "I want it very much."

He couldn't believe it. All his life people had told him that he was charmed, that things came easily to him. Right then, he was inclined to think they were right. In his mind he saw not just a comfortable house, but family vacations to Disney World, summer camps, travel sports. Big Will's parents were immigrants who had worked double shifts at maintenance and clerical jobs. They had done it for him—for him to get to a position where he could give his family nice things.

Katherine smiled magisterially. Big Will's response was just what she had intended. She knew that in Connecticut, unlike in Potterstown, he would be surrounded by opportunity, not only in retail but also in banking, insurance, defense contracting, pharmaceuticals. Seeing as how Town Square had been fortunate enough to nab Big Will when it did, it ought to do what it could to keep him. A well-crafted carrot indeed.

24

TWO DAYS AFTER corporate's visit, Meredith stopped smiling. Two days after that, Big Will called Movement in for another special morning meeting. This time, Meredith was nowhere to be seen. At his side stood Anita. "I want you all to officially meet your next store manager," he said.

Even though they already knew by then—they just knew, no matter how often Val exhorted them to stay hopeful—some of them gasped.

During break, Val said it must have been the drug thing. "What else could it have been?" she asked, glancing at Milo. It had to have been him.

Milo turned bright red.

Val leaned toward him. "Did you—" she began.

"What does it even matter?" Milo cut her off. "It was true about the pills, wasn't it? So who cares?"

Val was about to respond when Nicole angled her body so she blocked Val from Milo.

"Milo's right," Nicole said. "It doesn't matter. I don't think that's what made the difference. Anita was always a real possibility. We knew that from the beginning. What's the point of going over it again and again?"

Everyone was surprised. It was so unlike Nicole to assert herself like that, risk any of her own capital, for anyone—let alone for *Milo*.

Val backed down. Nicole nodded. Her eye happened to meet Raymond's. He smiled and nodded at her with something like approval. It was a silly thing—why should she care what Raymond thought?—but nevertheless that look pleased Nicole, made her feel like she'd done something good. Raymond might be a dork, but he was a nice guy.

At the end of the shift, Callie was walking out to her car when she overheard Big Will on his cell phone outside, talking to the district manager. Callie knew the call could be important to the others, so she put off going home. She leaned on her car and pretended to be absorbed in scrolling through Facebook on her phone. Big Will stood next to a streetlamp in the middle of the employee parking aisle and, unaware he wasn't alone outside, went over items for some sort of report or statement about Meredith. The phrase "poor management skills" came up. So did: "tendency to alienate," "lack of judgment," and "unwillingness to learn from others."

Callie immediately told Ruby and Nicole, who were getting ready to drive home together, what she'd heard. By the next day—Saturday—they had all accepted that it was Big Will himself who had come out against Meredith. It fit in with other bits of gossip Val and the others had picked up from the store's whisper network, about how Anita had been Big Will's own choice. Milo and the caffeine pills were forgotten. Their plan, they realized now, had been foiled by Big Will himself.

Val realized she had gotten it wrong, miscalculated.

"You were right," Val said to Raymond, at break on Monday.

Raymond looked puzzled.

"When we had our meeting, you said you thought maybe Big Will didn't really like Meredith and didn't want her to get promoted," Val explained. "I didn't see it."

"Did I?" Raymond shrugged self-deprecatingly. He could see how unhappy Val was about the plan's failure and shrank from rubbing in this small, inconsequential victory.

"I said that too," Ruby interjected. "About how Big Will didn't like her. Remember?" When no one backed her up, she continued. "As soon as we heard he was leaving, as soon as he made that first announcement, I said—I told you all—Big Will would never let them do it. Remember now?"

The others didn't but pretended they had because they liked Ruby—she was in some ways the group's center, the warmest and most socially adept of any of them. They didn't want to hurt her feelings.

This was a turning point for Val. In the days immediately following corporate's visit, when Meredith started to deflate almost before their eyes, Val had been in denial about the increasingly obvious fact that Meredith was getting passed over. Then, after Big Will's announcement made it official, she had focused on her anger at Milo. Now that it turned out that what happened hadn't been Milo's fault, there was nothing left to distract Val from the failure of the plan. She became increasingly depressed. As the days wore on, she found it to be more of a struggle to get out of bed when her alarm went off at three.

She was reminded of how bad she'd felt when she was a teenager, before she ran away for good, and during some of the darker periods in New Paltz, before she met Liz. For the first time since she and Liz had gotten together, that old sense of futility had crept over her, the feeling that nothing she did mattered. In the past, Val had learned this was just a feeling—not some sort of unalterable truth. She had in fact been able to change her life—she'd left home, found someone who loved her, made a better life for herself, hadn't she? But what if, in this case, the voice saying that there was no point in continuing to try was right? After all, after more than three years at Town Square, she still had the same job title as any eighteen-year-old new hire just here for the summer. It was beyond demoralizing. Val began to lose interest in the things she'd once cared about. In Graphic Tees, a shirt that said THE SECOND AMENDMENT IS MY BAG hung in a position of prominence for days without her seeming to notice. She thought about applying to United, joining Liz at the call center.

Diego, too, was struggling. The week after the plan failed, he drank heavily. His girlfriend had noticed that he had barely touched any alcohol the week of the overnights. He himself hadn't even realized, not until he started up again with a vengeance. He understood then that he drank, at least in part, to distract himself from the feeling of being stuck on a treadmill, working hard as if to prove a point: to prove that he was worth the expense and the trouble his father and grandparents had gone to in rescuing him from Belize as a small child and bringing him first to Honduras and then to the US. But what had he proven? What did it matter that in four years on the job he'd never once been late, if all it ever amounted to was an occasional compliment or pat on the back from Big Will? A 2 percent annual raise—and even that was conditioned on not getting written up? Without alcohol, the futility of it all became at times unbearable—especially when he was cooped up with two other people in a small, dark basement apartment with no outdoor space. Since he'd sworn off cheating—he'd promised himself he wasn't going to mess up this relationship the way he had so many past ones—a drink was about the only thing he had to look forward to.

At the other end of the happiness spectrum was Big Will, who continued to marvel at how well things had worked out. He had even been spared what had turned out to be the not-so-minor annoyance of having to decide who to promote to be group manager of Movement. Even though Big Will had been annoyed with Little Will for his indecision, when Big Will had tried to settle the matter himself, the question had turned out to be surprisingly vexing. (*Vex* had been the word-of-the-day a month ago.) Raymond and Nicole could be put off, that was easy enough. Nicole was young, and Raymond, though not much younger than Val, was so down on himself that Big Will felt confident he'd take almost any disappointment in stride, as no more than what he expected. Milo might get mad, but he was nevertheless a hard no, come what may, in terms of his reaction. He lacked the maturity, the temperament. So far so good. It was only when Big Will got to Val and Diego that the math became tricky. Either would be good at the job—but promoting one dramatically increased the odds that the other would quit in anger at being passed over.

In Big Will's experience, women usually bore disappointment better. But words had been spoken at Val's last performance review. He could try to chalk up any change of intention on his part to her outburst over the Employee of the Month incident, but who knew if that would satisfy her? All in all, Diego, who was insecure about his accent and his limited English writing skills, might be the less angry of the two. On the other hand, Val *was* more than ten years younger and had been at the store for three years to Diego's four. And while Diego was pretty chill, not really a political guy, every once in a while he'd make a remark about structural racism and its relationship to economic inequality that caused Big Will to look at him with surprise. Diego might conclude Val was getting promoted over him because she was white. Which could be bad. When it came down to it, Big Will wasn't sure what Diego would do, any more than he was sure what Val would do. And losing either of them right now—with the labor market as tight as it was—would be a real blow. Big Will had found that he was as little able to make up his mind as Little Will had been.

The strange thing was that, according to the business and econ classes Big Will had taken in college, this problem shouldn't exist. In school, he had learned that employers were eager to keep good employees and would spend what they needed to retain them: at an efficient firm, wages corresponded to productivity. But if that had ever been true in retail—and maybe it had only ever applied to white-collar workers?—it certainly wasn't how things worked at Town Square, especially not in the age of the online retailer. Not only were raises for the rank-and-file capped so low as to make them more like cost-of-living adjustments than performance-based rewards, promotions were tightly guarded. Big Will certainly didn't have the power to, say, promote both Val and Diego, create a new position for one in order to keep both happy and on the payroll—if he'd asked for permission to do that, Ryan would laugh in his face. Given the state of retail—for everyone but the online retailer—the tide was moving the other way, toward cutting the number of management positions in stores, not creating new ones just to keep good workers happy. Given everything, the only surefire way to keep both Diego and Val was to promote neither of them. Which, to Big Will's relief, was exactly what happened.

A FEW DAYS after Anita's promotion was announced, Ruby pulled Callie aside on their way into the morning meeting. "I wanted to ask you a favor," she said. "I was wondering if I could borrow twenty dollars. Just until we get paid on Friday. If you can't, that's okay. I understand, I just thought I'd ask. I'm a little short this week, is all."

They hadn't yet gotten their "big" paychecks, for the week of overnights, and wouldn't for several more days. Ruby's younger son and his girlfriend and their two kids were coming up from New Jersey. Ruby wanted very much to get her nails done—it was important to her that her kids and her daughter-in-law saw her a certain way, as a person who could afford a manicure. But she was short.

Callie said it was no problem.

"Thank you," Ruby said. "I appreciate it. I really do."

The next day Movement's schedule change was announced. As expected, people reacted badly to the news. They had lives beyond the store, complicated schedules that involved parents, children, babysitters. They couldn't just change things up at the drop of a hat.

For the next couple of weeks, the schedule change was pretty much all they talked about. That, and Raymond's strep throat and Lyme disease. The latter was a complete surprise, although it probably shouldn't have been. He'd probably gotten it on one of his landscaping gigs with Little Will. Raymond had thought his knees hurt because, at twenty-seven, he was getting older, but when his sore throat had persisted, he had used his big paycheck from the week of overnights to go to Urgent Care. Though he'd gotten hit with more than $1,100 in bills for the appointment and the prescriptions and the various tests and scans and facilities fees associated with it all, within forty-eight hours of getting on antibiotics, Raymond felt better than he had in months. Maybe that's why he wasn't as depressed as some of the others about the failure of the pro-Mer plan. Or maybe it was because deep down he'd never really thought he'd get the promotion. The only thing that bummed him out was that after the doctors' bills, there wasn't enough for a Chuck E. Cheese birthday party for his son. Maybe next year.

Then it was Big Will's last week, and his departure became the main event again.

Nicole wanted to talk to Big Will before he left. Like Raymond, Nicole had taken the failure of the plan relatively well—she, too, had never really expected to be made group manager. What she had enjoyed about being part of the pro-Mer group had been the feeling of working toward something: having a goal and solving problems along the way. She had felt energized during the week of overnights, and in the aftermath of the plan, she had begun to think more about college. She wondered if being in school might feel a little like that, if it might give her something to direct her energy toward. But she hadn't found the right moment to talk to Callie—it was rare that she and Callie were alone, without Ruby. Then she got the idea to ask Big Will. He probably knew even more than Callie did about college, and he was, after all, the person who had told her she was "very smart."

The first time Nicole tried to approach him, he was harried and distracted—"What's up, Nicole?" he said when she ventured tentatively into his office. He didn't even bother to set down the receiver of the phone, just cradled it between his head and shoulder while using his index finger to keep the hang-up button depressed. It was disconcerting. Nicole said she'd come back later when he wasn't so busy.

She returned the next day. Big Will wasn't on the phone, thankfully. She sat down on the love seat as she waited for him to finish typing something on his computer. He'd already started packing up his office, and while she waited, Nicole glanced at one of the open boxes near her feet. She saw the purple UConn pennant that used to hang on his corkboard. Poking out from underneath it was a photo she'd never noticed before. She nudged the pennant to the side so she could get a better look. The picture had obviously been taken at Big Will's college graduation. He and some of his friends were standing arm in arm in gowns with mortarboards on their heads, smiling. Nicole looked at their faces. These guys didn't look at all like the kind of people Nicole hung out with. They looked preppy and confident, like the rich kids from Potterstown High. Then Nicole realized that they *were* the rich kids from Potterstown High, just a few years older and in a different city and state. As soon as she realized this, Nicole remembered how she'd felt in high school. She thought of the time in social studies class she'd referred to people in Mexico as speaking Mexican. She could still hear the laughter. What if, when Big Will said she was smart, he didn't mean that kind of smart, college smart, like his friends? What if he thought she was ridiculous for imagining she could be one of them? She got up from the love seat, told Big Will it was nothing, and quickly left his office.

Big Will didn't press her. He was by this point so busy—getting things in order at the store, packing up his Potterstown apartment, driving back and forth to Connecticut to look at houses and make decisions about the wedding—that he was relieved when she left. The store had 150 employees, almost all of whom seemed to want something from him before he left: a reference, a promise to put in a good word about them to Anita, even—for some reason—reassurance that Anita was not going to do away with their free holiday meals. With so much to take care of, he forgot a lot of things, not just to find out what Nicole wanted. He also forgot to ask Anita to make sure that Raymond didn't get screwed again on health insurance next year—remind her that, for the sake of fairness, the short end of the stick should be given to someone else this time.

Big Will did do one thing before he left: advocate on behalf of Little Will. Having all but promised him a promotion when he had thought Meredith would become store manager, Big Will felt he owed Little Will something, and corporate allowed that "retention" was a reasonable priority, when it came to managers, just not the rank-and-file, whom it treated as interchangeable, unskilled—never mind that in reality the difference in productivity between, say, Ruby and Callie was tremendous. Big Will made a compelling case to Ryan that they didn't want to risk losing Little Will. Little Will might not be the most ambitious person, but he was hardworking and more than competent and beloved by the people of Movement, which was why Movement had the lowest turnover of any group at the store. Ryan was persuaded. Little Will would get a raise, an annual pay bump of $6K.

When Big Will told him the news, Little Will wasn't quite as pleased as he knew he ought to be. He tried to smile, but he could almost see his quit date receding further into the distance. The fact was, the more he made at Town Square, the harder it would be to justify leaving. Perhaps he'd never run his own business full-time, as his dad and grandfather had. Perhaps he'd be at Town Square until he died.

For Meredith, Little Will's raise felt like one more humiliation, as if corporate were going out of its way to heap rewards on everyone but her. She knew full well that she'd been blackballed, that it wasn't a matter of having to wait a year or two to become store manager. She saw the report that went into her file. Her career at Town Square was essentially over.

She began showing up later than ever and entirely stopped caring about the job, even the unload time. She was angry at Big Will and at corporate and at her so-called team, those ungrateful shits, who must have said all sorts of terrible things about her, who were happy enough to eat the breakfast she bought them right before knifing her in the back. She didn't believe Big Will when he told her that the interviews were good—she thought he was just trying to protect them for his own reasons. He was always so obsessed with the rank-and-file, with being popular with them. Narcissistic fuck.

Anger was better than the other thing she felt: shame. After her one-on-one interview with corporate, Meredith had texted her parents and sister that she'd nailed it, told them she was sure the top job was hers. How humiliating it had been to tell them a few days later that she hadn't gotten the promotion after all. Her mother had suggested that she go back to school, to become a teacher like her sister, if things weren't working out at Town Square. "I'm sure she would be happy to help you with the coursework," her mother said. A week earlier Meredith had been the daughter with the big job, the one rapidly climbing the corporate ladder, the one her parents bragged about. Now she was being counseled to go to her sister, tail between her legs.

Meanwhile, the bills were piling up. In retrospect, the Lake Placid vacation had been a mistake.

THE NEW HOURS were not going to work for Callie. She relied on her mother to babysit. But her mother was too sick to run after a two-year-old for hours. Four-to-eight only worked because Zoe was asleep for most of the time, waking up right around eight. Before the new hours went into effect, Callie put in her notice.

It was okay, she told the others. She'd finish her certificate program soon and get a good job as a sleep technologist. Then she'd put her daughter in a high-quality day care. "I totally get it," Val said. "Stimulation is so important for kids in the early years." But Val's voice caught as she spoke, and her big, childlike eyes were shiny. For an instant it looked to Callie like Val might cry. Even Callie, who hadn't known Val for long, could see that Val hadn't snapped back from the failure of the pro-Mer plan.

The others found a way to make the new hours work. Milo and Diego still came in half an hour before the others to set up the line, but Milo got special permission to work only until 8:30, so he could still make it in time to pick up his younger daughter before his ex left for her job at the drugstore. Leaving early meant he'd make less, but the fact that an exception was being made for him—and only for him—pleased him, confirming how important he was to the store. Nicole, who borrowed the Dingmobile to drive her and Ruby to work, no longer had time to give Ruby a ride home—if her mother was going to get to work on time, Nicole had to leave Town Square at ten exactly and head straight to her mother's. Raymond stepped up, said he would be Ruby's ride back.

On Big Will's last day, Nicole was hanging dresses in Women's at the end of the shift when she looked up to see Meredith standing by herself at the front of the store, looking outside through the glass doors. Backlit, her face partially turned away from Nicole, Meredith looked very small and very lonely. Then Nicole heard a peal of feminine laughter. It was Anita. She and Big Will were walking along the store's front corridor. Meredith heard, too. Nicole saw her wince. A strange feeling came over Nicole, almost like pity. Which made no sense. Because Meredith was a bitch. She deserved whatever she got. Yet it was hard for Nicole to muster the hostility she'd once felt.

The following day was Callie's last. They were all sad to see her go—even though she had only worked with them for six weeks, they all felt that it had been quite a six weeks. No one was as sad as Ruby, though. Callie, she said, might not be the brightest bulb, but she had a good heart.

They didn't expect to see Callie again. No one ever stayed in touch after they left Town Square. None of them had the money to get together at bars for happy hour drinks, and they were too old and embarrassed and nervous of the police to drink in parks or other public spaces. Mostly they drank—or smoked—at home. And at the moment none of them had the kind of home setups where they were comfortable inviting friends over. Ruby worried about her furniture, Diego worried about his girlfriend's mental health—strangers made her anxious, and besides he didn't want people to see her in one of her bad moods—Raymond was embarrassed about how out-of-it Cristina was, Milo didn't want the others to see how his mother treated him, Marcus was down on all of Nicole's guy friends because they were guys. Even Travis no longer had his own place with Jeanie. They'd been evicted from their apartment because of back rent. Jeanie had gone with the kids to her mother's. Travis wasn't allowed to live there with them—Jeanie's mom knew he used to deal and didn't like him. Which, Travis felt, was a little ironic since Jeanie didn't much like him these days because he no longer dealt. For now, Travis was staying on a buddy's couch.

The closest any of them came to hanging out was when Raymond and Ruby stopped at QuickChek for beers on their way home. They'd pull up to Ruby's place and sit in the car on the street outside and chat while they drank. Raymond couldn't speak for Ruby, but this half hour of conversation was often the best part of his day. Ruby had a rare quality of being both a good talker—lively, colorful, cheering—and a good listener.

STARTING THE UNLOAD at six instead of four had unintended consequences, the most significant of which involved vendors. The warehouse at store #1512 was not well configured to receive deliveries while the truck was being unloaded. This hadn't been an issue when Movement did the unload at four because vendors didn't start to arrive until six or so. Now, however, the line blocked their path from the delivery entrance at the back of the warehouse to the store. To get their carts through the warehouse, vendors had to stop the line, disconnect two sections of track, and pass through the gap.

On principle, Milo disliked stopping the line. And he saw the line as belonging to him. Meanwhile, most vendors behaved in what he thought was a high-handed manner, demanding, rather than requesting, that he stop throwing boxes so they could get through, as if they were the boss of him. Worse, they sometimes just broke the line on their own, without even asking him, just did it and expected Milo to notice and to stop throwing until they'd reconnected the thing. The way they acted reminded Milo of his mother's boyfriends, who'd move in with them and immediately start telling Milo what to do, as if it were their house and not Milo's.

A couple of weeks into the new schedule, a guy who delivered bread for a local outfit broke the line without asking. A big guy with a potbelly and gray hair pulled into a braid, he reminded Milo of a particularly mean boyfriend his mother had brought to live with them when

Milo was ten or so. When, for the third or fourth time, he broke the line without asking, Milo lost it. He slammed a box of HBA down as hard as he could down the line. It nearly hit the guy just as he was crossing through the gap. As the box crashed to the ground behind him, Milo rushed out of the truck, yelling and waving his arms.

"See, motherfucker," he yelled. "You need to ask me before you break my line, or this is what will happen. Anything that's broken in that box is on you. You're lucky you didn't get hit. Next time you might not be so lucky."

In Anita's office an hour later, Milo insisted this hadn't been a threat. He said he hadn't meant that he would purposely hit the vendor. It was a warning, intended to be helpful, letting the guy know he might accidentally get hit by a box if he didn't get the okay before breaking the line. Anita didn't buy it. She saw the incident as a clear violation of the store's zero-tolerance policy in regard to workplace violence. Her inclination was to fire Milo on the spot.

Meredith didn't try to talk her out of it. By then she was totally checked out—she didn't care one way or the other what happened to Milo. Little Will did try, even though he himself didn't know what the right thing was—deep down, he thought Anita was probably right, that it probably was a threat, whatever Milo said after the fact. He certainly couldn't deny that Milo had a problem with "emotional regulation," as Svetlana from HR liked to put it. And yet Little Will felt awful about it.

As he was escorted out of the building, Milo screamed at Meredith and Anita and Svetlana: "How the hell are you going to run this store without me? Who will throw the truck like I do?" Then he looked at Little Will and said what he'd been wanting to say to his face for years: "I know you're a snake. You pretend to be nice, but you don't fool me. I know that you fucked me over. I've always known."

After the door closed behind him, Milo stood outside the employee door, screaming more of the same. If it hadn't been for Raymond and Ruby and Diego, the police would have been called. But the three of them managed to talk Milo down, convince him that he'd be better off without this job, especially since with the new schedule he was only getting three hours a day anyway.

"Think of what the job is doing to your body," Ruby said. "Your back. Maybe it's a blessing in disguise."

"It'll give you more time for your comedy," Raymond pointed out.

"Didn't you say you wanted to become an Uber driver?" Diego asked. "Make your own hours?"

They got Milo into his car and watched him drive off.

The void left by Milo's absence made Callie's departure seem like nothing. However irritating he could be, Milo had felt like part of the store, part of them. After he was fired, Diego threw the truck, and Val came in early to help him set up. It wasn't the same. When she talked, Val expected to be answered. Milo's monologues first thing in the morning had been like the sound of traffic when you live next to a highway, something you learn to tune out, but that is, in its own way, soothing.

25

AT THE END of July, a few days after Milo was fired, it rained. Joyce gave Travis a ride. In the car, she told him that he reminded her of her grandson. "Not my oldest grandson—he's gay. Or so he says. We'll see. Sometimes I wonder if he just hasn't met the right girl yet. No, you remind me of his younger brother. He's got tattoos like you. Back when I was young, it was different—there wasn't this rage for tattoos. Now even my granddaughters are getting them. The world has changed—that's what I tell my husband Roy. The world has changed, and we've got to change, too."

The rain was beating down on the roof of Joyce's Hyundai. They were on Broadway, by the hospital, inching along behind a long line of cars waiting to get into the employee lot.

Travis mentioned to Joyce that his sister was a tech at the hospital. "She's the big success in the family," he said. Then he found himself telling Joyce that he was thinking about studying for the GED test. "It's about time I finally did it," he said.

He didn't say that he had more time now than he used to because his kids were no longer living with him, or that he was looking for a distraction because he was depressed without them, even if he hadn't been the best dad, even if he had utterly failed at being a provider. He hadn't told anyone at work about getting evicted, about Jeanie taking the kids to her mom's. He let Joyce think that his buddy's address was his, that Jeanie and the kids were right upstairs.

Joyce said that it was great about studying for the GED, and if she could help to let her know. "I did finish high school," she said, and laughed. "Of course back then there weren't computers or anything like that. It was different. I probably couldn't pass the test today."

When they passed the hospital, traffic cleared. They made it to Town Square with ten minutes to spare.

Two hours later, when it was time for break, the rain was still coming down.

Because of the change in hours, break was at eight—same time as the store opened. This was a drag in the rain. When the store was open to customers, the smokers weren't allowed to stand in front of the main entrance, under the overhang. They stood in their regular spot, just outside the employee entrance, holding umbrellas with one hand and their lit cigarettes with the other, their coffee cups set down on one of the benches or on the wide rim of the garbage can.

"Big Will set a day for his wedding," Ruby said. "I heard Anita got a 'Save the Date.'"

Nicole's cigarette went out. Travis handed her his lighter. She thanked him, then immediately edged away. She pretended not to see the momentary look of confusion and hurt that passed over his face. She'd been avoiding him for weeks.

After Nicole had told Marcus about how Travis had played football with Michael Vick and repeated some of his funnier stories, Nicole and Marcus had gotten into a big fight. Marcus was quick to feel jealous, especially lately. He was between jobs, and feeling adrift. Nicole loved Marcus. For the sake of their relationship, and their daughter, she thought it made sense to put some distance between herself and Travis. But she did feel a little wistful—not just for shooting the shit with Travis but for what things had been like only a few weeks ago.

It wasn't just Milo's absence or Callie's or Big Will's. It almost seemed to Nicole that the job had been more fun back when Meredith loomed over them, criticizing and threatening and yelling at them, exhorting them to go faster. Having a common enemy had given their days shape. Now Meredith was more pitiful than scary, like a sad ghost that haunted Logistics. Honestly it was hard for Nicole to remember if Meredith had ever really been frightening. Nicole wondered now if they had all perhaps exaggerated the threat Meredith posed, played it up for drama, because it was fun to have someone to hate. Had Nicole really been afraid of her—worried Meredith would fire her or write her up? Or had she always known on some level that Big Will wouldn't let Meredith do anything too bad? She really couldn't say, for sure. All she knew was that work now felt kind of slack, dull.

A car passed on its way to the main part of the parking lot, spraying water as it passed. Because it was after eight o'clock, the lot was busy. Seconds later, a blue sedan slowed to a stop in front of the employee entrance. The passenger door opened, and a woman from Harvest named Kathy stepped out. She waved goodbye to her boyfriend in the driver's seat of the sedan and started toward the employee door. Then she saw the people of Movement standing out front. She stopped, said she had something to tell them.

She huddled with Ruby—whom she was friendly with—under a big purple-and-white-striped golf umbrella that Diego had found in the store's lost-and-found and which, being a gentleman, he now held over the women. Kathy told Ruby that her sister, who worked at T.J.Maxx in the next shopping center over, saw Meredith there, interviewing for a job as an assistant manager. "My sister spoke to the manager," Kathy said, "and she thinks Meredith'll get it. Of course it's a smaller store. It'd be a pay cut for her." She shrugged. "Anyway, I thought you guys would want to know."

Then she ran into the store.

For a long moment, no one said anything at all.

No one needed Val to spell it out this time. They all knew that if Meredith left for T.J.Maxx, her job would open up. Which would mean Little Will would take over for her, and . . .

For a full minute they stood with their backs to the store, cigarettes and umbrellas in hand as SUVs and minivans splashed by. Their eyes were directed beyond the lot, beyond the valley into which Potterstown—where many of them had been born and had lived their whole lives—was tucked, toward the milky sky and grayish-white storm clouds that obscured the mountaintops. On the railroad tracks that ran parallel to 11W, behind the shopping centers, a freight train passed, its horn shrieking mournfully. But the people of Movement felt something they hadn't a few minutes before: hope.

Then it was time to go inside.

ACKNOWLEDGMENTS

I'VE BENEFITED SO much from the generosity of friends, family members, and fellow writers who read drafts of this manuscript over the years—several drafts in some cases. A heartfelt thank you to James Lasdun, Joshua Ferris, Casey Cep, Sam Graham-Felsen, Sheila Heti, Barbara Jones, Ilana Teitelbaum, Charles Finch, Laura Kipnis, Lydia Kiesling, Matthew Bonds, Jonathan Franzen, Karan Mahajan, Charles Bock, Michelle Orange, Robin Shutinya, Tashena Dixon, John Renner, Steve Waldman (a.k.a @interfluidity), and Zev Waldman.

I have to single out my dear friend Carlin Flora, who read every version of this novel, from first draft to the final manuscript and seemed to care about the story and the characters as much as I did. Her continual kindness, empathy, and enthusiasm are gifts that I cherish and depend on more than I can say.

My agent, Elyse Cheney, has been one of the most important people in my writing life for over a decade, a person whose judgment I trust and whose commitment to this book dates back to its earliest iteration. I'd also like to thank Adam Eaglin, Kassie Evashevski,

Natasha Fairweather, Grace Johnson, Beniamino Ambrosi, Isabel Mendia, and Claire Gillespie.

When Elyse sent this manuscript to editors, I asked her to send it to Matt Weiland because he struck me as the ideal editor for this novel. In a remarkable stroke of good fortune, Matt acquired the book. I'm indebted to his patience, his kindness, and most of all to his intellect and sensibility. I'd also like to thank the tremendous team at Norton, especially Huneeya Siddiqui, Erin Sinesky Lovett, Meredith McGinnis, Meredith Dowling, Amy Robbins, Don Rifkin, Julia Druskin, Derek Thornton, and Gregg Kulick.

My parents, Edward and Ina Waldman, are in many ways the moral force behind this book. My blind spots are my own, but the values they instilled in me inform how I see the world. I sent them the first draft four years ago and to my great relief they have believed in the book ever since.

My husband, Evan, is always my first and best reader, as well as my best friend and most trusted confidante. Thank you, Evan, for putting up with me through the long process of writing this book and for being my ballast for the last fifteen years. I love you dearly. Thank you also to our wonderful daughter, Isabel, for making the best of having not one but two writer parents.

Finally, thank you to Mikey, Lincoln, Cee Cee, Royal, Keith, Danielle, and Jess.

HELP WANTED

Adelle Waldman

READING GROUP GUIDE

HELP WANTED

Adelle Waldman

READING GROUP GUIDE

DISCUSSION QUESTIONS

1. Adelle Waldman uses a line from George Eliot's *Daniel Deronda* ("What makes life dreary is the want of motive") as an epigraph. What conflict does this quote suggest is at the heart of *Help Wanted*? What might Waldman be suggesting about striving and strivers?

2. How does Waldman begin generating suspense in the first paragraph of *Help Wanted*? How do "the time clocks"—watched by Town Square's top bosses, Meredith and Team Movement—function in chapter 1 and throughout this novel? How does urgency, both real and exaggerated, affect the mood in store #1512 and the momentum of *Help Wanted* overall?

3. Waldman brilliantly makes use of the objective correlative, listing merchandise Team Movement begins unloading and scanning each morning at 4 a.m. What emotions and ideas came to your mind in chapter 1 when Nicole falls "into a steady, almost somnambulant rhythm," scanning "a cordless vacuum cleaner, an infant car seat, several packages of paper towels fused together with shrink-wrap, a box containing tubs of protein powder" (p. 4), and so on? What might these items tell us about Town Square's customer base, big-box stores, and American values?

4. Meredith makes her "grand entrance" at the end of chapter 1 and the start of chapter 2. What was your first impression of her? How does Waldman convey the chasm between Meredith and Team Movement? Can Meredith rightly be described as "a villain" in this story?

5. Town Square's annual reports include photographs of the store manager (Big Will) "smiling kindly" while helping "a disabled veteran in a wheelchair retrieve a roll of paper towels from an upper shelf" and "looking cheerful but respectful" while fastening "a cardboard menorah to the top of a Hanukkah display" (p. 27). What is the effect of these details? In your opinion, is Town Square a "principled" big-box store? What do you think makes a store "ethical"? What, if anything, does a company like Town Square owe its employees and community?

6. How has Town Square changed since 2003? Why do you think the store slowly rolled back employee benefits? To what extent do you think the rollbacks were inevitable and necessary? How does Town Square's founding story and history influence Team Movement and heighten the conflict in *Help Wanted*?

7. The last sentence of chapter 5 is, "It was time for the roaches . . . to scatter" (p. 53). Why do you think Waldman chose "roaches" as a metaphor here? Whose perspective does she capture? Did you laugh? Why or why not?

8. Why does Milo, the "best thrower" (p. 78) on Team Movement, resent his current position? Why does Val believe she's entitled to Meredith's job? Why does Diego believe he's as likely to be promoted as Val? Can anyone on Team Movement really discern what it takes to climb Town Square's corporate ladder?

9. When Callie joins Team Movement, Little Will hands her a box cutter and jokes, "Hold on to it—it's the only thing Town Square will ever give you" (p. 61). Why do you suppose Little Will thinks this is funny? What does his "joke" reveal about the culture of Town Square? Does there seem to be a tier in Town Square's corporate structure where this kind of cynicism vanishes? Have you personally observed or experienced skepticism within a large company? How did you respond?

10. What motivates each of Team Movement's members? Who on the team most desires professional validation? Who longs to be better

understood and loved? Who wants a second chance in life? Who feels enormous pressure to take care of loved ones at home? Who views Town Square as a temporary gig? Who clings to the job as a chance at a better life?

11. Big Will has tried to impress upon Meredith that "in a city like Potterstown, finding people willing to work as an executive manager, for $80K or $85K, [isn't] exactly a challenge," but finding "good, reliable rank-and-file workers [is] a different story." What do you suppose is happening in the labor market that Big Will is alluding to, and are there parallels in real cities across the United States? Why can't Meredith see "what the trouble really look[s] like" (p. 100)? Why is Big Will loyal to Meredith even after realizing she lacks foresight, tact, and good judgment?

12. Diego doesn't think telling people from corporate the truth about Meredith is a good idea. He says to Nicole, "I think . . . it'll feel real good at first. . . . [But] I want you to think about what happens next. What I think is you'll wake up a few days later and realize nothing is different." Why exactly does Diego believe that complaining about Meredith is a losing game? Why does Nicole think otherwise but agree to stay mum about Meredith's actions? What would you do in Nicole's position?

13. Meredith recommends Travis for a promotion. She tells Big Will, "I know he hasn't been here long, but Travis is high-energy. He has the right attitude" (p. 173). What else do you think is behind Meredith's interest in promoting Travis? Do you think Meredith's behavior is unique? Or is Meredith a recognizable "type" in any bureaucracy?

14. Several of Team Movement's members express ideas about race and racism. How does Diego discuss "musical chairs" as an analogy for wealth distribution among white and Black Americans? Why does Raymond identify with Black people? Who on the team sees Raymond as a *person of color*? Who, on the other hand, thinks Raymond is "playing the race card"? How much does

race figure into friendships and sympathies on Team Movement and into decisions made by Town Square's management?

15. Val's job in the "pro-Mer plan" is to mess up Anita's tables right before corporate reps come into the store to evaluate merchandise displays. Why does Val have second thoughts about sabotaging Anita? What difference does Nicole's encouraging nod make at the last minute? What does Val's moment of decision reveal? How might you describe Val's eventual sweep of Anita's tables? An act of desperation? Solidarity? Something else?

16. During a meeting at Texas Roadhouse, Big Will elicits support from Katherine, "the highest-ranking person at the table." How does Katherine rationalize Big Will's delay in expressing concerns about Meredith? Describe Katherine's approach to managing employees at Town Square. Why does she extol the "well-crafted carrot" (pp. 246–247)? Have you ever observed a manager using praise to encourage and, at the same time, humble an employee?

17. How does store #1512 change after corporate leaves and Anita becomes store manager? What does Val realize about Big Will? How does Diego cope with feeling "stuck on a treadmill" (p. 259)? How does Milo's departure affect morning unloads? Why is Meredith overcome with regret? What has the team lost? What might they hope to reclaim?

18. Waldman leans into absurdity and humor, and yet *Help Wanted* can also be read as a serious moral inquiry into the lives of low-wage workers. What exactly are the functions of absurdity and humor in this novel? How does farce help Waldman movingly and memorably interrogate the effects of late capitalism?

19. Joshua Ferris praised *Help Wanted* for portraying "the tragic heroes of the gig economy." To what extent are low-wage, retail workers "tragic heroes" in this day and age? How has the "gig economy" changed American labor? How hopeful do you feel about "work" and today's retail industry? Where should we go from here?

SELECTED NORTON BOOKS WITH READING GROUP GUIDES AVAILABLE

For a complete list of Norton's works with reading group guides, please go to wwnorton.com/reading-guides.

Diana Abu-Jaber	*Life Without a Recipe*
Diane Ackerman	*The Zookeeper's Wife*
Michelle Adelman	*Piece of Mind*
Molly Antopol	*The UnAmericans*
Andrea Barrett	*Archangel*
Rowan Hisayo Buchanan	*Harmless Like You*
Ada Calhoun	*Wedding Toasts I'll Never Give*
Bonnie Jo Campbell	*Mothers, Tell Your Daughters*
	Once Upon a River
Lan Samantha Chang	*Inheritance*
Ann Cherian	*A Good Indian Wife*
Evgenia Citkowitz	*The Shades*
Amanda Coe	*The Love She Left Behind*
Michael Cox	*The Meaning of Night*
Jeremy Dauber	*Jewish Comedy*
Jared Diamond	*Guns, Germs, and Steel*
Caitlin Doughty	*From Here to Eternity*
Andre Dubus III	*House of Sand and Fog*
	Townie: A Memoir
Anne Enright	*The Forgotten Waltz*
	The Green Road
Amanda Filipacchi	*The Unfortunate Importance of Beauty*
Beth Ann Fennelly	*Heating & Cooling*
Betty Friedan	*The Feminine Mystique*
Maureen Gibbon	*Paris Red*
Stephen Greenblatt	*The Swerve*
Lawrence Hill	*The Illegal*
	Someone Knows My Name
Ann Hood	*The Book That Matters Most*
	The Obituary Writer
Dara Horn	*A Guide for the Perplexed*
Blair Hurley	*The Devoted*

Meghan Kenny	*The Driest Season*
Nicole Krauss	*The History of Love*
Don Lee	*The Collective*
Amy Liptrot	*The Outrun: A Memoir*
Donna M. Lucey	*Sargent's Women*
Bernard MacLaverty	*Midwinter Break*
Maaza Mengiste	*Beneath the Lion's Gaze*
Claire Messud	*The Burning Girl*
	When the World Was Steady
Liz Moore	*Heft*
	The Unseen World
Neel Mukherjee	*The Lives of Others*
	A State of Freedom
Janice P. Nimura	*Daughters of the Samurai*
Rachel Pearson	*No Apparent Distress*
Richard Powers	*Orfeo*
Kirstin Valdez Quade	*Night at the Fiestas*
Jean Rhys	*Wide Sargasso Sea*
Mary Roach	*Packing for Mars*
Somini Sengupta	*The End of Karma*
Akhil Sharma	*Family Life*
	A Life of Adventure and Delight
Joan Silber	*Fools*
Johanna Skibsrud	*Quartet for the End of Time*
Mark Slouka	*Brewster*
Kate Southwood	*Evensong*
Manil Suri	*The City of Devi*
	The Age of Shiva
Madeleine Thien	*Do Not Say We Have Nothing*
	Dogs at the Perimeter
Vu Tran	*Dragonfish*
Rose Tremain	*The American Lover*
	The Gustav Sonata
Brady Udall	*The Lonely Polygamist*
Brad Watson	*Miss Jane*
Constance Fenimore Woolson	*Miss Grief and Other Stories*

Available only on the Norton website